SNAKEBITE

PHANTOM QUEEN DIARIES BOOK 13

SHAYNE SILVERS

CAMERON O'CONNELL

ARGENTO PUBLISHING

CONTENTS

Shayne Silvers & Cameron O'Connell

Snakebite

The Phantom Queen Diaries Book 13

A TempleVerse Series

ISBN 13: 978-1-947709-90-4

© 2022, Shayne Silvers / Argento Publishing, LLC

info@shaynesilvers.com

SHAYNE AND CAMERON

Shayne Silvers, here.

Cameron O'Connell is one helluva writer, and he's worked tire-lessly to merge a story into the Temple Verse that would provide a different and unique *voice*, but a complementary *tone* to my other novels. *SOME* people might say I'm hard to work with. But certainly, Cameron would never...

Hey! Pipe down over there, author monkey! Get back to your writing cave and finish the next Phantom Queen Novel!

Ahem. Now, where was I?

This is book 13 in the Phantom Queen Diaries, which is a series that ties into the existing TempleVerse with Nate Temple and Callie Penrose. This series could also be read independently if one so chose. Then again, you, the reader, will get SO much more out of my existing books (and this series) by reading them all in tandem.

But that's not up to us. It's up to you, the reader.

You tell us...

1

I remembered *everything*.

And it all began with a door.

It wasn't a particularly noteworthy door. It had a mail slot made of brass and was painted a green so dark that it appeared black at night—which it was. The knob, also brass, turned easily in my hand, though I refrained from opening the door right away. Instead, I allowed myself a moment to survey the quiet residential street.

The light of a full moon was barely visible this close to the city of Boston with its skyglow and skyscrapers, though the bright yellow gas lamps that lined the streets lended the place plenty of cozy ambience. An old man walking his dog at the end of the block stopped to let the animal sniff at the base of a hedgerow while, farther down, a middle-aged couple were pulling their car into a shallow driveway. I recognized the man as a neighbor from my childhood, though I couldn't for the life of me recall his name.

With a sigh, I pressed my shoulder into the door and pushed. It opened, albeit with a groan of protest; a pile of mail and flyers and other such paraphernalia blocked the entrance—including a bulky package bound with paper and twine. I slipped through the narrow gap, shut the door, and fetched the parcel off the ground. Then, after turning on the hall light, I crept down the corridor and ventured into a living room full of ghosts.

Not actual ghosts; I'd yet to encounter any of those outside dreams and the occasional astral visitation. These were, in fact, white bed sheets draped over several items of furniture that had once belonged to my Aunt Dez, short for Desdemona. This was her house —our house, technically.

Of course, I hadn't stepped foot in it for a long time, not since her funeral. I'd had someone else come in and take care of the place in my absence, which explained the sheets as well as the empty spaces on the wall where paintings and portraits had once hung. Those I could see, stacked together against the wall beside the fireplace, their flimsy, brown paper backs belying the beautiful images that would be found on the other side.

I set the parcel down on a shrouded dresser and moved towards those frames, prying one of the larger, heavier numbers free with little difficulty—a perk of being inhumanly strong—and setting it down where the light from the hall could reach it.

The woman in the portrait was a lithe, dark-haired beauty with soft features and large eyes. The painting had been commissioned a long time ago, along with one of my mother that had hung in the hall upstairs for much of my life. Still, the portrait captured a great deal of my aunt's character: her wry smile, the hard glint in her eyes that spoke of a troubled past, the inquisitive tilt of her chin.

"Hello, Dez," I said in the accented voice I'd picked up from her, itself a strange blend of Irish and New Englander that would've marked me as a stranger in either place.

The portrait didn't respond. Not that I'd expected it to. Dez was dead—murdered in this very house in a room just above my head by a mythical being from another realm. It was still hard to believe. The part about her being gone, not the part about a fairy tale creature having been involved. I'd gotten quite used to the latter. In fact, at this point in my life I associated far less with normal people—those we called Regulars—than I did with the abnormal ones. The individuals we called Freaks.

Dez had been a Regular. Or at least that's what I'd always believed. My parents, on the other hand, had been anything but. It'd taken me years to figure that out, however. Indeed, I'd spent most my life thinking my mother a bit of a floozy who'd died giving birth to me and my father a deadbeat who either never knew I existed or simply hadn't cared. Instead, it turned out my mother was an ancient Celtic goddess and my father the most notorious wizard ever to have walked the planet.

Unfortunately, that knowledge hadn't really changed anything: my mother still hadn't been there to raise me, and I'd never laid direct eyes on my father. Sure, they probably had better excuses than most for abandoning their child, but that didn't make it suck any less.

I ran my fingers along the portrait's gilded frame, sighed, and wandered back over to the package. For a moment, I considered collecting the rest of the mail, turning on the lights, and sorting through it. But then I wasn't sure I could handle that just yet; no doubt there would be letters addressed to Dez dated prior to the news of her passing, not to mention letters of condolences sent to me.

So, rather than tackle that emotionally eviscerating chore, I snatched up the package, wrenched free the sheet covering my favorite chair, and took a seat. A hasty inspection revealed it had been addressed to me, though with no return address, it was hard to tell what it might contain. I held the parcel aloft, turning it about as though I might guess its contents.

Eventually, I gave up and peeled off the bits of tape securing each tidy fold, then removed the packaging altogether to reveal a slender wooden box with a silver clasp. There were no other marks and no decorations, nor was there a card or receipt of any kind. Warily, I rose, plugged in a nearby lamp, and turned on the light.

The box remained unchanged—non-threatening. And yet, I was exceptionally careful as I flicked open the clasp. After all, it would not have been the first time that something dangerous had come into my possession. In fact, in my previous line of work as a black magic antiques collector and occasional arms dealer, it had become rather commonplace.

I flipped open the box and took a step back, prepared for whatever might come leaping out. When nothing did, however, I returned to find the dried-up husk of some desiccated creature—presumably a snake, judging by the musky stench. I wasn't sure what to make of it, though I knew enough not to reach out and touch the thing; it was shocking how many ordinary, everyday items have some sort of curse on them, to say nothing of the truly occult shit people could find online and have delivered to your doorstep.

Still, it seemed harmless enough. My money was on one of those crazy, serpent-handling Pentacostals having shoved it through the door for kicks. That, or I'd accidentally subscribed to *Black Magic Magazine*. Either way, I quickly dismissed the box and its morbid contents, steeling myself instead for the emotional turmoil that lay ahead.

And that's when it struck.

The desiccated snakeskin sprang out of the box and latched onto my hand so fast that not even my finely-honed instincts were able to save me. Something sharp pierced the meat of my hand between my thumb and forefinger, sending waves of pain radiating up my arm. And not just pain, either, but cold—such cold as to rattle my bones.

I dropped the box, fell to one knee, and fought to pry the damned thing loose even as the numbness spread past my shoulder and across my chest. But it was no use; whatever this thing was, it had thoroughly embedded itself in my skin. The sensation spread to my hips, then my legs, at which point I collapsed onto the floor. The box lay beside me, overturned, which was when I noticed a white card taped to its base. With what strength I had left, I reached out and pried the note free, desperate to find out whether my ailment could somehow be reversed. Instead, I found a single phrase scribbled between the margins.

"*...the spell become flesh must be cast...*"

I scanned the odd phrase over and over again, hoping it might provide some clue as to what was happening to me. When it didn't, I knew I was in real trouble. This notion was only reinforced when I felt Areadbhar—my legendary spear and near constant companion over the past few weeks, currently locked away in her pebble form—pulse in my pocket. Clearly, she could sense it, too. I fumbled about in search of the stone only to feel it slip between my useless fingers. I flung my hand out to retrieve it, but only succeeded in sending the pebble skittering farther across the floor.

Dammit.

"Someone," I moaned. "Help me, please."

But no one came.

2

I must have slipped into unconsciousness at some point, because when I came to, night had become day. Stranger still, I found myself sprawled face down on a deserted shore littered with large black rocks rimmed in snow. Dark mountains rose to the east and west, their peaks wreathed in mist and fog—the same colorless haze that obscured the distant horizon—while to the south lay a blanket of snow that extended as far as my eyes could see. To the north lay a sea so bleak and uninviting it appeared almost purple, its waves pounding restlessly against the sand.

The wind coming off the water nipped at my skin as I sat up, biting at my exposed flesh and whipping my hair about with little concern for the effort it took to tame it. A hasty inspection revealed I'd been transported in the clothes and accessories I'd been wearing, my pockets mercifully unpicked.

Of Areadbhar in her pebble form, however, there was no sign.

As for my hand, I could see nothing to suggest an injury. Indeed, nothing about my situation seemed to explain who might have sent me to this place or why—assuming the bite of that cursed *thing* and my current whereabouts were somehow connected.

"Where the hell am I?" I asked through gritted teeth, forced to hug myself for warmth.

As if in reply, snow sloughed off the back of one of the mountains to the east, crashing into the sea below with a thunderous roar. I shivered, dimly aware that I might already be suffering from hypothermia, perhaps even frostbite, were I someone else. But then I wasn't, and the moment that thought occured to me, I remembered being durable was not all I had in my favor.

I flicked my hands about in a mad dance, gesturing first to my feet, then my legs, my torso, and so on until my fingers touched the crown of my forehead. It wasn't strictly necessary considering my outfit had once belonged to the Valkyrie Brunhilde and could be altered according to my whim alone, but I preferred the old fashioned way, if only because it made the process feel slightly more natural.

One spell at a time, as they say.

In any event, by the time I rose to my feet I wore so many layers of magically-sourced animal skins that I could have starred in an ad campaign for Cruella de Vil couture.

But hey, at least I was warm.

I hastily shoved my hands in the fur-lined pockets of my parka and was moments from turning to walk along the beach when the sea began to seethe some leagues beyond the break water. I took a step back as something gargantuan emerged from its depths, creating a swell so enormous it appeared like a mountain of water surging towards the shore.

I started to run, slowly at first, but picked up momentum until finally I was sprinting as fast as I could for the open plain in the hopes of avoiding the tidal wave. Of course, it was far too late for that.

The colossal wave crashed against the mountains on either side of the beach and swept into the bay with a deafening roar that drowned out the sound of my startled cry, the water snatching me off my feet and buffeting me about like a leaf caught in a hurricane. For what must have only been a moment but felt like an eternity, mine was a violent, turbulent existence. And then, so abruptly it was as though

I'd been struck on the back of the head and plunged into a bottomless pit, everything went dark.

And thus it was I found myself floating insensate in a lightless void, my body utterly unresponsive—though not unpleasantly so. Indeed, it felt rather like being caught between waking and a dream: an out-of-body experience mingled with coziness and transience. An agreeable experience, perhaps, were it not for the voice of a ghost echoing in my ears.

3

" . . . Your mother foresaw many possibilities when she bore you, not the least of which was that you—and, by extension, your interference—would be necessary. That you would be needed."

4

I jerked awake and found myself dressed in the clothes of a stranger, sitting at a bus stop—the aluminum bench enclosed in a grimy plexiglass box that had been plastered with posters featuring a rapper I vaguely remembered from my high school days who went by the name Tech N9ne. Across the street stood a squat 7-Eleven with bars on the windows and, beyond it, a scattered array of red brick buildings and congested tenements connected by a tangled mess of power lines just visible against a twilight sky.

I shook my head, trying to remember how I'd ended up here, but couldn't. In fact, I couldn't even be certain where here *was*; the skyline was utterly unfamiliar, though my modest surroundings suggested a less than desirable neighborhood in a major US city, and one in the midst of a heat wave.

This I could tell by the air, which was so heavy with humidity that I felt it clinging to my skin like cellophane—the sort of oppressive mugginess that made summer intolerable for all but the most cold-blooded. Which, in retrospect, was what alerted me to the cluster of young men lounging beneath a street light two blocks down on the other side of the road.

There were three of them in total, each uncommonly pale for this time of year and wearing some absurd assortment of dark denim jacket, hoodie, leather pants, and acid washed jeans. There was also something remarkably outdated about their hairstyles and choice of accessories—a sort of ragged, retro-look that reminded me of the early 2000s.

While I struggled to get my bearings, a sharp rap of knuckles against the plexiglass startled me so much that I nearly jumped out of my own skin. I whirled to find a burly, bearded man leaning against the transparent barricade, the hood of his unseasonable coat thrown up so that it cast a shadow across his face. I opened my mouth, prepared to lash out at the bastard for scaring me half to death, but he spoke first.

"The Church appreciates your tip, sister," he said, his voice both rough and oddly familiar as he turned, putting his back to me. "Keep an eye on those three for me, won't you? I'll take care of them once I've dealt with the ones in their little nest. God willing, I'll catch them all napping in their coffins."

Taken aback by the familiarity of his tone as much as by the words themselves, I had hardly begun to formulate a reply when he tossed something over to me—a five-decade rosary decorated with red beads, the chain so long I could have wound it around my hand three times over.

"If they move," he continued, still not looking at me, "I want you to follow them. Discreetly, of course. The rosary will make it easy to find you. If anything unexpected happens or they double back towards their hideout, break the chain. But whatever you do, don't lose it. A whole lot of prayers and a fair amount of magic went into making that thing."

Surprised by the admission, I held the rosary up for a closer inspection. The beads were ruby-red crystals cut into dainty spheres, while the crucifix itself was silver-plated, the figure of Jesus on the cross worn smooth with the passage of time and the frequent touch of hands. Still, there didn't seem anything particularly remarkable about it.

"Hold on," I said, lowering the prayer necklace, "I'm pretty sure ye have the wrong—"

But the man was already gone. Indeed, I saw that the sidewalk behind me was utterly deserted in both directions. Eerily so, in fact—like those scenes in a Western when the sheriff rides into a ghost town. I glanced warily down at the rosary and was debating whether to leave it on the bench beside me when I heard a bray of laughter from farther down the street.

I turned to find a pair of teenage girls with oddly distinct faces, each dressed as though they'd spent the day at a pool, riding their bikes along the opposite sidewalk. Both were blonde, though the taller of the two had hair so fair it was practically platinum. Moreover, they were both uncommonly pretty, especially for girls their age —a fact that did not escape the trio huddled beneath the halo of the street light.

I saw one nudge his companions as the girls approached, and soon all three had turned to clock the pair. The girls didn't seem particularly bothered by the attention at first; they rode on, smiling coyly, as though they'd come to expect such things—as no doubt they had from leering teenage boys. Indeed, it wasn't until they drew close enough to see exactly who was eyeing them that they began to slow, their expressions suddenly apprehensive.

As I watched, one of the men stepped forward and beckoned suggestively while behind him his friend shouted something far too crass to be called a greeting. The girls, who had stopped completely by this point, hastily turned their bikes around and started to peddle back the way they'd come. Unfortunately, that seemed to further entice the men; they began shouting, then running, and finally sprinting after the girls at a pace no ordinary human could have possibly sustained.

I cursed in alarm and surged to my feet as the teenagers turned down an alley with the men, who were not in fact men at all, hot on their heels. Checking to make sure I wouldn't get clipped by a passing car, I raced across the street after them. Of course, I wasn't sure what I planned to do once I reached them. Even now, it felt like I was experiencing some sort of strange, hyper-realistic fever dream. Still, there was simply no way I could sit idly by and let anything happen to those poor girls—not if I could do something about it.

I arrived at the mouth of the alley just in time to see one of the trio snatch the rear chassis of the taller girl's bike, sending the teenager flying over the handlebars to crash into a dumpster with a sickening crunch. The other girl had already been wrenched from her bike and was being held up against the wall, her top torn to shreds as they pawed at her. Anger washed over me in a white hot wave, and I subconsciously raised a hand as if I might call down lightning and smite the fuckers right then and there.

Only I couldn't.

Indeed, I found myself unable to do much of anything; no matter how much I willed my feet to move, they refused—almost as if there stood an invisible, impassable barrier between me and the alleyway. When that didn't work, I thought to scream, hoping to scare the fiends off or at least get their attention, but it was no use. No words came out.

Instead, I had no choice but to watch as the taller girl was yanked to her feet and pressed against the wall, the side of her face slick with blood from a cut above her eye. The bastard holding her leaned in close and licked her cheek, lapping at the dark fluid like a dog, his fangs forming an arch around his tongue.

A goddamned vampire.

It was at that moment that I remembered the rosary in my hand and recalled the message that had accompanied its arrival. My heart racing, I grabbed the chain in both hands and yanked with all my considerable strength, prying the links apart as if they were made of putty rather than precious metal. A subsequent pulse of energy sent a thrill through me, but I was barely able to take note of it before the vampire clutching the taller girl suddenly burst into flames.

The bloodsucker wailed as he released the girl and fell to his knees, the fire consuming him so thoroughly it was as if he'd been doused in gasoline. His companions, meanwhile, turned to watch—too startled perhaps to even consider putting him out.

"Sister, what's happening, why did you call me?" asked a voice over my shoulder.

I spun to find the hooded man brandishing a sword, its blade already slick with blood. Fortunately, he wasn't pointing it at, or even really looking at, me. Instead, his attention was drawn to the alleyway and the shrieking bloodsucker. The stranger, taking quick stock of the situation, took hold of my arm and guided me gently to a small recess near the alley entrance. I tensed, expecting to meet the resistance I'd experienced earlier, but felt nothing.

"You've more than done your part, sister," he whispered conspiratorially. "I'll take it from here. When the coast is clear, I want you to get away from this place. The local authorities will no doubt be suspicious of any bystanders, especially in a neighborhood like this."

"But I'm not—" I began.

The man squeezed my arm and stepped past before I could say more, striding into the alley with grim purpose. The two remaining vampires, seeing him coming, exchanged glances and rushed forward with their fangs bared and their hands raised like claws. Not that it did them any good; the hooded man danced just out of reach, swinging his sword in a deadly arc that sent both their heads tumbling neatly from their necks.

At that precise moment, however, my attention was diverted by the resounding clang of metal overhead as a crow landed on the railing of a nearby fire escape.

"Stupid bird," I hissed, startled.

The crow simply cocked its head at me.

I rolled my eyes and turned back to the scene in the alley to find the hooded man had sheathed his sword and given his coat to the girl whose top had been ruined. I could see he and the taller girl were engaged in some sort of discussion, though I had no clue what they might be saying to one another.

Resolved to catch at least a part of their conversation in the dim hope that it might reveal how I'd come to end up here as well as the reason the hooded man kept calling me "sister," I crept forward, keeping to the shadows of the alley until I was finally within earshot.

"...been tracking them for days," the hooded man was saying, his cragged, weathered face and shorn head—both of which I felt I recognized—visible now that he'd removed his coat.

"Vampires aren't real," replied the girl, though the bloodstains on her face and the pile of ash at her feet seemed to directly contradict that statement.

"Neither are wizards, girl," came the reply.

"Exactly. What's your name? What did you do to them?"

The man chuckled. "My name is Roland Haviar. And it looks like I may be in town longer than I originally planned. Kansas City... might be fun."

It wasn't until that moment, in the dark with the stench of barbecued vampire and the metallic tang of spilled blood still lingering in the air, that I finally realized why all three had seemed so familiar.

First, there was the hooded man, Roland Haviar, a Shepherd-turned-vampire I'd met in New York City what seemed like forever ago. Only back then his eyes had been bright red, not brown, and his face a decade older at least. And then there was Claire, the half-naked girl currently huddled beneath Roland's coat, who had ironically been wearing even less when we had first met—though the Claire I'd met was not an awkward girl on the cusp of womanhood but a lascivious young lady in her mid-to-late twenties.

And finally there was the platinum-haired child, who was the spitting image of a very powerful and talented individual I was destined to meet on a wild girls-night-out in Vegas, provided you aged her up to the point she was legally old enough to drink.

Callie Penrose.

Which begged the question: what the actual *fuck* was going on?

5

Unfortunately, just as I was about to emerge from the shadows and demand answers to the dozens of questions my revelations had raised, Roland pressed a hand to both girls' backs and teleported all three from the alley using magic. I hissed at their abrupt departure, annoyed that I'd missed my opportunity to find out precisely what had happened here, not to mention my role in it.

I rose and meandered towards the mouth of the alley as those questions continued bouncing around inside my head. For starters, how had I ended up in Kansas City of all places? And why had those three appeared so much younger than the Callie, Claire, and Roland I knew? Was that why Roland hadn't recognized me? Except he *had* recognized me—only as someone else. His so-called sister. No, not his sister. *A* sister.

I paused to eye the broken rosary as if it might hold the answers I sought, but of course it didn't. I sighed, slipped the prayer necklace into a pocket where it rested alongside another object I'd been given not so long ago under equally mysterious circumstances, and took a quick look around to get my bearings before deciding my next move.

And that's when I first noticed the storm.

It advanced hungrily across the sky, so immense it was visible even through the narrow gap between the buildings, the black storm clouds spewing forth as though they'd been summoned by a vengeful god. Scarlet lightning danced within those roiling clouds, turning them pink in places and a bloody crimson in others. Stranger still, the edges of the storm had a shape to it—a vaguely equine mold that reminded me of a horse and rider come to trample the world to dust.

I shuddered and took a nervous step backwards, inadvertently bumping into something. I stumbled and groped for the wall as the object I'd collided with—a person, as it turned out—stepped into the light, revealing a shrouded figure dressed in a black velvet cloak with a train made entirely of black feathers. The newcomer looked past me, staring up at that horrendous storm from the shadows of their cowl before speaking in a husky, melodious voice that could only have belonged to a woman.

"And I saw, and behold a Dark Horse."

I shivered, recognizing the phrase from its Biblical source material at once, even if it was bastardized. The original passage was from Revelations and referred to a pale horse, otherwise known as the Horseman of Death—an acquaintance and occasional poker buddy of mine, I might add. But there *was* something foreboding about that storm. Something that spoke of dour prophecies and irrevocable fates.

Screw it. I'd had enough of this fever dream or out of body experience or whatever the hell this was. It was high time someone told me what was really going on, and I didn't particularly care who so long as they spoke fast.

"What the hell is goin' on?" I demanded of the newcomer, shrilly. "And what was that supposed to mean, anyway? About the Dark Horse."

"It means it's time to go."

She snapped her fingers, and my whole world went black once more.

6

"You never control your dreams. You control yourself within a dream. The sooner you learn that, the better."

7

When I came to this time, I found myself leaning over a rust-speckled railing overlooking the dingy green waters of Boston's Seaport district as it had appeared back when I was a child—nothing but plots of dying grass tucked between empty parking lots and ugly concrete buildings. One such plot could be seen some ten yards off to my right, though it had clearly been converted for a special occasion of some sort. A large pavilion had been erected, and a couple hundred people milled about beneath its crisp white tent, eyeing the wares on display while dozens of vendors looked on.

Judging from the low-sitting sun casting long shadows across the ground, I guessed it to be early morning. It was also chilly, the New England wind as brisk and bracing as it ever was in the months leading up to winter. Fortunately, I seemed appropriately bundled up for the time of year, albeit in an unfashionably large trench coat I'd never have chosen for myself.

Disturbed and confused, I abandoned the railing to stare out at the city I called home, scanning the horizon line for the buildings that should have been there but weren't. Gone was the gleaming Millenium Tower, the R2-D2 building in the Prudential Center, the financial district's One Lincoln, and even the Atlantic Wharf—all of which were either built, or at least completed, in the last twenty years.

Which raised the questions: had I been teleported solely from Kansas City to Boston, or had I been thrown back in time, as well? And, more importantly, for what purpose?

Regrettably, whatever conclusions I might have drawn from further study were disregarded the instant a child came sprinting past, her red locks fluttering madly in the wind as she chased what appeared to be an insect, or perhaps some other nimble, flying creature. Indeed, so fixated was she that the girl took no notice of the adult version of herself standing not ten feet away.

I reached out to touch myself, in the most appropriate way of course, but it was too late; the girl had already gone racing towards the pavilion in pursuit of her prey. And so I stood there with my hand outstretched, my heart thundering in my chest, unable to wrap my head around the sheer impossibility of what I'd just witnessed.

Startled by the sudden bleating of a fog horn, I dropped my arm and took off after my younger self, weaving between bystanders as I tracked her—easier said than done, even with our conspicuous ginger mop to guide me. Along the way, however, I passed a sign that made me stop in my tracks. "Souvenirs from Salem," it read in a thick, spooky font, with "Presented by the Witches of Ipswich" written neatly below.

I remembered that sign.

Indeed, I could recall much of that entire day. The whole affair had been a surprise, if memory served. Dez had woken me up early, fetching my cranky self out of bed in the wee hours of the morning on a Saturday with the promise of a candy apple and perhaps a toy from what she called the "witches tent." It had all seemed terribly exciting at first, especially that bit about the apple. At least until we arrived, at which point Dez revealed she planned to meet up with a few of her church friends while I spent the afternoon in the company of their obnoxious offspring.

Naturally, I'd broken away as soon as I could, far more content to roam the area on my own in spite of the dangers. Of course, times were different then; the threat of abduction was not yet so common as to thwart a child's attempts at wandering off on one's own. In any case, these were the events that led up to the moment I first spotted the winged creature with the face and body of a young woman fluttering around the pavilion.

Years later, I would know the Faeling by its proper classification: a pixie. But, as a child, I remembered thinking only that Dez would never believe I'd seen such a thing unless I caught her—and so our chase had begun. A chase it seemed my younger self was still in the middle of.

Which meant *it* hadn't happened yet.

Coming back to the moment at hand, I cursed and hurried onward, headed for the rearmost part of the tent where the crowds were thinnest. It was there, where the so-called witches kept the more expensive merchandise, that I knew I'd find her. Because that was where the pixie had fled, and where I as a child had stumbled across my very first genuine magical artifact.

An artifact I was destined to steal.

8

Even now, I couldn't tell you why I did it. Perhaps it was merely a compulsion—the sort every child contends with when confronted by the lure of a pretty bauble. Or perhaps I sensed there was something more to the object. Either way, when I first laid eyes on the cup, I knew I had to have it, consequences be damned.

For a moment, I considered trying to prevent the theft, if only to salvage what little moral fiber I had left after all these years. Unfortunately, it seemed I was already too late to intervene; a shout of alarm sounded as I reached the rear stalls, accompanied by the gasps and muttered curses of those who happened to get in the way of my younger self as she tore through the crowd with the cup clenched in her tiny fist.

The stall owner—a buxom young woman sporting a low-brimmed newsie cap and knitted scarf—came racing after the girl, flinging her hand out and shouting something unintelligible. To my surprise, a pulse of energy accompanied the motion, followed by a fierce wind that should have sent my younger self flying, but instead toppled a table full of leather goods—the spell's effect no doubt nullified by the shield that had once protected me from such things.

Several bystanders cried out at the disturbance, their sudden frenzy making it harder for the stall owner to keep track of me, or her, or whatever as she bounded forward and was eventually swallowed up by the milling crowds. Still, the woman wasn't to be deterred; she strode after her prey with all the determination of an executioner.

I, meanwhile, frowned.

My memories of this time—of my theft and subsequent flight— were chaotic at best. And yet, I could still remember looking over my shoulder as I caught my breath and seeing someone distracting the stall owner long enough for me to get away with my prize. Someone tall, in a baggy khaki coat...and yet there was no one fitting that description in sight.

Unless...

I took off after the stall owner, managing to head her off just as she was about to spot the miniature version of me leaning against a tent pole and gulping air.

"Excuse me," I said, angling my body so that my younger self would remain hidden from sight. "D'ye work here, by chance?"

To my surprise, the stall owner smiled.

Stranger still, it was a smile I recognized.

"Well hello, lover," the stall owner replied, peeling away the hat and scarf that had momentarily obscured her features, revealing the face of a stunningly attractive, raven-haired enchantress. "Fancy seeing you here."

9

"**M**organ?" I asked, so shocked my voice registered perhaps an octave higher than normal. "Morgan le Fay?"

The enchantress grimaced. "I've told you not to call me that, Archwizard."

"Archwizard?"

"What? Do you not go by that title, anymore? I suppose it *is* a more modern era, befitting of new and improved nomenclature. I've taken a shine to 'High Priestess,' myself. It's how this local coven addresses their leader. A charming designation, don't you think? You know how much I appreciate these mortals and their overt religious overtones."

I nodded absentmindedly for want of a reply, my mind whirling with the implications of running into Morgan le Fay—an immortal enchantress and self-professed paternal Godmother I'd last laid eyes on while helping a preternatural branch of the FBI solve a particularly complicated murder case in Branson, Missouri—here in Boston on the very same day my younger self stole her first magical object.

What were the odds?

"You didn't happen to see a little girl run past here, by the way, did you?" Morgan asked, craning her neck to see past my shoulder. "She's made off with that cup Galahad gave me. You remember the one."

I blanched at the mention of a Knight of the Round Table in conjunction with a cup of any description, though of course I knew for a fact my younger self hadn't absconded with the Holy Grail; if she had, I imagined the sale would have set me up for life.

"I didn't see anyone," I lied.

"Shame. Oh well. It'll make its way back to me, one day. They almost always do."

I nodded as if that made sense. "So...what are ye doin' here?"

The enchantress cocked an eyebrow. "Trading spells and selling potions, what else? And what's with the accent? Don't tell me you've gone native since wandering off to that island of savages."

"Tradin' spells with whom?" I asked, ignoring her second question.

"The Faerie Chancery, of course."

I snapped my fingers. "That's why the pixie was here."

"Not just pixies. Kobolds, brownies, sprites...they've all been by. Even my sister and the Green Knight himself made an appearance. She's still not your biggest fan, you know. Probably best you don't stick around too long."

Her sister...did she mean Morgause? The old Adjudicator? I frowned, wondering what beef the legendary enchantress could possibly have with me. Indeed, the fact that Morgause even knew who I was came a little as a surprise.

"Why? What did I do to her?"

Morgan pursed her lips. "Like you don't know. Anyway, I expect you came here to collect that scroll you asked me to track down for you? You're lucky I happen to have it with me, you know. A decade is a long time to hold onto anything, let alone some random scrap of parchment."

"Parchment?"

"Mmhmm. Vellum, in fact. High quality stuff, nothing like those wretched modern sheets of paper. I do wish these mortals would go back to making things that last, don't you?"

Morgan sighed and waved for me to follow without waiting for a reply, and together the two of us retraced our steps until we stood before the table full of treasures my younger self had been drawn to. I tried not to stare at the place where the cup had sat, and instead eyed a collection of bracelets on display—several of which mirrored the one Morgan had given me to contain my godlike powers. The very one I wore now, as a matter of fact.

While Morgan rummaged about, I picked up a shard of glass that had been fixed to a bit of inscribed wood and bound with gold-plated wire. "What's this do?"

"Absolutely nothing," she replied. "But if any of those kooky, new age soccer moms ask, it blesses their house with positive energy and will ensure all their children go to college. They simply adore that prophetic tripe."

Amused, I set the shard back down.

"Here we are," Morgan said at last, passing me a scroll sealed with a red silk ribbon tied in a bow.

"T'anks. But, um...what is it?"

"You don't remember?"

I shook my head.

"You've started slipping in your old age." Morgan clucked her tongue. "'A spell to overcome the influence of the moon.' I believe those were your words. Though I can't imagine why you'd want to have anything to do with *them*. I never was a fan of their kind. But then, I've always preferred my men the way I prefer my coffee."

"Sold to ye by a Colombian?" I ventured.

"Weak and pale."

I snickered as I slipped the scroll into the inner lining of my coat, though I had to admit I wasn't sure exactly what she was talking about. Or, for that matter, just who it was the infamous enchantress kept mistaking me for—a question I'd delayed asking in the hopes I might be able to use context clues instead. Resolved to find out, I had

only just opened my mouth to ask when I caught sight of my reflection in the glass shard I held in my hand.

Only it wasn't my reflection I saw.

It was a man's.

"What the fu—"

A hand snatched my arm and tugged, drawing me back into
darkness.

"Calvin and Makayla Temple...Your mother never trusted them, not entirely, but she saw the necessity in what they were doing. In what they asked of her and the wizard...to provide them with a protector. For their son. Nathin Laurent Temple."

11

The screech of iron hinges brought me back as a pair of enormous, ostentatious gates swung wide in welcome to reveal a paved road slithering off into the trees. A similarly massive wall stood on either side of those gates, guarded by a pair of naked sentinels armed with swords and shields—one masculine in every sense of the word, the other lithe and beautiful.

Beneath me idled a half-ton's worth of motorcycle capable of pumping out at least 1000cc judging by the full throated rumble of its flat-twin engine. Mercifully, the kickstand was taking most of that weight, saving me the trouble of fighting to keep the massive thing upright.

"Welcome to Chateau Falco," said a faintly robotic voice from the intercom system attached to the gate. "Please proceed with care as you make your way up the drive."

Chateau Falco...hadn't I heard that name before, somewhere?

"Wait, I don't—"

The intercom clicked off before I could finish. Clearly I hadn't been expected to reply, or perhaps the person on the other end was simply rude. Either way, I wasn't sure what to do next. A glance over my shoulder revealed the same paved road going in the opposite direction, although this one intersected a two-lane highway perhaps a half-mile farther down.

So, I could either go back the way I'd come, or I could pass through those gates and follow the directions I'd been given. Exasperated, I raised my face to the sky and let out a long groan. It was only as I brought my attention back down, in fact, that I realized I was wearing what amounted to a black leather onesie complete with padded gloves, double-breasted jacket, skintight pants, and thicksoled boots. The helmet, carbon fiber and also black, hung from the handle bar with its clear plastic visor slid back.

Feeling a little like a Bond villain, I snatched the helmet and slipped it on. The fit was snug, but not uncomfortable. Then, worried the gates might shut on me soon if I didn't go through them, I hoisted the bike, dislodged the kickstand, and throttled the engine.

Fortunately, the subsequent journey was not unpleasant; I'd always enjoyed riding motorcycles, even if they sometimes paled in comparison to the joys of zooming down the I-95 in a high-performance sports car. Of course, it helped that spring was in full swing wherever it was I'd ended up. Dogwood trees in full bloom lined either side of the road, their white petals floating in the light breeze. Indeed, it was an idyllic ride, and one I would have thoroughly enjoyed under ordinary circumstances.

In fact, by the time I reached my intended destination I found my mood had markedly improved. Which was perhaps all that saved me from cursing the moment I laid eyes on the sprawling, four-story mansion at the top of the drive.

Chateau Falco.

Nate's home. I recognized it from the news and my own attempts at researching the wizard, back when he was on my long list of potential enemies. Of course, there was something odd about it I couldn't quite place—like a famous painting with a small, seemingly innocuous piece missing.

I circled round the artisanal fountain in the center of the drive, wary of the water spewing from its jets as I parked the bike, slid off its back, and removed my helmet to stare up at the gaudy, colonial monstrosity. Pictures hadn't done it justice. But then, in the photos online I could have sworn there'd been a modest observatory sitting atop the west wing of the house. An observatory that was conspicuously absent.

Before I could speculate further, however, the front doors swung open and a dead woman emerged.

"Over here!" cried Makayla Temple, waving animatedly to me from the top of the portico.

The woman playing tour guide as we meandered through the Temple's ancestral home was not, as it turned out, deceased, but rather a younger version of the spirit I'd met in the Underworld some months back. A younger, *livelier* version.

"Chateau Falco has an east and west wing," she was explaining, "each with a sizable library. I'm not sure how many bedrooms there are in total. Maybe twenty, and at least half as many bathrooms. There are three kitchens, though we only use the one unless we're hosting guests. Over that way is the theater. Calvin's great uncle was very fond of the cinema, apparently. The greenhouse you'll have seen on the way in is his great grandmother's doing. Bit of a green thumb, by all accounts."

"No observatory?" I asked, numbly.

"No, but what a good idea! I'll have to mention that to Calvin. He's always enjoyed a bit of star gazing."

We continued on like this for a while, with Makayla pointing out the mansion's finer features: the pipes that ran beneath the marble floors to keep them warm during the winter months, the remarkable craftsmanship that extended from banisters to busts, and of course the numerous displays of art—a collection which included water-worn statues of gargoyles that I could have sworn I'd seen nestled between the buttresses of Notre Dame.

But then, I supposed that *was* possible. After all, while the famous cathedral was a preeminent house of worship, it was said the Temples were richer than God.

And what better way to prove it than to nick His things?

I froze.

Had one of those gargoyles just blinked at me? I squinted suspiciously, only to see the grotesque creature's bat-like wings flex ever so slightly. I stifled a startled cry.

Makayla tittered joyously. "Oh, don't mind them. They don't attack." She furrowed a brow. "Well, not that often. One of Calvin's many creations. He's a tinkerer, you see. Not quite a Maker, but he does like to pay homage to the greats, as he says. Men, what can you do?"

I nodded along as though this was all perfectly natural, though that didn't stop me from giving the statues a wide berth. Makayla, meanwhile, reached out to pet a scaled Stryga as we passed, and I swear I saw the monster's tail wag back and forth like a loyal dog's.

I shuddered as we ascended a large and winding stairway, the lush carpet muffling our steps. Once again, I found myself wondering just who my host had mistaken me for, to say nothing of how I'd ended up here in the first place. I'd begun to strongly suspect these were not dreams after all, but rather actual events I was being made privy to. The question was why.

"Who d'ye t'ink I—" I began.

"We're here," Makayla interjected, her hand on the knob of a door just to the right of the staircase. "Oh, sorry, did you say something?"

I opened my mouth to repeat my question, but then thought better of it. Whatever *this* was, I didn't get the sense there was any malice in it. Perhaps it would be better to play along for the time being, at least until I knew more. After all, there might be risks associated with revealing my true identity that I couldn't anticipate.

What if the Temples decided I was an imposter and opted to have me thrown out rather than help me sort through the confusion? Or worse, what if they lashed out, instead? Going toe-to-toe with a pair of powerful wizards on their home turf...no thank you.

"Nothin'," I said, gesturing for her to continue what she'd been doing. "It wasn't important."

Makayla flashed me a questioning look but went ahead and knocked. "Calvin? It's us."

"What's the password?" came the reply.

"He thinks he's very funny," Makayla whispered to me. Then, in a louder voice, "You better be decent! We're coming in."

"I make no promises."

Makayla rolled her eyes. Cigar smoke, wispy and aromatic, wafted out to greet us as she opened the door. The room itself was dominated by an enormous desk, beyond which stood a man silhouetted by the light of an open window. Calvin Temple turned, and I was struck by the marked resemblance to his son—much more pronounced without the additional years weighing on his face.

The wizard smiled and hurriedly put out his cigar, waving for us to join him inside. "Sorry about that. I had a few things to wrap up before we see the boys. I trust Makayla kept you entertained with anecdotes about our humble family home?"

"A few," I replied.

"Good, good. I swear, if these walls could talk..." Calvin rapped a knuckle against the nearest one and winked at his wife. "Did Makayla tell you the one about old Abelard and his second cousin twice removed?"

"I didn't think that was an appropriate story to tell a guest," Makayla interjected, sternly, though the twitch of her lips suggested otherwise.

"Poisoned his tea," Calvin whispered conspiratorially behind a raised hand, his eyes twinkling with mischief. "Apparently he was astral projecting places he shouldn't have been. I'm sure you know what I mean."

"Calvin," Makayla chastised.

Calvin shrugged. "Just goes to show that no matter how ancient or 'pure' the bloodline, there's always a chance they'll end up making a mess of things. Speaking of, should we be on? The longer we wait, the more likely Wylde will have turned our backyard into a battlefield."

"Wylde?" I echoed.

"Nate," Makayla clarified, staring pointedly at her husband. "He means Nate."

Calvin arched an eyebrow, his gaze growing distant and pensive, as if he were entertaining a philosophical question of great importance. "Do I?"

13

Together, the three of us left Chateau Falco behind for the thriving woods that covered the estate, following a dirt trail that appeared to have been recently cleared. We spoke very little as we walked—me because I wasn't sure what I *could* say without incriminating myself, while the other two seemed lost in thought. After several more minutes of silence, I caught the sound of laughter and a squeal of excitement drifting through the air.

"That'll be the boys," Makayla informed me. "They've taken to playing make-believe out here. Calvin even helped them build a fort."

"I *supervised*," Calvin amended, dryly. "The end result was all their doing."

We rounded a bend in the trail and came upon a clearing at the center of which stood a two-tiered treehouse fashioned out of timber and fortified with sheet metal. The words "Chateau Defiance" had been painted across a plank in bold red letters and hung above a narrow set of stairs for all to see.

Two little boys squared off at the top level, their faces ruddy with dirt and snot and sweat. Both boys were blonde, though only the one on the right—a stocky and uncommonly pale lad—was destined to stay that way. The other—olive-skinned and rake thin—would not.

"Nate," I said aloud, recognizing at once the wizard's diminutive features. "But...who's the other boy?"

Calvin smirked. "That would be Gunnar."

Ah, yes, of course. Gunnar Randulf, Nate's best friend from childhood. I supposed I should have known. Indeed, I'd even met the former Alpha Werewolf once, although at the time he'd been a great deal...hairier. Not to mention larger.

"He's the one we told you about," Makayla said, taking the conversational baton from her husband. "The one we were hoping you could help. I...don't suppose you stumbled across anything?"

I frowned. "Stumbled across what, exactly?"

"Something that could make it easier for the child to control the change," she supplied, helpfully. "As things stand, the boy is a slave to his...well, I wouldn't call it a curse. But it certainly won't make his life any easier."

"Ye mean him bein' a werewolf?"

Makayla nodded.

"Ye t'ink there might be a way to control it?"

"We hope there is," Calvin clarified. "It's not just for Gunnar's sake, you understand. Wylde...Nate...is having trouble adjusting to this world. Its rules. Its...rigidity. That's partly why we want to help Gunnar. If the boy can learn to master his baser urges and repress his wild side, perhaps he can help our son to do the same."

I coughed a laugh into my fist; judging from what I knew of Nate Temple, I could be reasonably certain his parents had failed to restrain his "baser urges." Still, I could appreciate what the Temples were hoping to achieve. I simply wasn't sure how I was supposed to help.

"I'm not—" I began.

Before I could finish, little Nate clapped his hands together and threw them towards the sky with a primal shout. For a moment, it seemed like nothing was going to happen. Then, just as I was about to turn away, I saw something forming between the boy's hands. A tiny, glowing orb wreathed in wisps of smoke. No, not smoke...clouds.

Unfortunately, it only lasted for a few seconds before winking out of existence.

Nate sagged and gave his friend a weak smile full of missing teeth. Gunnar returned the gesture, called out a challenge, and soon both children were chasing one another as though nothing strange had happened.

I blinked in stunned disbelief. Had Nate just tried to conjure up a fucking *moon*? I mean sure, he hadn't exactly succeeded, but he'd gotten a whole lot closer than he had any right to. And I was pretty damned sure that wasn't something any ordinary wizard could do.

"Hold on," I said, squinting at the place where the orb had hung. "What the hell was that?"

Calvin was busy massaging the bridge of his nose. "Magic. Sort of."

"He gets it from his father," Makayla added, smirking. "Too clever by half, the both of them."

Calvin snorted. "Podsnappery. I don't recall ever summoning a moon in my backyard just so I could help my best friend shift."

"There, there." Makayla patted his shoulder. "Some of us are just late bloomers, dear. There's no shame in it."

Calvin shrugged her off with a wry smile.

I, however, was too busy thinking about the moon to appreciate the banter. Not the moon Nate had just conjured out of thin air, but the one Morgan le Fay had so recently mentioned.

"Surely not," I muttered.

Perhaps alerted by my tone, the two Temples turned to me as one, their expressions expectant. Rather than elaborate, however, I unzipped my leather jacket and probed at the lining within. It was there, tucked away in a pocket, that I found a rolled up sheet of paper. No, not paper, I amended.

Vellum.

"I t'ink this might be what you're lookin' for," I said as I produced the scroll and handed it over for their perusal. The Temples exchanged looks but wasted little time before untying the ribbon and unraveling the scroll.

"Oh, my!" Makayla cried. "How remarkable. Wherever did you find such a thing?"

"From an enchantress," I answered, honestly.

"It really could work," Calvin acknowledged, one finger perched on his lips. "A tattoo. So simple, and yet also quite brilliant. These symbols are ancient. Much closer to rune magic than anything you'd find in the Academy's libraries."

"It *will* work," Makayla replied. "I know it will. Thank you! You have no idea what this will mean for Gunnar. A werewolf who can control when and where he shifts is sure to become a king among his packmates."

At that moment, Calvin and Makayla's son let out a shout and kicked his companion full on in the chest, sending the poor boy soaring off the upper level to land on his back with a sickening thud. I sucked in a breath, dreading the possibility that Nate had just killed his best friend and that it was somehow my fault for interfering— that whatever was happening here had more in common with *The Butterfly Effect* than *Back to the Future*.

Before I could get too worked up, however, the young werewolf leapt to his feet with an explosive laugh, brushed off his pants, and went racing after Nate, who was already squealing with laughter as he fled.

I sighed in relief.

"I t'ink I may have some idea," I replied at last, my mind's eye picturing the Alpha Werewolf lording over his pack in his bipedal form. "But you're welcome."

Makayla flashed me a smile and grabbed her husband's arm. "Come on, Calvin, we should go and tell the boys. They'll be thrilled."

"You go on ahead, dear. I've got something I need to talk to our friend about. I won't be long."

Makayla squeezed Calvin's arm affectionately, took the scroll, and bounded off towards the fort like someone half her age.

"She seems happy," I noted.

"She does, doesn't she?"

"Sorry?"

"It's nothing. Forget it."

"Okay," I drawled, mindful of the wizard's suddenly grave expression. "So...what was it ye wanted to say to me?"

Calvin shook himself. "I wanted you to know that I've done what you asked. The entrance to the Elder Realm is shut, and can only be opened once Makayla and I are gone. As for the rest, I've already begun laying the foundations. The Table has been installed per your wishes, and the relevant parties forewarned."

I frowned, wishing I had even the faintest clue what the Temple patriarch was blabbing about. Unfortunately, it all sounded like gibberish to me. Maybe he was building something? That would explain the bit about laying foundations and installing a table. The forewarned parties could be his neighbors—though what any of that had to do with this so-called Elder Realm was beyond me.

"Sounds good," I replied evenly, worried I'd give myself away if I said anything more specific.

Calvin nodded. "The key to open the seal will be a code of my own devising, though I'll have to break it into parts to keep it from falling into the wrong hands."

"Naturally."

"When the time comes for the way to be closed again, you need only say the words 'I will show you fear in a handful of dust.' I trust you'll know when to use it."

"Uh huh..."

Calvin fell silent for a moment, his gaze locked on his wife and the two boys as they huddled around the scroll. "Do you think he'll have what it takes to survive what's coming?"

"Well, I—"

"Actually, nevermind. It was a silly question. We've come too far to turn back now, haven't we, old friend?"

Calvin clasped a hand on my shoulder, shook me gently, and smiled. Then, he went to join his family, leaving me to speculate over his final words. Sadly, I had neither the context nor the capacity to dissect them.

And so, feeling more muddled than ever since I began leaping through time and space, I thrust my hands into the pockets of my jacket and leaned against a tree. Or at least I tried; one pocket proved too full to accommodate my hand.

"Oh, right," I said aloud, "the rosary."

Only it wasn't just the rosary. There was also the object I'd kept on my person ever since leaving the Underworld—a gift given to me by the Temples themselves under equally mysterious circumstances, albeit in a far less idyllic location. A gift that, perhaps, they'd want returned?

"Now is not the time."

"Jesus Christ!" I swore, disturbed by the unexpected presence of the shrouded woman at my side, her outmoded outfit even more out of place here in the harsh light of day than it had been back in the alley. "D'ye enjoy sneakin' up on me like that?"

"Perhaps if you were more observant, we wouldn't have this problem."

I rolled my eyes. "Don't give me that shite. Are ye the one doin' this? Sendin' me from one place to the next? And what the hell d'ye mean 'now isn't the time?'"

Rather than reply, the shrouded woman gestured for me to look up. As if on cue, an enormous stormcloud appeared and began to charge across the sky, obscuring the sun so thoroughly it was as if darkness itself had fallen. A great gust of wind came roaring across the treetops, sending twigs and leaves flying in its wake.

"Stop it!" I shouted, angrily. "Whatever it is ye t'ink you're doin', stop it!"

The shrouded woman had to shout to be heard over the crash of thunder. "The storm does not belong to me! It's chasing you. The question is, would you rather stay here and weather it on your own, or would you rather come with me?"

"And go where?"

"Somewhere the storm will have trouble finding you. Somewhere you will be needed, as you were needed here."

"Needed for what?"

The shrouded woman said nothing, but instead reached out for me the way one might a lover. I hesitated, my gaze oscillating between her gloved hand and the oncoming storm. Even now, I could sense the raw hunger that drove it—a need so perversely strong that it made my skin crawl.

"Ah, fuck it," I hissed.

And I took her hand.

14

"You have been given a gift, yes? Use it, and eventually you will come to understand what you are capable of, and what your true purpose is."

15

Her hand fell away, and I stumbled backwards, nearly tripping over a divan in the process. Once I'd regained my footing, I saw we no longer stood beneath the canopy of a towering oak tree, but beneath that of a spacious Bedouin tent. It was a jarring transition; where moments ago there had been dirt and rocks and trees, there were now hand-woven carpets, clay pots, tasseled pillows, and sturdy poles—the dappled sunlight replaced by the orange glow of a gas lantern dangling from an iron hook.

"Where the hell are we, now?" I asked, forced to raise my voice over the sound of what I could only assume was a ferocious storm raging outside.

"Somewhere in the Saharan desert," replied the shrouded woman. "And caught in the eye of a particularly nasty sandstorm, by the sounds of it."

Now that she mentioned it, I realized what I'd mistaken for gusting rain might in fact have been sand and dust whirling madly about. Not that she'd adequately answered my question.

"I meant why here?" I clarified.

"Because it's where you're meant to be."

"That's not an answer."

The shrouded woman shrugged but said nothing, her expression obscured beneath the shadows of her cowl. Indeed, I could deduce nothing from looking at her except that she was of average height and especially fond of the color black; she wore a black velvet gown beneath the cloak, complete with gloves of the same material.

I decided to change my approach.

"Who are ye, anyway?"

"Who I am doesn't matter."

I scoffed at that. "It matters to me, or I wouldn't be askin'. Surely ye have a name?"

"Once, perhaps. But no, not anymore."

"Look," I said, disgusted, "enough of the runaround. Either ye tell me who ye are, or I'll...I'll..."

"Or you'll what?"

"Or I'll beat the livin' shit out of ye. How's that?"

"Is that all? If so, you're welcome to try."

For a moment, I actually considered following through on my threat. Regrettably, I could tell from her tone that a fight wouldn't solve this particular problem; the only people unfazed by the threat of violence were either total nutters or already acclimated to it, and she didn't strike me as the crazy type.

I sighed. "Fine then, have it your way. I'll just give ye a name, since ye won't tell me. How about...Simourney Griever?"

She just stared at me.

"No? Then how about Whoa, Black Betty."

"Why would—"

"Bam-ba-lam."

The mirthless spectre shook her head and waved me off. "Call me whatever you like. It doesn't matter."

"Mourna Lisa it is."

The shrouded woman, who I'd actually decided to call Veil if only for simplicity's sake, went on as though I hadn't spoken. "The storm should not be able to find you here. Not for a while, anyway."

"About that. What the hell was that t'ing, anyway? It's no ordinary storm, obviously."

"No, it isn't. I suppose you'd call it a sending of sorts. It's an immensely powerful spell fueled by death magic. One designed to fulfill a very specific purpose."

"Which is?"

"To find you, apparently."

"Why me?"

"That I don't know. Not yet, anyway."

I rolled my eyes. "Sure ye don't. Then what about that phrase ye used for it? Dark Horse? What's that about?"

"It's an archaic term for that sort of spell, as well as for the type of person who might cast it, amongst other things."

"And who would that be?"

"I already told you, I do not know."

While I sensed she might be lying about that, it wasn't like I could debate the point—not unless I was willing to punctuate my argument with my fists. Instead, I weighed the dozens of questions my little forays through time and space had incurred.

"Then maybe ye can tell me what is happenin' to me, instead?" I asked, hoping to tackle the most outstanding item first. "I told meself this must all be some sort of fever dream, especially in the beginning. But I can't see how that could possibly be the case. There are way too many details. Too much I could never have conjured up, even in me wildest dreams."

Veil nodded. "You're correct. All that you have witnessed and done so far has indeed happened just as you saw it."

"But how? And why?"

"That I cannot say."

"Can't?" I growled, taking a threatening step forward. "Or won't?"

"Can't," she replied, firmly. "It is my duty to ensure you reach your intended destinations, not to reveal the path you must walk. What I can tell you, however, is that the path will be one of your own choosing. I am not here to interfere, only to escort. And perhaps to educate."

"Educate?"

"Of course. Free will is a minefield that makes casualties of us all, which means the best way to avoid blowing yourself up is to find out where the landmines are buried."

"Or maybe don't walk out into a minefield," I joked.

Veil nodded. "The coward's way out. Always a popular choice."

"That was supposed to be a joke. I am *not* a—"

The shrouded woman raised a finger in warning. "I'd wait a while before you finish that sentence. The lies we tell ourselves are often best kept *to* ourselves."

"What the hell is that supposed to mean?"

"It means you will have many choices to make before this is all said and done, and that not every decision comes without a price."

"Could ye possibly *be* more cryptic?"

Veil said nothing.

I sighed and threw up my hands. "Fine. Have it your way. So, what kind of decisions are we talkin'? Which restaurant to go to for brunch on a Sunday? What to pack for a trip to Vegas? Which shoes to wear for a blind date?"

"Not exactly. More like the spur of the moment kind. The kind all of us must make under duress. Whether or not to chase after a group of malcontents bent on doing harm, for instance. Or perhaps whether or not to intervene on behalf of an afflicted child."

"Oh, come on," I replied, seeing at once where she was going. "Those weren't decisions. Those were like...common sense. I mean—"

Veil halted me with a hand. "Unconscious or not, your actions were your own. Whether it's to stop and pick up a piece of trash littering the ground or leaping in front of a bus to save a child makes no difference. We are each compelled to do as we desire in the moment."

"Okay...but what if I'd chosen to do nothin'? What then?"

Veil shrugged. "That, too, would have been a choice. Though one you'd probably have regretted."

I wanted to deny it, but I couldn't exactly refute her claim. There was simply no way I'd have abandoned those girls to their fates no matter who they'd been, just as there was no way I'd have let my younger self get caught red-handed if I could prevent it. As for my brief exchange with the Temples, well, I could honestly say I hadn't even considered holding back the scroll—not when they so clearly needed it.

"Be that as it may," I replied after a moment's hesitation, "why should I go along with whatever this is? For all I know, this could be an elaborate trap. Ye could be trickin' me somehow, or leadin' me into a life-threatenin' situation, or messin' with me mind."

"And does it feel like that's what's happening here?"

"No," I admitted. "But then I'd be a fool not to at least suspect somethin' like that was goin' on, especially without proof to the contrary. Maybe if ye told me who ye really were, or whose brilliant idea this was in the first place..."

"I cannot." Veil raised a palm to silence my rebuttal before I could begin. "Though I *can* assure you that you will discover the answers to those questions on your own, in due time."

"How reassurin'," I drawled. "Could ye at least tell me how much longer we're goin' to play this little game before ye send me back home? Ye *do* plan on sendin' me back, right?"

Whatever Veil's reply might have been, however, was delayed by a conspicuous sound—or rather the unexpected absence of one—as the storm outside died down completely.

"Does that mean the sandstorm's over?" I asked, my voice booming in the sudden silence that had descended all around us.

"No," Veil replied, her spectral figure becoming more and more transparent by the second. "I believe it means your guests have finally arrived. Which is my cue to leave. Good luck, and remember: whatever choices you make from here on out, you alone will have to live with the consequences."

"Wait, where are ye—"

But she was already gone.

16

Two silhouettes appeared on the other side of the tent within seconds of Veil's departure, the pair huddled so close together it was tough to tell at first whether it was one individual or two. My so-called guests, according to Veil. Unsure what to expect or even what to do, I busied myself by tidying up—stacking pillows, gathering pots, and aligning rugs until the place stopped screaming Bohemian-chic.

"Hello?" called a man's gravelly voice just as I'd finished straightening the divan. "Is anyone home?"

"There is," I confirmed, approaching the entrance warily. "And who are ye?"

"My name is Titus, and beside me is my wife, Constance. We were told we might find shelter here."

I frowned. Their names were unfamiliar to me, though I supposed that wasn't terribly surprising; I couldn't think of anyone I knew on this continent, let alone a married couple seeking shelter in the third largest desert on the planet, during a sandstorm. The question was, what were they seeking shelter from?

"Please," he went on, presumably taking my prolonged silence for reticence. "We have come a very long way, and my wife needs rest. She's almost nine months pregnant."

"Well ye could've just led with that," I grumbled as I peeled back the tent flap and gestured for the mysterious pair to come inside.

As they crossed the threshold, however, the wind started to pick back up, which meant I was suddenly too busy attending to the tent to take stock of my newly welcomed guests.

By the time I'd finished, the husband was busy lowering his tremendously pregnant wife onto the divan. The woman, Constance, hissed as she sank back onto her haunches, the sheer size of her belly making it difficult to sit upright. Instead, she teetered to the side, propped up by pillows provided by her husband.

They were clearly a doting couple—the sort who could display affection without advertising it. Attractive, too. Titus was taller than I was by a few inches, his frame so large I could see it bulging beneath his poncho. A beige shawl covered his neck and head, though the few strands of hair poking out from beneath it were uncommonly pale, pairing remarkably well with his bright blue eyes.

Constance, meanwhile, was the sort of woman who defied pregnancy; despite her enormous belly, she had the lean silhouette of a runner. Indeed, she seemed especially suited to the condition, if only because the color in her cheeks brought out the light in her eyes. Her hair, visible now that she'd stripped off her own shawl, was a rich and vibrant gold.

"Enough, Titus," she said, patting her husband's arm. "Sit down. You should rest, too."

"Of course, dear."

But Titus stayed standing, and I noticed his right hand remained hidden beneath his poncho as he took a look around. Meanwhile, the storm outside continued to beat against the tent, the wind howling like a pack of wild dogs.

"So, tell me," I began, "what brings the two of ye all this way out here?"

"We could ask the same of you," Titus replied. "What's a witch like you doing camped in the middle of the desert?"

A witch? I glanced down at myself, noticing for the first time the peculiar outfit I wore—a scandalous display of sheer silk and light cotton sashes. Indeed, so many beads hung from my neck I felt like a Mardi Gras float. Still, I didn't exactly scream Hocus Pocus. More like Hoe-cus Poke-us, if you catch my drift. So why call me a witch?

"Titus," Constance interjected, sternly. "There's no need for that. She was merely asking a question. I'm sorry, you'll have to forgive my husband. He was raised to be a tad...overzealous. And we aren't exactly in the habit of answering probing questions posed to us by strangers."

"I see," I replied, nodding. "Still, I t'ink it's only fair to wonder what exactly it is the two of ye are seekin' shelter from. Is it the storm? Or somethin' more?"

Constance's eyes narrowed. "What makes you think that?"

"Him, mostly." I pointed at Titus. "Or whatever it is he keeps fondlin' beneath that poncho. In my experience, shite weather forecasts call for a coat and umbrella, not a weapon. Unless ye t'ink ye can take a pot shot at Mother Nature, in which case more power to ye."

"It could be you I'm worried about," Titus replied, defiantly.

"Aye, it could be. But, if it was, I expect you'd have drawn already. After all, ye had plenty of time to do so while I was seein' to the tent. Your wife saw to that when she canceled the spell keepin' the storm at bay."

Constance frowned. "How'd you know?"

"Your clothes, mostly. You're both clean as a whistle, when ye should be covered in the stuff. Plus, it all seemed rather too convenient. The storm stoppin' and startin' up again like that. Magic seemed the likeliest explanation. I'm guessin' you're some kind of wizard, then?"

The couple exchanged looks.

Constance sighed. "He did warn us you'd be smart.".

"He?"

"The one who sent us. Another wizard, and someone I trust. He insisted that if we were ever in trouble we should find our way here.

He said whomever we stumbled across would keep us safe. And that they'd be clever."

"A wizard, huh?" I scowled, wishing that description narrowed down the possibilities to more than a few dozen people with whom I was acquainted. "And does this wizard have a name?"

"He does, but I'm certain he'd be cross if I were to share it with you. No offense."

I shrugged. "None taken. It's the answer I expected, to be honest. But that still leaves me earlier question. What exactly are the two of ye runnin' from?"

"Not what," Constance corrected. "Whom."

"The Nephilim," Titus explained. "They're—"

I raised a hand, cutting him off. "Angelic half-breeds. Heaven's frontline soldiers. Aye, I've run across the fanatic bastards once before."

Titus coughed into his fist. "I was actually going to say they're my brothers and sisters."

Of course they were. In hindsight, I could certainly see the resemblance; that near perfect physique and stunningly handsome bone structure was a trait all the Nephilim seemed to share. The difference between good genes and God genes, I supposed.

"Ah, sorry about that."

"It's fine. They are fanatics. And technically we're all bastards."

"They don't exactly approve of our union," Constance added. "Hence the theatrics. They nearly caught up with us back in Rome, so I brought us here."

"And thoroughly exhausted yourself in the process." Titus reached out to take his wife's hand. "Which I've repeatedly asked you to stop doing. I really could have handled them."

"I know, dear. I know."

And yet, for all her bravado, I could tell Constance wasn't so sure. There was a worn out look to them both that suggested sleepless nights and far too little rest. It was there in the bags beneath their eyes, the faint quiver of their clutched hands. They'd been on the run so long they probably couldn't even see it, but I knew from experience that they had only a few days left in them before the mistakes started to pile up.

Not that it would help much to warn them.

"How far along are ye?" I asked Constance, instead, hoping to change the subject to something a little less miserable.

The wizard snickered. "Far enough to feel like a human minivan driving around on flat tires. The baby will be here soon, if that's what you mean. A few more weeks at most."

"D'ye know the sex?"

"A girl," Titus replied, flashing a rare smile.

"That's nice. And how about a name? Have ye picked one out yet?"

Constance nodded. "Excalibur."

"Well...that's, uh, nice. Original."

Constance smirked at my awkwardness. "It's asking a lot, is what it is. But don't worry. She'll live up to it."

Her husband nodded his agreement.

"Right," I replied. "Well, that's great, then. And are ye plannin' to have her while you're on the run? Or, what I mean is, d'ye have some-place safe to go?"

Titus cocked his head. "Why do you think we're here?"

"Oh! Well, I...uh..."

"He's kidding," Constance assured me. "No. We have...friends who intend to help us. Powerful friends. We've already made the arrangements to stay with them until the baby's born. They're actu-ally our next stop, once we've rested here for a bit."

"Glad to hear it. Not that ye wouldn't have been welcome here. But, as ye can see, this isn't much of a maternity ward."

Not to mention the fact that I had no intention of hanging around for weeks to help deliver some stranger's baby, I added silently.

"Don't worry, I wouldn't want a total stranger delivering my baby, either," Constance said, clearly reading my mind. "Besides, that's not a target I'd willingly paint on anyone's back, let alone someone who's been kind to us."

I frowned, wondering if that had something to do with their

pursuers, or something else altogether. Not that the Nephilim weren't bad enough on their own. I'd dealt with them before, back in the day. I'd been visiting Manhattan on behalf of a friend and ended up embroiled in a convoluted power struggle between a scheming, skin-stealing demon and the Heavenly host—most of which seemed to consist of half-human, half-angel hybrids willing to go blade-to-claw against their unholy counterparts.

The question was, why were the Nephilim hunting one of their own? Surely fraternization with a wizard of the opposite sex wasn't against their Biblical by-laws. I meant, what ever happened to be fruitful and multiply? Or were Angelic mongrels exempt from that particular decree?

Before I could voice these thoughts, however, the three of us were spooked by what sounded eerily like a sonic boom—a thunderous cacophony that made the ground beneath our feet tremble.

"What the hell was that?" I wondered aloud.

"That's them," Titus replied hoarsely, his gaze drawn immediately to his prostrated, pregnant wife. "They've found us."

17

"Those goddamned bastards!"

"Titus, enough."

"Three times in less than a week," Titus continued, "and now twice in the same day. They must have found a new way to track us."

"Or they knew where we were headed, somehow," his wife added. "Either way, that's something we'll have to deal with later. Right now, we need to move."

The three of us were huddled together in the dark, having extinguished the lantern so as to evade the attention of the Nephilim scouts; it was their sudden arrival which had generated the cacophonous boom—a clap of thunder that signaled nothing but terror whenever it was heard, according to the married couple.

Though I wasn't sure they'd be able to spot me in the dim light provided by the faint glow of magic radiating from Constance's palm, I held up both hands in objection. "Wait, please. Stop and t'ink about what you're doin'. Ye aren't exactly in any condition to flee, either of ye. What we need is to come up with a plan, or some kind of distraction."

"We?" Constance sounded surprised. "There is no we. Of course we appreciate you taking us in, but the only path forward for you now is to run as far as you can from here and pray they don't follow."

"Or maybe don't pray at all," Titus suggested bitterly.

Yikes. A freaking *Nephilim* suffering from a crisis of faith—talk about losing your religion.

"Besides," Constance went on, "we already have a plan. All we need to do is head east until we reach the edge of the storm. I sent word to a...friend of mine to expect us in case we didn't find shelter here with you. He should still be waiting for us."

"And then what?" I asked.

"And then the Nephilim will be the least of our problems," Titus replied, sounding less than pleased by the prospect of meeting this so-called friend. Jealous, perhaps?

Constance patted his shoulder. "It can't be helped, dear. Thanks to Sanguina, I barely have enough magic left to keep the storm at bay, and we know they can track my Gateways. Now it seems even shadow walking isn't safe. This is our best chance. Maybe our only chance."

"Yes, you're right. Of course you're right."

"Hold on," I interjected. "Let me get this straight. Your plan is to go back out into the storm and head east for what could be miles, all while fendin' off any Nephilim ye come across along the way. That is until ye meet up with this friend of yours, at which point you'll be safe."

"Relatively safe," Titus replied.

"Why relatively?"

"He's saying the greater demon you know is sometimes better than the demon you don't," Constance replied. "Not that it's any concern of yours."

"And why wouldn't it be a concern of mine? I'm goin' with ye, after all."

"Excuse me?"

"At least as far as the storm's edge," I clarified. "After that, I imagine I'll be able to find me own way."

Sadly, it seemed Titus was having none of it; the black sheep of the family was shaking his head so hard back and forth I thought he might be having a seizure.

"I don't think you understand," he said. "My brothers and sisters are ruthless. They'll mow you down simply for sheltering us, not to mention what they'd do if you were spotted aiding our escape. Besides, protecting my wife will be hard enough without having to keep an eye on you, too."

I snorted an indelicate laugh. "Who said I needed ye to keep an eye on me? Ye may not have heard me before, but this wouldn't be the first time I've tangled with the Nephilim. Probably won't be the last, either, the way t'ings are shakin' out."

Not to mention the probability that *this* was what I'd been sent here to do, I added silently. After all, it wasn't like I was about to allow a woman in her third trimester and her husband to go traipsing off into the desert with targets painted on their backs—not when I could potentially step in and prevent it. As for the reason the Nephilim were after them...well, my gut said these two weren't the bad sort, and I'd learned a long time ago to trust my instincts in situations like these.

"False bravado won't save you when the time comes," Titus warned, sternly. "And neither will I. The safety of my wife and unborn child is what matters. Nothing else."

"Appreciate the pep talk. Now, d'ye have any extra weapons under that poncho ye wouldn't mind partin' with, or do I have to go out there and wail on your family with me bare hands?"

Titus grumbled something unintelligible, but I could hear him shifting about in the dark before he pressed something small and pathetically lightweight into my hand.

"A knife?" I asked, raising the blade. "Really?"

"That's all I'm willing to part with. Of course, if that doesn't work for you, you could always forget this foolishness and run."

"My husband is right," Constance insisted. "You'd be risking your life for a pair of total strangers. I cannot tell you how much we appreciate your offer, but it's not necessary. We can manage on our own."

I sighed, feeling a little like the scrawny kid no one wanted to pick to play dodgeball, or maybe the poor guy who keeps getting turned down for being too "nice."

"Look," I said, sharply, "have either of ye ever duked it out with a Firbolg with a devourer for an eye? Maybe taken down an undead Faelin' monster? A Master vampire? How about a god? Ever killed one of those? No? Then maybe ye should just say 't'anks for taggin' along' and move on so we can get the hell out of here before they find us debatin' who comes and who goes. Sound good?"

"You cannot honestly expect us to believe—" Titus began.

"And here, ye can have your little Swiss army knife back," I interrupted, passing him the blade. "I'm sure if and when your brothers and sisters come out to play, *they* won't mind sharin' their toys."

"Did you really kill a god?" Constance interjected, her voice strained as though she were suffering from a discomfort of some kind.

"I mean I had *help*."

Constance grunted. "And why would you want to help us? You barely know us."

I shrugged. "I know that ye love each other, and that you're pregnant and in trouble. That, if you're wrong and ye can't handle t'ings on your own, it could jeopardize not only your lives but your baby's life, as well. What else is there to know?"

The couple shifted their weight and exchanged a look I couldn't read on account of the darkness.

"Fine," Titus allowed. "But you have to agree to do what I say, when I say. We can't afford you taking any unnecessary risks."

I flashed him a thumbs up he couldn't see. "It's your show, Jesus Christ Superstar. Just lead the way."

18

Wary of any potential ambush, we snuck out only once we were sure no one had stumbled across our tent. Thankfully, it seemed the vicious sandstorm had provided ample cover. Grit and dust permeated the air, so thick we'd have choked on the stuff were it not for Constance, who was busy holding back the storm. The wizard had fashioned a faintly shimmering dome out of thin air, and it was within this magic bubble we traveled—able to see the raging storm, but incapable of feeling or even hearing it.

Titus took point while I took the rear, effectively putting Constance between us for her protection. Unfortunately, our pace was plodding at best. The terrain was especially tricky to navigate, the footing uncertain in every sense of the word. Personally, I couldn't have imagined a worse scenario for Constance; the woman's stamina was already being taxed by the spell, not to mention her prior physical limitations.

Indeed, the farther we went along, the clearer her struggle became.

"Titus," I called, my voice startlingly loud in the tight confines of our sealed space. "Shite, sorry. Titus?"

"What is it?"

"This isn't goin' to work."

The reformed Nephilim grunted. "It's too late to turn back now. Don't worry, if they haven't found us yet, it means they are probably as blind in this storm as we are. More so, probably."

"It's not that. It's your wife."

"Hmm? Constance, dear, how are you doing back there?"

"I'm fine."

"You're not fine," I insisted. "You're barely managin' to put one foot in front of the other. Ye should at least take your husband's arm. If ye collapse, we may all end up with lungs full of sand."

"I need my hands free," Titus replied, though I noticed he too sounded worried. "Why don't you—"

Titus clammed up as one of our pursuers stumbled blindly into our private little oasis. Positively caked in dust, the Nephilim scout sputtered at us in surprise and hefted his weapon—a gladius so freshly oiled that grit had formed a thick patina along the blade.

Titus intercepted the intruder immediately, dancing nimbly around his wife to catch the scout's wrist in mid-swing. He twisted it so savagely I could've sworn I heard the Nephilim's bones snap. The sword fell from the scout's numb fingertips, the blade sinking hilt-deep into the sand. Sensing his opportunity, Titus stepped in close and thrust his dagger into his assailant's belly several times before flinging the intruder back out into the storm.

"I take back what I said about your knife," I told him in the hushed silence that followed. "It's a very nice knife."

Titus grunted. "There'll be others where he came from. We need to be on our guard and move quickly."

Constance and I nodded in agreement, though I could tell the strain of our present circumstances was really beginning to take its toll on the poor woman; she'd gone pale, her eyes unfocused. Titus must have noticed, too, because he hastily stepped forward to take her hand.

Which was when the next Nephilim struck.

This one, armed with a Roman pilum, punched through

Constance's bubble at a trot and kept right on coming, lunging at the couple as if he intended to run them both through with his spear. Titus, thinking quickly, spun around to shield his wife from the blow.

Only the blow never landed.

With the Nephilim fully committed to his thrust, I doubted he even noticed me until I shoulder tackled him to the sand. The spear tumbled from his grasp to land somewhere behind us, but I wasn't concerned about the weapon. My goal was submission, plain and simple. To that end, I rolled away from my opponent, stripped off one of the cotton sashes, and rushed him from behind. Only this time I didn't tackle the bastard, but instead looped the sash around his throat and pulled with everything I had.

Now, ordinarily even that wouldn't have been enough to subdue a Heavenly half-breed; I'd seen them hold their own against terrifying demons thrice their size with twice as many limbs. Indeed, back then it had been all I could do to stay out of the way. But that was a long time ago, before I'd traveled to Fae and discovered my true heritage, before I'd traveled to Circe's island and unlocked my true potential, and before I'd gained access to Brunhilde's armor with all its physical endowments.

I could feel the armor's influence even now, underneath the strange clothes and disturbingly convincing illusions—augmenting my strength and reflexes to such a degree that I could not only keep up with a soldier of God, but put one to sleep with a simple application of leverage.

"Hope ye said your prayers," I said through gritted teeth. "Because it's time for ye to go night-night."

The Nephilim reached up to claw feebly at my arms, but I held fast, oblivious to the feeling of his fingernails gouging into my bare skin. Five seconds passed. Then ten. Finally, at fifteen, his head drooped and his hands fell limp to his sides.

I waited another couple heartbeats before releasing the sorry bastard to crumple face first into the sand with his ass in the air.

When at last I turned back around, I found Constance standing nearby, offering me a tired smile full of gratitude. Her husband, however, looked down on the results of my little bout with an expression of open respect.

He cleared his throat. "I'm really glad you decided to tag along. Thank you."

I grinned and punched his shoulder playfully. "You're welcome. Ye were right before, though, the longer we hang around in one place, the likelier it is they'll find us. We should hurry up and go while we still can."

Titus nodded. "You're right."

Unfortunately, one glance at Constance was enough to guarantee that would be easier said than done; the wizard was hunched in on herself in pain, her eyes pinched shut. Frankly, given her tormented expression, I was impressed she'd managed to keep the magic flowing.

"Oh no, Constance, are you alright?" Titus asked, taking her hand.

"I'm fine," she lied. "It's just a contraction. She's right up against my ribs, I think."

"Is there anything I can do?"

Constance shook her head.

"How many more Nephilim are out there?" I interrupted, wondering if we might be better served putting up a fight than running, especially with Constance in her current condition.

"The scouts usually travel in groups of five or six."

"Really? That's all? Well then maybe we could—"

"But they aren't the problem," Titus elaborated before I could propose an alternative plan. "The scouts aren't warriors. They're more like spies. They have thinner blood, which means they're primarily suited to blend in and locate targets, not to fight. The soldiers, on the other hand, are properly trained."

"I take it that means we should be expectin' company?"

"It's not unlikely, especially if the scouts fail to report in right away. Usually, they'd send in one or two soldiers at most to deal with a problem like this—"

"Like when they sent you to deal with me," Constance interjected with a weak laugh, her color slowly returning.

"Yes, dear," replied her husband. "Sadly, I don't think they'll find it in their hearts to spare us the way I did you. And I doubt they'll only send a few."

Constance snickered. "Me either. Not after what we did to the last bunch."

"Alright, new plan," I said as I plucked the defeated Nephilim's spear from the sand. "Titus, ye stay by your wife and make sure she doesn't fall. I'll—"

"Actually," Titus interrupted, "I think I should carry her. If we run, there's a chance we clear the storm before the soldiers arrive. Assuming you can stand the indignity, my love..."

"Desperate times, desperate measures, is that it?" Constance sighed. "Fine. Just don't you dare drop me. And I don't want to hear any complaints if I vomit on you."

"I wouldn't dream of it, dear," replied her husband.

They really were a lovely couple.

19

We took off at a trot with Constance nestled in her husband's arms, leaving the fallen Nephilim behind to be swallowed up by the storm. The wizard didn't seem too thrilled by the constant jostling, but she managed to maintain her magic field nonetheless. We saw no immediate sign of the remaining Nephilim scouts, though I couldn't say I was surprised; between the lack of visibility and the sheer size of the desert, I imagined they'd have had an easier time finding a New York Giants fan in a Southie bar than tracking us down while we were on the move.

Of course, those odds increased with every passing moment.

"How much farther until we reach the edge of the storm, d'ye t'ink?" I called.

"I'm not sure," Titus replied. "Had you turned us away, our plan was to rendezvous somewhere to the east."

"Somewhere to the...ye do realize this is one of the largest deserts in the world, right?"

"It shouldn't matter. Once we're out in the open, I'm sure he'll find us."

"Find us, how?"

Titus sniffed. "If I knew the answer to that, we wouldn't be in this situation."

"I don't follow."

"It's not important. All you need to know is that my brothers and sisters aren't the only ones keeping tabs on us."

"I see. And why is that, again?"

"We already told you, they—"

"Don't like the idea of the two of ye bein' together, aye. I got that, Romeo and Juliet. Now why do I feel like that's not all there is to it?"

Titus fell silent rather than reply, which told me my hunch was very likely spot on. Unfortunately, a hunch was all I had; whatever the pair were up to, I could only guess it had something to do with the eternal war between Heaven and Hell. A war I only knew about thanks to my brief stint in Manhattan...and, you know, my Catholic upbringing.

That said, I felt a sort of empathy for these two that I couldn't rightly explain. Perhaps it was the closet romantic in me rooting for a young couple on the lam, or perhaps I was simply relieved to discover Veil hadn't lied, and that I was indeed allowed to do as I saw fit—even if that entailed strangling the Spy Who Saved Me.

"We aren't far," Constance chimed in weakly after a few moments. "The wind has changed. I can feel it. The storm is headed west now, which means it should pass over us soon. We should be seeing him shortly."

"Aye? Well, that's good news."

Titus, however, didn't seem so certain. "That means our cover will be gone soon, as well. You're sure he'll find us in time?"

"We're bonded, Titus. Besides, we both know how much he is willing to risk for Lily's sake. He'll be there. I'm sure of it."

20

Unfortunately, it appeared Constance was wrong.

When at last we reached a clear patch of desert, the wizard dropped her shield and promptly leaned on her husband, where she remained for several minutes before suggesting we march up the slope of the largest dune we could find in search of their would-be savior. From its crest, however, we saw nothing but more sand dunes snaking out towards the horizon like an ochre ocean frozen in time.

After leaving the pitch black darkness of the storm behind, I was pleasantly surprised to find the sun had yet to set—leaving the sky a soft, cloudless shade of muted purple. Sadly, what little satisfaction I'd gleaned from the spectacular view was being offset by the mounting tension in the air.

Titus squinted, his handsome face bathed in orange light, and folded his arms across his chest. "Is it possible he failed to receive your message?"

"Possible," Constance replied. "But unlikely."

"Can't you feel him with your bond?"

"I...already tried. He isn't here. Or if he was, he's gone now."

The Nephilim muttered a curse under his breath.

"Titus—"

"No," he snapped. "I knew we should never have trusted a demon. This is *their* fault. They should never have pushed you to cut ties with Solomon. If he were here—"

"Titus! That's enough!"

Constance shot me a look as if to say "you didn't hear that." I raised both hands in mock surrender. Not that it made much difference to me, either way; I hadn't the faintest idea what they were talking about. I was, however, on Titus' side in at least one respect: things were looking a bit grim for us. At this point, it was clear that no help was coming.

But then...maybe I was the help? Perhaps I was meant to be the savior of this situation. After all, why else would Veil have dumped me here? Of course it was also possible I was moments away from tossing back a double-shot of hubris, no chaser.

Either way, with no one coming to the rescue and our pursuers due to emerge from the storm at any moment, it seemed like things couldn't possibly get worse.

But of course they could.

And they did.

Constance, having turned back to look the way we'd come, cried out in sudden alarm. Titus and I spun with our weapons raised, prepared to fight, only there were no enemies to be found. Indeed, for the moment all seemed peaceful—the desert sands empty, the dunes backlit by the falling sun. Titus slid his blade back into its sheath and sidled up next to his wife.

"Constance, what is it?"

"Contraction," she hissed, clutching at her swollen belly. "A big one. Titus...I think she's coming early."

Titus blanched. "Now?"

Constance grimaced. "Not now. But soon."

Before her husband could reply, a thunderous crack rent the sky, followed by a blinding light and what I could have sworn was the bleating of trumpets. I shielded my eyes until the light faded, then lowered my arm to find a towering being shrouded in dust standing some fifty yards away. Behind him extended an enormous pair of wings fashioned from bleached bone, while in his hands he held a length of chain made entirely of flame.

"Who the fuck is that?"

"Ramiel," whispered an awed Titus. "God's Thunder, and the Archangel of Hope. No wonder Samael never showed."

I grunted, not the least bit impressed with Titus' bad habit of Biblical name-dropping. In my, admittedly limited, experience, angels were pompous elitists with their halos shoved so far up their asses they could see light at the end of the tunnel. "Not a friend of yours, I take it?"

"No," he replied, his face so pale I thought he might faint at any moment. "More like an ancestor. A notoriously preachy, powerful ancestor."

Constance cried out again as the Archangel began marching menacingly towards us, only this time she was in such pain she was unable to support herself. The wizard collapsed into her husband's arms, and the couple sank to their knees in the sand. Titus looked up at me as he cradled his wife, his gaze desperate and pleading. Unfortunately, there was only so much I could do to help.

"The best I can do is buy ye some time," I told the poor Nephilim. "Maybe enough to put some distance between ye and Assrael."

"It's not...oh, Assrael. Like Azriel. Clever."

I shrugged. "It was either that or the Angel in the Outhouse."

Titus snorted, though I could tell from his troubled expression how little he thought of their chances now that one of Heaven's finest had taken up the chase—not to mention Constance's current condition. At this point, the question wasn't whether they'd be captured, but when.

I cracked my neck as the colossal figure neared. "I don't suppose ye have any tips for fightin' an Archangel?"

"Yeah," Titus replied. "Don't do it."

"I was afraid you'd say that." I moved to coil a finger beneath the bracelet around my wrist, preparing myself mentally for the sudden release of power bound to accompany its removal—an exercise I'd gone through several times since receiving the powerful artifact—only to find it missing.

"Wait!" Constance latched a hand onto my forearm, her grip so tight I could practically feel my bones grinding together. "Her magic. I can feel—"

A wave of scalding heat poured along my flesh where her hand touched, followed almost immediately by a frigid blast of cold. Silver light began to emanate from that hand, then radiate up the wizard's arm to eventually surround her in a metallic penumbra. Constance groaned, then screamed, as raw power coursed through her body.

Seeing this, the Archangel took to the air, but it was too late; Constance had already flung out a hand and sent all that roaring power out into the aether, tearing a hole in the fabric of space. A portal, otherwise known as a Gateway—although this particular portal was hemmed in silver flame that danced like glinting steel shards.

Stranger still, I'd seen its like before.

"Is that...?" I muttered, so distracted by the naggingly familiar sight that I didn't even notice Titus scooping the two of us up and rushing through the Gateway until I was parallel with the ground and being bounced around.

"Oy!" I yelped. "Put me down!"

Titus obliged, tossing me to the ground as the Gateway snapped shut behind us. I landed hard but remarkably unscathed, my arms and legs pricked by blades of freshly mown grass, the scent of which was heavy in the night air.

I rolled over, took a look around, and found myself strewn across a strikingly familiar lawn that gave way to an even more familiar mansion. I sat up, too stunned to speak. Lit up as it was, Chateau Falco appeared less stately and more glamorous, like something out of a Baz Lurhmann film. Moreover, there was a completely different energy about the place from when I was last here. A turbulent, feral energy—the sort that had the hairs on the back of my neck standing straight up.

"You did great, my love," Titus said as he gently lowered his wife to her feet, seemingly oblivious to whatever I was sensing. "I had no idea you could still manage a Gateway. But it won't take them long to follow us. Not with Remiel on the prowl. We have to try and—"

Constance raised a hand.

"Not...this time," she interjected, her breathing ragged. "They won't be able...to follow us through...that Gateway. Something... different about it."

I'd climbed to my feet and only just opened my mouth to ask Constance to elaborate on that when the doors to the mansion were thrown open and an all-too-familiar figure came rushing out wearing a rather scandalous bit of negligée. Makayla Temple, looking even younger and in fact quite fit as she raced across the lawn, took one look at Constance before calling to another figure in the doorway.

"Prepare the parlor. We have guests."

The figure vanished inside.

With that done, Makayla hurried over, spared Titus a cursory smile, and took Constance's hand. "Don't take this the wrong way, hon, but you don't look so great."

"Contractions," Constance replied through gritted teeth.

Makayla's eyes widened. "How far apart?"

"Not...sure."

"We weren't exactly able to keep an accurate count," I offered, helpfully. "But, if I had to guess, I'd say ten, maybe fifteen minutes?"

Makayla shot me a guarded look that jived very poorly with the peppy, bubbly wizard I'd met a mere hour ago when giving her Gunnar's rune.

"And who is this?" she asked, the wizard's voice hissing like a dagger sliding across velvet—and I was the velvet.

"She's not an enemy, Makayla," Titus assured her, saving me the trouble of having to answer the loaded question. "She sheltered us and then helped us escape at the risk of her own life."

Makayla looked as though she might argue, but Constance chose that moment to utter another long and wretched moan. Her grip on Makayla's hand tightened and stayed that way for perhaps a full minute before the contraction passed and she was able to let go.

Once Constance was breathing normally again and Makayla had regained use of her hand, the owner of the mansion swept out an arm towards the gaping doorway. "Let's get you inside. Calvin is with the Archwizard, dismantling the sword. They should be finished soon."

Constance and Titus exchanged startled glances.

"Already?" Titus asked.

Makayla smirked. "Quite the coincidence, isn't it? Him showing up the same night you do."

"I don't believe in coincidences," Constance replied, though for some reason her gaze was locked on me when she said it. "How about you?"

I pointed at myself.

The wizard nodded.

I paused to think about that—about the fact that I'd ended up outside Chateau Falco yet again, only this time in the company of two individuals on Heaven's Evange-hit-list. About the fact that one of those individuals was pregnant and able to produce a Gateway that happened to be identical to one I'd seen before. About the fact that my every decision, freely made or not, seemed to be leading me down remarkably similar paths.

"Ye want to know if I believe in coincidences?" I snorted a laugh. "Yeah...after the day I've had? Not a fuckin' chance."

21

I f my reply bothered the trio, they at least had the grace not to show it. Indeed, Constance seemed pleased by my candor; she flashed me a wry smile as she turned to take the hands of her husband and friend, neither of whom seemed to know what to make of our little exchange.

Together, the four of us began making our laborious way across the impeccably manicured lawn when I spotted a telltale flash of red lightning some miles in the distance. The others must have missed it, because none of them said a word as they continued to shuffle towards the entrance. I lagged back, realizing with a sinking feeling in my gut that my time here was coming to an end.

Constance must have noticed, however, because she stopped. "What is it? Is something wrong?"

"I'm afraid I can't come with ye."

"Why not?"

I let my eyes wander in the direction of the oncoming storm—the spell Veil had dubbed the Dark Horse. It was moving slower than usual but was certain to arrive with the same force as before, accompanied by that bloodcurdling miasma.

Assuming I stuck around.

I debated how much or how little to tell the wizard before settling on an extremely shortened version of the truth. "Because ye don't need me anymore, and because me bein' here might put all of ye at risk. I'm not sure for what exactly, but the only way to be sure is for me to go."

I expected the wizard to argue or at least question me further, but she didn't—almost as if she'd expected something like this to happen. Instead, Constance waddled away from her companions and held a hand out to me. I closed the distance between us and took it.

Constance squeezed my fingers. "We cannot thank you enough for what you've done. On behalf of myself, my husband, and our little girl, please know that what you've done for us tonight will never be forgotten."

"Don't mention it." I ducked my head to avoid making eye contact. "So...ye still plannin' on namin' her Excalibur?"

"We are." Constance released my hand and cradled her swollen belly. "Excalibur Solomon."

"Solomon?"

"I know, I know," Constance assured me. "Not exactly the least conspicuous surname. But it's a legacy we fully expect her to live up to."

"Well, I can't wait to meet her one day," I said, though I strongly suspected I already had. Of course, that might have been wishful thinking on my part; if I was right, it meant Constance would soon be giving birth to a healthy baby girl with platinum blonde hair and the ability to produce a silver-trimmed Gateway. A girl who would one day come to my rescue as I had just come to hers.

"Neither can we," she replied. "Though I hope that if and when you do, she isn't causing too much trouble. With a name like hers, I expect she may turn out to be quite the handful."

She had no idea.

I grinned. "Aye, you're probably right about that. But I wouldn't worry too much. I'm sure little Callie will grow up just fine."

Constance cocked her head. "Callie?"

"Oh, sorry. I meant Excalibur."

"No, I like it. Callie. It's very pretty."

Titus stepped up alongside his wife. "It's a good nickname. But we really should get you inside and settled, dear, while we can."

"He's right," I chimed in, my heart racing a little at the thought that I might have inadvertently given Calle Penrose's biological parents the nickname she'd later use in life. "The two of ye have more important t'ings to worry about right now than names."

For some reason, this made Constance laugh. She patted my arm, told me to take care, and allowed her husband to lead her away. Titus flashed me a thankful smile over his shoulder, to which I offered him a thumbs up. Makayla, meanwhile, lingered behind, watching the couple with an implacable expression on her face. An odd blend of pity and something far less charitable—something I might have called envy if I hadn't known any better. But what could Nate's mother possibly be envious of?

Unfortunately, I wouldn't be getting the chance to ask her, because it was at that moment that I felt Veil's hand settle on my shoulder.

"Time to go."

22

"... Whe they love, mortals love with a ferocity the gods cannot match. This is perhaps why the gods so often deal in vengeance and spite; those are emotions that can be held onto. That can grow without being nurtured. Even the shallowest love can become hate if left unattended."

23

Squeals of childish laughter and the high-pitched squeak of sneakers on tile snapped me back to yet another new reality, and I found myself standing in the middle of a dormitory hallway as a cluster of prepubescent boys came stampeding through a pair of double doors. They raced past with all the grace of drunken foals, howling with manic glee. I scowled after them, irritated by their lack of decorum, especially in a place as prestigious as this.

And prestigious it was; not too dissimilar from some of Boston's oldest and most luxurious hotels, the dormitory's hallway practically oozed old money. Hand-crafted baseboards rimmed a dark green carpet littered with blazing patches of sunlight courtesy of floor-to-ceiling windows, while tasteful sconces lined the walls to provide added ambience. Sturdy oak doors filled the remaining gaps, each bearing a name plaque to reveal the identity of the occupants within as well as a strange crest branded into the wood—an open palm positioned above a pair of crossed staffs, all of which encircled by the words *dum vivimus servimus*.

"Serve while we live," I translated aloud, exercising the dead language skills that had been drilled into me in Catholic school. "Huh. Well, remind me not to drink any of *their* Kool-Aid."

Just as I was about to wander farther down the hall in search of someone who could tell me where I'd ended up, a caustic odor hit my nostrils—the stench of something burning. I scented the air and discovered the smell originating from beyond the doors through which the boys had emerged. Had those little bastards set fire to something before running off? They'd certainly seemed chuffed enough with themselves.

Ruled by a nagging curiosity and a faint sense of self-preservation, I hastily propped open one of the doors to have a peek. Within, I found a boys locker room, complete with tile floors, urinals, sinks, and hard plastic benches. Further back, I could make out rows of shower heads beyond a waist-high wall, and it was from that direction the smoke drifted. Mercifully, the locker room appeared otherwise unoccupied, which saved me the trouble of having to explain why I slipped through the door.

"Wh-Who's there?"

I froze. The voice was thready and obviously distraught, which was perhaps why I decided to ignore my better judgment and creep farther into the room. I didn't respond, but instead sought out the source of the smoke, which soon led me to a smoldering trash can. Little remained of whatever had been discarded—nothing but a few chunks of sizzling leather and charred buttons.

"I'm warning you," the speaker went on. "If you don't get the hell out here, I'll...I'll make you sorry."

With the fire due to burn itself out sooner rather than later, I disregarded the trash can and turned towards the sound of the voice, lured perhaps by the pain and anguish in it. I hadn't gone far when I found its owner: naked and shivering, the young boy had tucked himself into the smallest ball he could manage in the corner of the shower, his head buried in his arms. Scalding hot water sprayed against his flushed back, the steam creating a faint haze that partially concealed his slender body. I noticed the water beneath him was tinged pink as it raced towards the drain in the middle of the floor. Blood, most likely.

"Are ye okay?"

The boy flinched.

"Don't worry," I assured him. "I'm not here to hurt ye."

"Oh yeah?" The boy scoffed and sniffled, his expression hidden beneath a curtain of soaking wet hair. "Then what are you doing here?"

"I smelled smoke."

The boy grunted. "My clothes. They thought it'd be funny to light them on fire and see if I could put it out."

"What, with your bare hands?"

The boy looked up, then, and I found my disgust for the situation supplanted by an entirely different sensation: recognition. Except that wasn't it, really; I'd never seen this child before in my life, nor had I met him as an adult, as far as I could tell. It was more a sense of kinship, or perhaps he simply reminded me of someone I knew? Either way, I doubt I would ever forget the sight of this child with his bloody nose and red-rimmed eyes.

"No, of course not," he replied. "With magic, obviously."

"Magic?"

The boy tensed, his expression suddenly wary. "Who are you? You look like a teacher, but I've never seen you before, and the Academy doesn't allow visitors. Are you an alumni?"

The Academy? That was a name I hadn't heard in a while; the school was notorious for churning out wizards, most of whom turned out to be assholes, in my humble opinion. The question was, how had I ended up here? And did he say I looked like a teacher?

I frowned and was about to ask a follow-up question when I happened to spot a mirror out of the corner of my eye. I craned my neck until I could see my reflection—only of course it wasn't mine. Instead, I found myself looking into the eyes of a stooped, middle-aged man with thinning gray hair sporting a cheap, three-piece suit. Which I supposed explained why the kid hadn't scrambled to cover himself up or screamed at me to go away.

"Yikes, talk about a downgrade," I muttered.

"What did you say?"

"Nothin', nevermind. Anyway, no. I'm not an alumni."

"Then what..." The boy's eyes lit up. "Wait! Are you a Justice?"

"One of those masked fuckers who go around stickin' their noses in other people's business? Hell no." I shook my head adamantly. "Not a chance."

"Oh," he replied, looking crestfallen.

"Why? Would ye have preferred if I was?"

"No. I mean, maybe. It's just...I heard the Justices go after wizards who abuse their powers. And I thought..."

"That I might teach the boys who lit your clothes on fire a lesson for ye? Maybe drag 'em out into the hall and rough 'em up a bit?"

The boy bit his lip but nodded. "Something like that."

"And would that make ye feel better, ye t'ink?"

To his credit, the kid actually stopped to consider the question before replying. "I'm not sure," he admitted. "But I doubt it would make me feel worse."

I grunted a laugh at that. "You've probably got a point, there. Tell ye what, how about I find ye some clothes, and then we can worry about plottin' your revenge?"

"There's nothing to worry about," he assured me, the sudden heat in his voice fiercer than the water that beat across his bare shoulders. "I'll settle the score, eventually. They think they can bully me because I have trouble with the basics, but I've already forgotten more than those idiots will ever know about magic."

"Is that right? Well, I'm glad to hear it. Still, it might be a good idea to get dressed before the hot water runs out or your skin gets all pruny, don't ye t'ink?"

The boy hesitated, then nodded.

"Excellent. Any idea where I can find ye another set of clothes? Or maybe a towel?"

"No. They took the towels."

"Of course they did. Are any of these lockers theirs?"

The boy pointed. "That's one of them, yeah."

I nodded and approached the locker he'd indicated. A slick metal combination lock had been thrust through the opening, thereby securing it from would-be thieves. Of course, I wasn't an ordinary thief.

I reached out, took hold of the lock, and wrenched it hard enough to snap the top off the damned thing like a candy cane. That done, I tossed the lock over my shoulder and began rifling through the locker's meager contents. Eventually, I found a pair of gym shorts and a t-shirt—both clean, thank the Lord.

"Will these work?" I asked, hoisting the garments for the kid to see.

"How'd you do that? With the lock, I mean? You didn't use magic, or I'd have been able to tell."

"D'ye want the clothes or not?"

He nodded and began to unfold himself, which I took as my cue to look away. I held out the shorts and shirt with my back turned, and waited until he gave me the all clear before facing me again. The clothes clung to his body for a moment, his damp skin soaking right through the fabric. Then, almost miraculously, steam began to pour off his body until both he and his outfit were bone dry.

"Impressive," I noted.

The boy had the grace to look embarrassed. "I've never had a problem with heat."

"And does that have anythin' to do with why they lit your clothes on fire? Ye rubbed their noses in it, so they decided to bloody yours?"

"Maybe."

"Hmm."

"It's not my fault I'm better at it than they are," he said, sullenly.

"Never said it was."

"Well, whatever. Could you...I mean, would you mind walking me back to my room? Just in case they're still hanging around out there."

"Sure." I didn't bother mentioning that I'd seen his tormentors run off like a gang of howling monkeys—there was no need. Besides, I could tell he simply wanted to keep me around until he felt safe, and that was something I could hardly deny the poor kid. "Oy. What's your name, anyway?"

"It's Aiden."

24

Aiden's room was in no way typical of a boy his age, which I'd have put somewhere between twelve and thirteen. Of course, the same could be said of the building itself; since leaving the locker room, we'd passed a handful of adjoining hallways filled with all manner of artifacts from life-size statues of armored knights standing guard along the walls to massive tomes set out on marble pedestals. Admittedly, the medieval aesthetic was all very impressive, if a bit stuffy—reminding me in some ways of Chateau Falco with a lot less soul.

"I'm going to change through here," Aiden informed me. He tilted his head towards an en suite bathroom, his arms full of fresh new clothes.

"Aye. Sounds good."

Once he'd closed and locked the door, I returned to studying the room. As I'd noted before, the space was uncommonly neat—far neater than it had any right to be, frankly, considering. Indeed, everything seemed to have been laid out with almost military precision: the writing desk held a single unmarked notebook and pen, the bed was made so tight I could have bounced a quarter off the comforter, and the only personal effects were a solitary picture frame on the wall and what appeared to be a letter tri-folded and tucked under the lamp on the nightstand.

After checking to make sure the boy was still preoccupied, I crept over to the side of the bed and probed at the letter. It was hand-written in cursive on old, surprisingly thick paper—all but illegible, in fact, aside from a remarkably large, looping signature at the bottom.

"Castor Queen," I read with a pensive frown. "Yikes. *Someone's* parents clearly didn't love them."

I carefully replaced the flap I'd lifted and turned to study the picture frame. Within sat a grainy Polaroid with a date scribbled across the bottom. The subjects were a man and woman with their backs turned to the camera, their arms linked like lovers, though the woman had turned her head just enough to reveal a lovely if not unfamiliar profile. I squinted, trying to place her, but couldn't.

Just as I was about to turn my attention to the man in the photo-graph, I heard the door handle rattle, at which point I had no choice but to step back into the middle of the room lest Aiden find me snooping.

"I just realized you never gave me your name," Aiden said as he emerged, his expression skeptical. The boy wore a boarding school-style uniform, including a dark blue blazer, grey sweater, and garish red tie. Dressed as he was, it made me rethink his age. He might be as old as fifteen, I decided, if a bit on the slight side.

"No," I replied. "I didn't."

"Okay...so, what are you doing here, then?"

"Ye invited me."

"Not here, here. I'm talking about the Academy. I want to know what you were doing before you found me."

"Oh, ye know. Wanderin' the halls, lookin' for answers. Or that was the plan, anyway."

Though I could tell he wanted me to elaborate, I didn't. Frankly, I still had no idea why I'd been sent to this particular time and place, though I suspected it had something to do with Aiden, himself. Unfortunately, not only couldn't I prove it, but it was beginning to feel as though rolling with the paradoxical punches was the best I could manage for the time being.

Which I loathed, obviously.

"Until you found me," Aiden said, bringing me back to the moment at hand.

I shrugged, then nodded.

"Why do I feel like you're avoiding the subject?"

"Probably because ye aren't stupid. Speakin' of which, what's with this room?"

"Huh? What about it?"

"I mean, where are all the posters of half-naked girls and professional athletes or whatever it is kids your age are into? Look at your closet for cryin' out loud. Your hangers are so evenly spaced ye may as well have used a ruler."

Aiden blushed. "I like things organized."

"Mmm."

"Whatever, I don't care what you think."

"Clearly."

The boy glared at me. "'The only difference between a mob and a trained army is organization.' Calvin Coolidge said that, you know."

"The president?"

Aiden nodded.

"Huh." I cocked an eyebrow. "And are ye plannin' to lead an army, one day?"

Aiden looked away, his expression abruptly grave. "So what if I am?"

Interesting.

"Then can I give ye some advice?" I asked. "It'll apply to this place, too."

"Sure."

"Play dumb."

"Huh?" Aiden gaped at me.

"Okay, maybe not dumb. But definitely less..." I gestured at his immaculate room. "Whatever this is. Gettin' along with people is first and foremost about understandin' what they want from ye. For some, it's a lackey. Someone who will fall in line with their head down. For others, it's a leader. Someone who will stand up for 'em, or fight when a fight is called for."

"I am no one's lackey."

"Aye. And that's the problem. You're too rigid. Maybe ye don't want those other boys to like ye, and that's fine. I don't blame ye. They seem like a bunch of little assholes. But if me experience of late has taught me anythin', it's that people can't take from ye what they don't know ye have. Gettin' angry or upset won't save ye from the likes of those boys, and neither will gettin' even. Ye have to anticipate and act methodically, not react."

"Easier said than done," Aiden muttered.

"No doubt. But I never said it would be easy. Very few of us come out of the box with that kind of ruthless practicality. Most come out either too hot or too cold. We rage at shite we can't change or let others walk all over us. But that doesn't mean we can't learn. That we can't grow."

Too late, I realized I wasn't only speaking to Aiden, but also to myself. After all, I *had* changed over these past few years—how could I not? Where once I might have lashed out, I was beginning to see that there were many ways to resolve conflicts. Ways that didn't always involve violence, or me running my smart mouth.

"So you're saying I shouldn't get back at them for what they did?" Aiden asked.

"I'm sayin' *what's the point*? D'ye want 'em to suffer, or d'ye want 'em to leave ye be? Or maybe what ye really want is to be in charge, eh? To be the one tellin' 'em what to do."

"And how would I do that?"

"Ye make a plan. Ye take all this organization of yours and apply it. But ye have to t'ink seventeen steps ahead. Ye have to learn to be patient. The more seeds ye sow, the better the harvest."

"You make it sound so simple, but I think we both know it's not."

"Ye won't know unless ye try. The sooner ye get into the habit of findin' out what others want, the sooner ye can give it to 'em. For a price, of course."

Aiden grunted, but I could tell from the pensive look on his face that he was considering my advice. Of course, there was no way to know whether he'd take it. He was right: everything I'd told him was far easier said than done. Except I was right, too. Standing up to one's bullies was all well and good in theory, but bullies at their core were still just people. And people could be reasoned with, or strong-armed, or blackmailed.

There was, after all, more than one way to skin a chimaera.

"By the way," I went on, "that picture on your wall. Are those your parents?"

Aiden sniffed, derisively. "So they tell me."

"Oh, I'm sorry. Are they..."

"Dead? No. At least, I don't think they are." Aiden unhooked the picture and held it at arm's reach, his mouth set in a grim line. "I don't know anything about them, except that they left me to be raised by someone else."

"Castor Queen?" I said without thinking.

Aiden stiffened. "How do you know that name?"

"Oh, right. Sorry, I just happened to see it written on the letter by your bed."

"Get out."

"Wha—"

"I said get out, before I make you get out."

The boy stood resolute, and I could see heat cascading off his hands in waves. Small arcs of lightning danced across his knuckles, and I could have sworn I saw his eyes flare pure white for just a moment. I wasn't frightened of the kid, of course, but I had to admit I wasn't eager to see what he could do with his blood up. Of course, that raised the question, if he could make me hesitate, why hadn't the other boys?

"I can't get kicked out," Aiden explained, reading my expression. "I don't have anywhere else to go, and hurting the other students is against the rules. But you aren't a student, or an alumni, or a Justice. You said so yourself. Which means you must be working for *him*."

"Him? Him, who?"

"You know who. Now, I'm giving you three seconds to leave, or things are going to get very ugly very fast."

"Listen, I don't—"

"One."

"Seriously? A countdown? What is this, *Tombstone*?"

"Two."

I threw my hands up in the air, sensing any further attempts to convince the boy of my innocence would only prove futile. "Okay, okay, fine. I'm leavin'. Just remember what I said, alright? I meant it."

I had already opened the door and was just about to turn back for one quick glance when I heard Aiden speak again, and an invisible force lashed out at me like an errant gust of wind. The blast sent me stumbling out into the hall, where I had no choice but to duck lest the boy fire off any further attacks. Instead, the door slammed violently shut in my face.

"You really do have quite the way with people, don't you?"

I flinched and spun just in time to see Veil hovering less than a foot away, one arm extended as though reaching for me. I tried to dodge, but it was too late; her gloved hand settled on my shoulder, and the hallway vanished from sight.

25

" ... W *hat is life without uncertainty?"*

26

Something small and furry slapped me across the face. Not hard, but with enough oomph to bring me gasping to my senses. I tried to sit up, only to find myself restrained—my wrists and ankles bound to a stone table by leather straps covered in strange runes written in what appeared to be dried blood. I panicked and thrashed, reminded of a time not so long ago when I'd been similarly treated by a mad scientist in the bowels of Helheim. Of course, back then I'd been stripped out of my armor, whereas now I seemed to be wearing a rather expensive pantsuit.

"Relax," came a soft and vaguely recognizable voice from just outside my peripheral vision, its soothing cadence accompanied by a puff of smoke. "I just wanted to make sure you were real."

"Who's there?" I demanded. "Where am I? Why d'ye have me tied down?"

"I'll answer your questions," the voice replied, airily, "once you've answered mine."

"And what's your question?"

"Who *really* killed Kennedy?"

"What? How should I know?!"

The speaker tsked. "Well *somebody* has to!"

I muttered a curse under my breath and craned my neck to catch sight of the speaker, but instead managed to get a good look at the room I was in—although I could tell at once that the word "cave" was a more accurate description. Unfortunately, what I saw did *not* put me at ease.

A pair of tables about the same height as the one I lay upon sat side by side against the far rock wall, their surfaces covered in an array of horrifying and occasionally bizarre devices not unlike a dentist's tray. Knives of varying sizes and shapes lay alongside painted masks and shrunken heads. Dirty needles leaned out of a whiskey glass like so many pens, and a rack of labeled vials lined the wall, their liquids ranging from pitch black to sickening yellow. There were handheld saws and screws as long as my forearm, leather bondage gear, and a slightly moist ball gag.

On the opposite wall stood a bookshelf loaded with ancient books, their spines weathered and peeling, while beside it hunkered a small desk occupied by a single, solitary tome speckled dark brown from a spray of blood from some time ago. The same color decorated the walls on either side, though these marks were not random so much as eclectic: a myriad arrangement of crude symbols that made me wriggle with discomfort.

"Okay, what in the actual fu—" I began.

The scrunched up, fur-covered face of a wizened old bear appeared directly above my own, his black, beady little eyes peering into mine from upside down. As I watched, he raised a paw coated in some sticky substance to his muzzle and began licking it clean like a demented Winnie-the-Pooh.

"What are you doing in there?" asked the bear. "That's not your body. Get out."

"What are ye doin' here?" I gaped at the creature.

A gob of wet saliva spattered into my forehead.

"Ugh! What the hell, Starlight?!"

A bright pink tongue whipped out to flick across the werebear's dainty claws, and I caught the heady scent of hash mingled with the nutty odor of honey. The wizard bear I'd met in Alaska not long after Callie rescued me from a firefight in Boston cocked his head.

"You know it's considered rude to borrow someone's body without their permission," he replied. "At least that's what they keep telling me when I do it."

"How about tyin' 'em down? Wouldn't ye say that's *more* rude?"

Starlight disappeared from sight rather than reply, and I could hear him stepping down off a bench to retrieve something that scraped across the floor. He wandered around the edge of the table until he came back into view, this time clutching a glass cylinder almost as tall as he was. I stared in mute fascination as the bear conjured a tiny flame and held it over a slide packed to the brim with marijuana.

"Are ye serious right now? Untie me, ye little dope addict!"

Starlight ignored me, shoved his muzzle into the mouth of the bong and took a deep inhale. Smoke flooded the cylinder, then vanished as Starlight yanked out the slide. The bear's head rocked back, where it stayed for several seconds before he exhaled. An enormous plume of smoke went soaring towards the roof of the cave where it hung like fog.

"Oy! Starlight! I'm tellin' ye, ye better let me out or—"

The bear held up a paw for silence, and for some reason I obeyed. Starlight shuffled over to his torture tables and slipped his bong under one of them, then waddled over to where I lay. Before I knew it, he'd climbed up onto my table and plopped himself down next to me.

"What are ye—"

"Shhh!" Starlight held a paw to his muzzle. "We have company."

"I don't—"

The bear lurched forward and planted both his paws over my mouth. I debated trying to bite the fuzzy sucker but ultimately decided against it; whatever he was up to, it wouldn't benefit me to piss him off. What I needed was for him to let me go, and the only way to make that happen was to assure him I wasn't a threat. Besides, I had to admit I was curious.

Who was the quasi-prophetic pothead expecting?

The answer: my old friend, Alucard Morningstar.

The vampire crept silently through an alcove to enter this section of the cave, his roguishly handsome face utterly unchanged from when I'd last seen him. Not that I was surprised; vampires were notoriously static in that regard. What did surprise me was the furtive way he moved about the room, noting the torture implements with a visible shudder but without ever once spotting Starlight and me.

I felt a pang of something like regret as I watched him glide throughout the room, reminded of the brief time we'd spent together. Dark-haired and dark eyed, the Daywalker from New Orleans had a drawl that could warm a girl all the way down to her...toes, stopping for an euphoric bender halfway there. Moreover, he was tough and savage enough to not only survive in our world, but thrive. Indeed, if he hadn't been a vampire whose loyalty was so closely linked to Nate Temple at a time when I needed someone loyal only to me, I liked to think we might have had something.

But that had been years ago now, and far too much had changed for me to wonder what might have been. Besides, I wasn't in my own body, which meant Alucard wouldn't recognize me even if I were to announce myself. Assuming he could even see me, which seemed increasingly doubtful as he continued his tour of the cave.

"Ah hah!" Alucard said, at last. "There you are, sweetheart. I've been looking for you everywhere."

For a moment I thought he might be talking to me, but then I saw the vampire had crossed the room to stand beside the bookshelf and was peering down at the desk. He carefully slid both hands beneath the blood-speckled book I'd noticed earlier and hefted it like he expected an alarm to go off. When it didn't, he grinned and snapped it shut, revealing a cover which read *Bioloki*. Within seconds he'd tucked the crumbling tome under one arm and slunk back out the way he'd come, all without sparing us a single glance.

I waited for several heartbeats for Starlight to remove his sticky little paws and explain what had just happened, but he didn't. In fact, I swore I could hear the tiny bastard snoring.

Screw it.

I bit his paw.

Starlight jerked upright, cradling his smarting paw and blinking at me with all the comprehension of an inebriated goat. He turned to look left, then right. "Oh, did the Daywalker leave already? I really hope he stole that book like he was supposed to."

27

I spent the next ten minutes trying to get straight answers out of the bear from Kansas City but I only managed to gather a handful of pertinent details. Firstly, it seemed Starlight had cast some sort of absurdly powerful invisibility spell to keep our presence hidden from a vampire with inhuman senses. Secondly, he'd done it on purpose; less than a full minute after Alucard left, he'd popped out to "snitch to the White Rose" before reappearing five minutes later and fetching his bong.

He held it now, tilted so he could reach its mouth while sitting on the floor of the cave. As for my release, he appeared content to leave me to rot—though I was relieved he seemed more interested in getting stoned than peeling off my fingernails or rubbing me down with bear scat or whatever twisted nonsense he usually got up to in this room.

"Ye could at least tie me to a chair or somethin'," I suggested. "This table isn't exactly ergonomic, and I can't feel me toes."

Starlight, ignoring my complaints as he had everything else I'd said since his return, released another plume of smoke into the air.

"Why didn't ye chase after him personally?" I asked. "Alucard, I mean."

The bear snorted. "When you can't be in two places at once, you send someone capable in your stead. Every wizard knows that."

"Except I'm not a wizard, at all. I'm—"

"I know what you are," Starlight interjected, cutting me off. He began packing his slide with even more herb, though he paused momentarily when he caught me looking. "I grew this batch myself, you know."

I sighed. "Ye don't say."

"I call it Snakebite."

I perked up at that, reminded of my brief return to my childhood home and the subsequent trap that had landed me here. The question was, did Starlight know anything about that? The bear definitely had an unusual, if not outright prescient, mind. He'd proven as much to me when we'd last met, when he'd provided me with the means to confront my mother's ghost for the very first time.

Plus, he was the only one who'd noticed I didn't belong, and that list included both Nate *and* Callie's parents, not to mention the powerful enchantress, Morgan le Fey.

"Any particular reason ye call it that?" I asked.

Rather than reply, Starlight flopped onto his back like a child, his furry little limbs akimbo. "Do you think organ donors who become zombies can feel their missing parts?"

"Sorry, what?"

"I bet they can." Starlight's ear twitched as he stared glassy-eyed up at the ceiling. "Is cereal soup? What about a hotdog? Would you say it's a sandwich?"

"I guess, technically."

Starlight nodded. "If I ate myself, do you think I'd be twice as big, or disappear?"

"Um, I'm pretty sure that's physically impossible."

The bear raised his paw to his face as if considering whether or not to try it anyway. "Why do round pizzas come in square boxes?"

"That's...actually not a bad question," I admitted. "But hold on, what was it ye were sayin' earlier, about your weed?"

Starlight lifted his head. "Who said it was weed?"

"I guess I just assumed."

The head flopped back down. "Then you assumed wrong. This stuff comes from a magically engineered plant I've been growing."

"A *magically* engineered plant?"

"Mmhmm. It's like a pale, scaly little tree."

"Seriously?"

"Seriously." Starlight held a paw to his heart. "I swear on my mother's teats."

Gross.

"And it gets ye high?" I asked.

"Ohhhh yeah. All it takes is the right material, and I got mine from the biggest snake you've ever seen in your life in exchange for some premium Wonderland shrooms. That's where I got that musty old book, too, come to think of it."

"Wait, back up. What does a giant snake need with mushrooms?"

Unfortunately, it appeared Starlight had lost interest in our conversation; the diminutive bear sat back up and proceeded to take his biggest hit yet. Except this time, rather than inhaling, he blew the smoke directly at me.

"Oy!" I snapped, coughing. "Stop that."

Starlight ignored me and did it again, producing yet more smoke in the process. In fact, he repeated this so many times that I soon ended up surrounded by a thick cloud of the stuff. I tried holding my breath at first, but in the end I had no choice but to inhale.

He'd Bill Clinton'd me.

The bear, partially obscured by the haze of vaporous smoke drifting throughout the room, set the bong aside.

"It's funny where we put things so we'll remember where to find them," he observed, idly. "Keys under the mat. Shoes by the door. Skeletons in the closet."

I frowned. "What's that supposed to—"

"Of course, not everything we leave behind is meant to be retrieved. A baby girl on the steps of a church, for instance, or a boy with chaos in his veins. Or perhaps a son who will never grow into the man he was meant to be so long as his parents live."

"Listen, I have no idea what you're talkin' about, but maybe if ye let me go—"

"If only you had the means to ensure their survival," Starlight went on, his silhouette getting murkier with each passing moment. "To see that they are safe and taken in by the right people, supported by the right friends, given the right advice at precisely the right moment. Of course, that would take a miracle. A miracle...or *magic*."

I scowled, wishing I had even some idea what the bear was babbling about. Unfortunately, I could feel the insidious smoke invading my lungs and dulling my senses, lulling me into a sort of anesthetized stupor.

"Only magic alone wouldn't be enough, would it? You'd also need foresight. And power. Enough power to make sure that everything that *had* to happen, would happen. But the sacrifice...such *sacrifice*. And the *lies*. Such bold, magnificent lies."

Starlight's voice fell silent, and I realized I could no longer see him in the white mist that surrounded me. In fact, I could no longer make out any of the furniture except the table I lay upon. It was a surreal feeling, like being thrust into a cloud.

"They dubbed it The Tale of Three Catalysts," Starlight continued, his disembodied voice fainter and fainter until it was little more than a whisper. "But it wasn't true. There were always only ever two. The Alpha and the Omega. The two whose destiny it is to break and reshape the world. But first, they needed the right tools, handed to them at just the right time. The lifeblood of an Archwizard, the bones of their ancestors, the wisdom of their elders and their elder's Elders...the list goes on and on."

"I...seriously don't know...what you're talkin' about," I managed to say between yawns.

"You will. In fact, one day it'll all seem so obvious that if it were a snake it would've *bitten you*."

I shuddered at the last two words and twisted my head around, acutely aware that I was being watched. At first,I could almost have sworn I'd imagined it; the smoke obscured everything. But then the cloud parted, and behind it I saw a single, solitary orb rimmed in beautifully articulated, albino scales. The blood-red eye of a reptile so enormous I swore I could almost make out my own reflection in its shard-like pupil.

Until it blinked.

I opened my mouth to scream for help, but the instant I turned away, the presence vanished and the room appeared as it had but a few minutes ago—the air free of smoke or indeed an odor of any kind. Starlight sat at one of the tables with his back turned towards me, fondling something disturbingly phallic in shape and size. He glanced back at me over his shoulder and raised a paw in greeting.

"Welcome back. Your friend over there has been waiting for you to wake up for, like, ages."

"Friend? What friend?"

"I think he means me." I gasped to find Veil looming over me at the foot of the table with her arms folded. The black-clad figure tilted her head. "Did you have a nice nap?"

"I'm sorry?"

"I asked if you slept well."

"I heard ye. I just don't know what the hell you're talkin' about. I wasn't asleep. That little bastard over there drugged me and then started sayin' all this stuff about Alphas and Omegas and destiny and—"

"Is that true?" Veil asked Starlight, cutting me off.

Starlight tilted his head. "That depends. If it grows from the ground and you set it on fire and it just so happens to make you count every one of your bones while you marvel about how impossibly configured our bodies are with all our veins and our muscles and how we manage to breathe without consciously thinking about it, but then you *do* think about it and you realize you've forgotten to breathe for a while, so you go ahead and do that and then...sorry, what was the question again?"

"I wanted to know if it was true that you drugged—"

"Drugs! That's right! I mean, what even *are* drugs but the keys to the doors we lock inside our own minds? The ciphers we use to translate our most cryptic thoughts? The—"

Veil held up a hand. "Enough. Tell me the truth, how high are you right now?"

"So, so high," he whispered in a sacredly faithful tone. "You have no idea. Like, I swear I can see three of you right now." The bear pointed with a single claw. "Uh huh. One, two, and the shade makes three."

Veil stiffened. "Very high, indeed. Well, in any case, I believe it's time for us to be on our way."

"Oh snap, me too!" Starlight exclaimed, and then he promptly fell off his stool with a loud *umph*. He scrambled back to his feet and patted his haunches as though he might have lost them in the fall. "I almost forgot, I have to see a Horseman about a book! But hey...be sure to leave that body behind when you two go, alright? It took me a long time to track down the Illuminati's press secretary, and she still hasn't confirmed whether or not Avril Lavigne is a clone."

"Noted," Veil replied, sounding bemused.

"Oh, and by the way," Starlight said as he waddled over to retrieve his bong. "Say hello to Danu for me, would you? And remind the Dagda he still owes me a pipe. Actually, maybe when this is all over, the four of us could get together and scarf down some of that good stuff, just like we did back in—"

"I have no idea what you're talking about, bear."

"Right, right. My bad. I'm just *so* stoned, you know?"

Veil sighed. "Forget about it."

Fortunately, it seemed Starlight already had; the bear was very intently studying his own paws. "Can anyone else hear my nails growing? Actually, no, don't answer that. Instead, could I ask you something that's *really* been bugging me?"

Veil sighed. "Fine. What is it?"

"Do you think fish ever get thirsty?"

Veil muttered something inaudible under her breath and—before I could weigh in on the subject or even begin lodging a complaint about how I'd been treated—reached out to grab me by the ankle.

28

"...Y ou belong to both worlds. You will be tempted to choose between the mortal realm and Fae, but you must be true to yourself and to those you profess to care about. Otherwise, when the time comes, you will be lost and unable to save them."

29

I awoke shivering and surrounded by a thick grey mist, the prow of a boat rocking gently beneath me. But at least I was finally free; I hastily checked my wrists and ankles for restraints and was elated to find them unshackled. Unfortunately, my relief did not last long, as the dreary combination of dense fog and dark skies soon had me wishing for the relative warmth and comfort of Starlight's torture cave.

"Where the hell am I now?" I asked, my mind still racing with the implications of all that had been said in Starlight's cave, especially during the drug-induced haze.

I'd claimed not to understand it all, and of course I hadn't, but that didn't mean I was stupid. I knew that Callie would end up abandoned on the front steps of a church in Kansas City. She'd told me as much not long after we first met. I also knew Nate's parents had died some years back, leaving behind an orphaned billionaire and—for the first couple months following their tragic murder, at least—the mainstream media's most eligible bachelor.

The question was, did that have anything to do with all that other stuff he'd spouted, or was the bear just stoned off his ass and spouting nonsense? And what was with that nonsense he'd spouted at Veil? Obviously he thought they'd met before, but when and where?

A hooded figure leaned forward and startled the crap out of me, his enormous bulk emerging from the mist as surely as if he'd materialized out of thin air. "Did you say something?"

"I...uh..."

"You look cold. Here, take this."

The figure removed his cloak before I could say anything and flung it over me like a blanket, revealing what could only generously be called a face; russet-toned and unusually proportioned, the creature sported a squat, vaguely feline nose, thick lips, and a pair of tapering ears that jutted out from either side of his head.

"You're a hobgoblin," I said, surprised.

The Faeling grimaced. "I'd prefer it if you didn't call me that. My friends call me Worricow."

"Sure t'ing. Worricow, it is."

The hobgoblin, who I'd recognized thanks to my mercifully brief forays into the political quagmire that was the Faerie Chancery, settled back onto his haunches. The mist quickly flooded the gap between us, but now that I knew he was there, I could at least make out his silhouette. Glad for the warmth of the gifted cloak, I drew it tight around my shoulders, pleased to note it smelled of wild berries and tree bark as opposed to blood or sex—sometimes more commonly known as *Eau du Faeling*.

"Better?" Worricow asked.

"Much. T'anks."

"You are welcome."

Silence descended once more, and that's when I realized I could hear muted voices off to my left and right, though their words were drowned out by the creak of oars lapping against calm waters. Indeed, we were suddenly surrounded by the constant clamor of plunks and swishes. I wasn't sure how I'd missed them before. The fog, perhaps, distorting sounds?

"Who's out there?" I asked the hobgoblin.

"The other exiles." One of Worricow's ears twitched. "We must be leaving the mists behind. I can finally hear the other boats."

"Sorry, what was that ye said about exiles?"

"Ah...you must be one of those."

"One of whom?"

"The ones who claim they left our home of their own accord."

"Our home...meanin' Fae," I ventured.

"Of course."

So, that meant he thought I was a Faeling, like him. Out of curiosity, I held open the cloak and peered down at myself. Unfortunately, I wasn't able to glean much; I wore a very plain tunic, nondescript breeches, and a pair of worn leather boots. To put it bluntly, if this were a video game, I'd swear I was starting at level 1.

"Beginner gear acquired," I muttered under my breath.

"What was that?"

"Nothin', I was just talkin' to meself. Anyway...ye were sayin' somethin' about leavin' the mists behind?"

"Just that we should be reaching our destination, soon."

"Ah, right. Our destination. That place...what was its name again?"

"The crossing. To join up with Mordred's forces before they invade the Summer Lands. Weren't you at the Chancery gathering?"

"Oh, no, I was. Totally. I was just makin' sure ye knew where we were headed. The crossin'. To meet up with Mordred. Of course."

"There's no need to be so nervous." Worricow smiled, flashing tusks. "The Usurper is sure to welcome us with open arms."

I waved that away. "Who me? I'm not nervous. Why would I be nervous? I'm fine."

Inwardly, however, I *was* panicking. What the hell was Veil thinking leaving me trapped on a boat with an unfamiliar Faeling? And why were we headed to link up with the forces of a notorious traitor like Mordred? While the knight's lineage was very much up for debate among scholars, Mordred's bad reputation was supported by the vast majority of sources—a consensus drawn from his wide-ranging attempts to steal King Arthur's rightful throne for himself.

Honestly, I wasn't sure what to make of any of it; the last time I'd even heard Mordred's name mentioned, it had been from the lips of his mother, Morgause, as she prepared to assault an entire bar full of Faelings. Oh yes, and let's not forget yours truly. In fact, that had been the first and last time I saw the enchantress, not to mention her fellow Adjudicator, Sir Bredbeddle, better known as the Green Knight.

The pair had gone missing not shortly thereafter in search of her son, never to be heard from again.

"Mordred..." I began, reminded of Morgause's words back then. "He came back from the dead , right?"

Worricow nodded idly, his gaze locked on the horizon where the mist was thinnest. "Escaped his cell in Hell. Rumor has it he plans to free the Vanquished, somehow. That he plans to take back everything that was stolen from us."

"D'ye say 'the Vanquished'?"

Worricow nodded, apparently not seeing the need to elaborate. Strange, considering I couldn't recall any mention of said individuals —nor for that matter had I heard any rumors of Mordred's plans during my increasingly brief stints in Boston. Of course, it was entirely possible this could be a more contemporary period in time, perhaps even current.

"How long ago did he escape?" I asked, hoping to get some sort of reference point.

Worricow shrugged. "Not long."

So, probably *not* current then. Though, to be honest, I had only a rough idea how long it'd been since my first and only visit to the *El Fae*—the underground speakeasy beneath the law offices of *Hansel, Hansel, & Gretel*.

Since then, I'd traveled to Fae and unwillingly participated in a war, flown to Moscow to rescue friends only to tangle with a shadowy sect within the Russian government, dropped in on the Otherworld and temporarily lost my mind, sailed across the Eighth Sea while following in Odysseus' legendary footsteps, visited both the Underworld and the Norse Realm, and all that before *finally* returning home.

And even then my stay had been remarkably short-lived.

And now here I was, being chucked about through space and time without even the slightest concern for my feelings on the matter.

Almost as if *fate* didn't want me returning to Boston.

Not that I could prove it.

"So, how much long—" I began.

Worricow cut me off by standing to point towards the horizon, where a landmass was beginning to take shape. I frowned, not sure just what to make of what I was seeing.

"Is that..."

Worricow nodded.

The crossing, as the Faeling had called it, was in fact an island in the middle of a vast lake—albeit unlike any I'd seen before. Whereas most I'd seen were either rimmed by sandy beaches or cragged cliffs, this isle was more like a floating plateau bounded by a sheer limestone escarpment and topped with moss-covered caprock. Stranger still, there were no man-made structures in sight, nor indeed any signs of habitation; certainly nothing to suggest an occupying force of any kind.

I frowned. "Are we early?"

The Faeling beside me shook his head, though he seemed uncertain. "They must have crossed already. That, or..."

"Or what?"

"Nothing. We must be patient. The Usurper's mother will have a plan, I'm sure."

"The...ye mean Morgause?"

"Who else?"

I gaped at him. "Morgause is *here*?"

"Of course. Who did you think was in command of all these boats?"

30

Now that the fog had lifted completely, I could see what Worricow meant; a dozen boats carrying all manner of Faelings both large and small drifted towards the island en masse, powered by an enchantment that kept their oars churning to the same rhythm. Most of the passengers appeared to have imitated my companion—donning loose-fitting garments that made it difficult to tell what manner of creature lurked beneath.

Difficult, but not impossible.

By my count, there were at least three trolls in a boat by themselves, the half dozen hobgoblins on our boat, a smattering of pointy-eared elves, a pack of snarling Barghests, and a handful of scaly-skinned kobolds. All in all, not exactly an army. Still, it was a remarkably diverse collection of mythical beings. Which was to say nothing of the pair who occupied the lead vessel.

The former Adjudicators stood side by side at the prow of their boat like they were Washington crossing the godsdamned Delaware. Not that I could blame them; if I looked half as good as they did even half the time, I'd have had my portrait painted twice a week for posterity alone.

Morgause, who'd traded in all the leather and chrome she'd had on display when we last met for a belted wrap dress with a plunging neckline, sported an effortlessly trim, supermodel physique—the sort that made the rest of us wish we'd been born with a gene that let us actually *enjoy* salad. Oh yeah, and let's not forget the flawless, ageless complexion of a Beverly Hills dermatologist.

Sir Bredbeddle, on the other hand, was as aesthetically pleasing and well-proportioned a man as any I'd ever seen—assuming that man had pale green skin. With a beard made of knotted twigs, a leafy mane where his hair should have been, and teeth carved from a tree, Bred was a specimen unique even to the Fae.

Unlike Morgause, the Green Knight appeared exactly as I'd last seen him: covered head to toe in layer of armor with tree limbs poking out from between the plates like jagged barbs, a crowned helmet affixed with enormous antlers clutched in his gauntleted fist, and a wickedly curved axe swinging from his hip.

So, it seemed I'd inadvertently stumbled upon the missing members of the Chancery's search party—a contingent that, as far as I knew, had mysteriously disappeared, never to be seen again.

Except by me, apparently.

What were the odds?

Before I could dwell too much on that question, however, the Green Knight shouted out a command, and I caught him flinging a hand towards the island. His enchanting companion nodded vehemently and clutched at a stone dangling from a necklace at her throat. She began chanting in a strange and guttural tongue.

I nearly stumbled as all twelve boats slowed, their oars no longer rowing of their own accord. For a moment, there was no sound but the startled cries of a few Faelings and the babble of Morgause's rambling incantations. Nothing to see but the deserted island and a still, grey lake beneath an equally monochromatic sky. Then Morgause's magic began to ripple the air around her as if she were some sort of mirage while overhead the heavens darkened.

Then, like a gust of wind slamming against a window pane, there came a great and terrible rumble at our backs. I whirled to find a swell of water approaching—not a tidal wave, but an actual hump rising from the middle of the lake like something out of *Jaws*. The swell grew and overtook our boat before any of us could react, and suddenly I found myself hundreds if not thousands of feet in the air and racing towards the island on the back of a massive wave, my body pinned against Worricow's as I tumbled backwards.

The swell carried us all the way to the island before it crashed against the sides of the plateau and sent all our boats careening onto the caprock. Miraculously, most managed to tip onto their sides and skid only a few dozen feet before coming to a grinding halt. A few, however, landed prow-first, their keels digging deep furrows in the earth before flipping like overturned cars.

Ours was one of the latter.

Flung headfirst to the ground, I rolled end over end until I finally came to a stop feeling like I'd leapt from a moving train. Fortunately, I was a whole lot more durable than I looked and managed to climb to my feet with hardly a scratch. Not everyone else was so lucky; a few of the Faelings appeared to be nursing minor injuries, while others seemed downright hobbled.

"Ye okay?" I asked, seeing Worricow limping over.

"I thought that might be my line," he replied. "You took a nasty fall."

"It's fine. I yelled 'parkour' beforehand."

Worricow either didn't appreciate the joke or didn't get it. Instead, he went shuffling after the others, all of whom seemed intent on linking up with the de facto leaders of this odd expedition. I considered calling after the hobgoblin and asking what this was all about but assumed it might make me look even more suspicious, so I followed him instead.

I found all those who'd been caught up in Morgause's reckless spell gathered some thirty yards inland, their expressions rapt as the enchantress paced back and forth, addressing them like the field commander of some small but elite military unit, or the general manager of a retail outlet on Black Friday.

"What lies beyond this place," she said, "is the home you all long for. A home you were denied, or perhaps one where you no longer felt welcome. Regardless, it is a home you will call your own once more as soon as my son ascends to his rightful place on the Throne Outside Time. And it is for this purpose that we, together, shall fight in his name!"

A rousing chorus of cheers greeted the news.

"You all know me," Sir Bred interjected as the cries quieted. "You know that I once challenged King Arthur of Camelot. That I vowed to trade lethal blows with one of his finest, Gawain, in order to test his resolve. That I would sacrifice my own head to discover a knight's true mettle. And so you must believe me when I tell you that Mordred, no matter his methods, is worthy of our loyalty and our lives."

The Fae clapped politely when it was clear he'd finished, seemingly preferring talk of fighting for a cause than dying for a knight most of them had likely never met. Still, Sir Bred seemed satisfied; he donned his helmet and turned to the enchantress, who in turn raised her hands to the sky in a familiar gesture.

"That witch better not be about to call another wave," I muttered under my breath.

Fortunately, that wasn't what Morgause had in mind. Instead, the enchantress flung both arms down to her sides, her magic tearing a hole in the fabric of space to reveal a Gateway unlike any I'd ever seen. In fact, I wasn't sure it was a Gateway at all, but a genuine partition between two completely different worlds—the first a lonely plateau in the middle of a gigantic lake, the second a black sand beach laden with obsidian rocks.

The two Adjudicators exchanged a single look before marching through the opening, at which point the remaining Fae had no choice but to follow or be left behind. This they did—rushing after their leaders in a mad dash that suggested they'd all recovered fairly well from their wounds. I, of course, stayed right where I was.

But then I knew something they didn't.

Because I'd seen that beach before.

31

"You don't wish to join them?"

I spun, startled to find a dour figure looming over my shoulder and staring at the doorway-sized tear in the sky. Veil matched the stark landscape of the plateau, like a corpse bride celebrating her destination wedding. I, meanwhile, did my best to resist the urge to jab her solar plexus with an elbow to give myself some space.

"Not on your life," I replied, instead.

"Why not?"

"Because *that* isn't Fae."

I pointed at the black sand beach, beyond which rose a path between a breathtaking series of lichen-coated ridges. It was on that beach that I'd first met my one and only canine companion—a colossal hound who went by the name Cathal when he wasn't busy talking smack and generally grouching his way through life.

"Well no, it wouldn't be. Not from here."

"What does that mean? And where's *here*?"

Veil knelt and settled a hand on the ground like a mother searching for a heartbeat in her child's breast. "All that remains of

Ynys Afallon, where the Sword was forged before being thrust into Stone. The Isle of Fruit Trees and the Sanctuary of Kings."

I frowned, my memory tickled by the strange terminology. "The Isle of Fruit Trees...d'ye mean Avalon?"

Veil lowered her head as though saying a silent prayer.

"As in *the* Avalon?" I went on. "Ye can't be serious. This place? But it's so..."

"Desolate?" Veil rose to survey the landscape. "Once, long ago, this island rose hundreds of feet higher than we are now. This flat plain was full of hills and apple orchards, while at the isle's heart lay a castle carved from stone that shone like the moon."

"What happened?"

"What always happens. Someone took one look at this wondrous place and saw a beautiful flower they wanted to pluck for themselves. And so they did."

I scowled, wondering how literal I was supposed to take Veil's analogy. After all, it certainly appeared as though someone had come along and cut the top of the island—assuming Veil's description had merit. I still wasn't sure what to make of her, or indeed how much she seemed to know.

"Why d'ye send me here?" I asked after a moment's silence. "What's the point of all this?"

"You tell me."

"If I knew, I wouldn't be askin'."

Veil just looked at me. Or at least I thought she was; it was tough to tell beneath all that impenetrable darkness she had on.

I rolled my eyes in exasperation. "Fine. As far as I can tell, it all has somethin' to do with the Temples. Or Callie Penrose, maybe? Or...hell, I don't know."

The truth was, I was still struggling to figure out what linked these various experiences. After everything I'd seen and done—or had done to me, in Starlight's case—the only common denominator was Veil. Well, her and that awful storm, though even it didn't appear in every instance. Perhaps it had difficulty tracking me down at times? Veil had certainly suggested as much, earlier.

I could've sworn I heard Veil's condescending smile in her tone when she replied at last.

"Trying to solve that puzzle won't get you anywhere," she said. "Not that I expect you to listen."

"I could stop ye, I'll have ye know. From layin' your hands on me. What then?

"Are you saying you'd rather stay in that body you've borrowed, stranded alone on a barren island in the middle of nowhere? It's a bold choice, but if that's what you want..."

"I'm not stranded, or alone," I countered. "I could always follow after the others. The portal's still open."

"Then do it."

I muttered a curse.

"What's wrong? I thought you were going after them."

"I can't," I replied through gritted teeth.

"Why not?"

"Because *that* isn't Fae. It's the Otherworld."

"So?"

"So, the last time I stepped foot on Otherworld soil, I lost all sense of who I was, and I have no interest in doin' that again. Never again."

"Never is an awfully long time," noted Veil, cryptically. "And what about those who crossed over? Aren't you worried about what will happen to them?"

"Why should I be? They knew where they were goin'...didn't they?"

"Perhaps." Veil tilted her head. "Avalon itself was lost to all but myth many centuries ago, but the power of this place remains. Its connection to Tír na Nóg is well known to those who seek a bridge between the realms. On the other hand, the Otherworld's curse is formidable. Far more so than those poor creatures could ever comprehend."

"Hold on, I don't understand. Are ye sayin' they're in danger?"

"I cannot say. Likely no more so than they would otherwise be. Less so, perhaps, than if they were to have joined forces with the

Fugitive. Though it is a shame they'll be stuck forever once that portal closes."

Stuck forever...the words echoed inside my mind, their implications sending shivers up my spine. Damn it all. Of course. *This* was where Sir Bred and Morgause had run off to, and why they'd never returned. They'd gotten themselves trapped in the Otherworld chasing after Mordred. Or...had they?

"What if I went after 'em?" I asked. "Could I convince 'em to come back in time?"

"I think that depends on how persuasive you are, not to mention how long the portal remains open. But yes, it's possible."

I started to take an involuntary step forward.

"However," Veil went on, "recalling them would have its fair share of unintended consequences."

"Consequences like what?"

"There's no way to be certain. Not everything that happens can be chalked up to destiny, or some mysterious hand of fate. Often what we call fate is nothing more than a collection of average, ordinary individuals making random, uninformed choices. It's haphazard and messy. Like a minefield."

"Aye, because *this* feels like total happenstance," I replied, swatting at my chest before pointing to the portal. "Give me a break."

Veil shrugged. "Not everyone is blessed with ignorance. To whom much is given—"

"Much is expected. Aye, I've heard it before."

"Actually, I was going to say 'much can be taken away.' But fine, if that's what you prefer. Either way, the choice to chase after them is yours. You might even succeed in bringing them back, but at what cost?"

I considered that for a moment, though for the life of me I couldn't see how retrieving the Adjudicators would do anything but good. Their disappearance had caused a tidal wave of repercussions that included unstable power vaccums within the Chancery, a spate of gruesome murders that went unchecked and undetected for weeks, and even—inadvertently—the rise of a god I would one day have to slay. Had they been around to enforce the Chancery's laws and police its citizens, none of that would've happened.

But then, what if I was looking at this all wrong? Maybe it wasn't about Boston, or the Chancery, or even the Fae. Maybe this was about me. Narcissistic, sure, but it did occur to me that the Adjudicators' absence had paved the way for my friendship with both Scathach and Robin Redcap, as well as my discovery of the tortured monster my old friend Ryan O'Rye had become—a revelation that would one day lead to a cat-and-mouse game across entire realms. There was also the matter of my brief trip to Scotland and extensive stay in the Otherworld, neither of which would've taken place had I not gotten involved in Chancery politics...which was to say nothing of meeting Morgan le Fay or the Velez siblings or Petal or anyone else I'd come across since.

Had Morgause and Sir Bredbeddle never vanished, what *would* my life look like?

And would I even recognize it?

"What's happenin' to 'em on the other side?" I asked. "Or are ye goin' to insist ye don't know, like always?"

Veil made a show of shrugging.

I gritted my teeth. "Are they safe, at least?"

"I cannot say. Though I can speculate, if you'd like."

"I'll take it."

"Very well. I believe it's possible that those Fae were sent to Tír na Nóg for altruistic reasons. That perhaps Mordred knew the risk he was taking when he escaped from Hell, and that he hoped to keep his mother and her people out of it. Which would suggest they are safer in the Otherworld than they might otherwise have been."

I nodded, relieved by her logic.

"Of course it's also possible they were lured here under false pretenses, perhaps even fed bad information, and that even now they are suffering horribly gruesome deaths."

"Seriously? Ye couldn't just have let me have that?"

"I'm not interested in easing your mind or alleviating your conscience. When this is all over, feel free to find yourself a therapist or a priest. Maybe they'll help you. I'm simply here to see what you decide."

I glared at the shrouded woman. "I am really startin' to dislike ye."

"I take it that means you've come to a resolution?"

I had, though I wasn't terribly proud of myself. In fact, I was a little sick to my stomach for what it implied about me as a person.

"I'll let 'em be," I replied after a lengthy pause.

"Understood."

I turned away from the portal entirely to face the shrouded figure, my hands balled into fists at my sides. "I'm gettin' tired of this bull-shit. I want to know where we're goin' next. I'm through with wakin' up in strange places in someone else's body, bein' asked to play a role I never signed up for."

"I don't recall you being asked to do anything of the sort."

"Ye know what I mean. Apart from Bud-a-Bear, no one seems to see me for who I really am, which means I don't stand a chance in hell of tryin' to convince 'em that I'm not who they t'ink I am."

"Fair enough. Though I wonder whether you've considered why that is."

"I don't care," I snapped. "I may not be able to stop ye from sendin' me to all these places, but I *can* start tellin' people who I really am. Even if they refuse to believe me."

Veil shrugged. "If that's what you want."

"Ye wouldn't try to stop me?"

"Nope."

I scowled, wishing not for the first time I could read that enigmatic expression behind her cowl. "So, where are we goin', then?"

"I'm afraid I have no idea. Your destinations are a mystery to us both until the very moment you arrive. If they weren't, you...*this* wouldn't be necessary."

I gaped at her. "Ye seriously expect me to believe you're goin' into this as blind as I am? Aren't ye supposed to be me guide or whatever?"

"On the contrary, I'm following *you*."

"But you're the one who controls when we leave," I countered.

"Is the person who turns the page responsible for writing the book?"

I frowned, struck by the peculiar phrasing and all it implied. "You're sayin' ye aren't the one pullin' the strings? That what is happenin' to me is outside of your control?"

But Veil was already shaking her head. "I'm saying this isn't happening *to* you. It's happening *because* of you."

"Because of me? How's that?"

Veil fell silent.

"Ye can't tell me that, either," I finished for her, unable to hide my mounting exasperation. "This is total bullshit, ye know that right?"

She shrugged. "I am afraid there are simply some things that must first be experienced to be understood."

Unfortunately, I couldn't refute that claim; I'd dealt with my fair share of improbable truths, few of which I'd considered remotely plausible until I'd been confronted by them. The existence of monsters and holy relics, of higher powers and alien realms—not exactly the sort of stuff you'd expect to find in a standard, peer-reviewed textbook. Still, there was a massive difference between asking me to acknowledge that fact and asking me to accept it.

Not that it seemed I had a choice, either way.

"Fine," I replied at last. "But I hope ye know that when I find whoever's responsible for this, they're goin' to pay. And when that happens, ye best stay out of me way."

Veil inclined her head. "I wouldn't dream of interfering."

"...Blessed you with a power too great to be let loose on the world. And so your mother bound you with her own life-force, containing your ability to move through time until you could use it responsibly."

W hen I opened my eyes again, I found myself in the captain's quarters aboard a ship and tied to a leather chair with a very sharp, very shiny sword hovering inches from my unprotected throat. I flinched backwards and cursed, my body suddenly coursing with adrenaline.

"Ye have got to be kiddin' me," I hissed as I struggled in vain against my restraints. "Not this shite again. Veil, get your ass out here right now. I mean it!"

"Don't move, and stop talking."

I did as I was told.

One, because the edge of that blade was now pressed against my jugular. And two, because I recognized the voice. Both it and the sword, a pirate's cutlass with an ostentatious hand guard, belonged to a young man with pitch black hair and penetrating blue eyes. The young man's name was James Pan, a surname derived from his adopted father, the legendary Peter Pan. The other belonged to his real father, Captain James Hook.

Beside James Pan stood Tiger Lily, a menacing figure decked out in furs, her razor sharp teeth hidden behind a grim scowl that matched the death mask she'd painted over an otherwise attractive face. Over the brave's shoulder hovered the murderous pixie known as Tinkerbell, her lithe little body thrumming pink with power.

Seeing them all gathered together again for the first time in so long, I let out a little sigh of relief. It'd been ages since I'd laid eyes on any of them—not since I'd taken Circe's potion and headed to the Underworld in the hopes of thwarting a madman and saving my friend. Indeed, last I'd heard, the trio of Neverlanders had linked up with my canine companion, Cathal, and the floating island who'd dubbed herself NeverEden. Or at least I prayed that they had; no matter how justified my reasons, I realized I still felt guilty for leaving them behind.

In fact, now that I finally had the chance to speak with them again, I desperately wanted to apologize. Not to mention fill them in on what had happened since then. Unfortunately, now didn't seem like the right time. As in *literally* not the right time, if my hunch was correct.

"Is this the Jolly Roger?" I asked in disbelief, looking around. The last time I'd seen this ship it'd been anchored off the coast of Aeaea, and this particular room had been in far rougher shape—a result of being dashed against the side of an island and repaired by some well-meaning giants.

"See? The Manling knows where he is," Tiger Lily growled. "I told you. He snuck aboard on purpose."

He? I frowned. Was Tiger Lily referring to me? I glanced down and saw that I did indeed have on men's clothes, including a heavy leather duster, a black t-shirt, a pair of dark washed jeans, and a pair of comically clunky cowboy boots that would be impossible to run away in.

Fantastic.

"Yes, you did," James replied, evenly. When the boy turned next to me, he spoke in a stilted baritone meant no doubt to make him seem more intimidating. "We're glad you have woken up, since it means you can finally explain how you managed to stow away aboard this ship, not to mention what you were planning to do before you got caught."

So, that's how it was. I sighed, promising myself silently that when I found whoever was responsible for putting me in these compromising positions, I was going to make them suffer. I mean, forcing me to inhabit a whole new and unfamiliar body was bad enough, but sending me to one who'd managed to alienate my friends to the point of incarceration before I ever arrived? That was just cruel.

"He isn't talking," noted Tinkerbell.

"Cut off his toes," Tiger Lily suggested. "Manlings hate it when you take their toes."

While James considered his companion's horrifying but not inaccurate proposal, I took the opportunity to get my bearings. Judging by the gentle light streaming through the portholes and the briny odor that permeated the air, I had to assume we were out on the open sea just after dawn. We were also anchored, or at the very least not sailing —I could tell that much by the way the ship lurched with each passing wave.

Unfortunately, there wasn't much else to be gleaned from my surroundings alone, which left me with little choice but to ask a probing question of my own. A question which had been nagging at me since I'd arrived.

"Exactly how long has it been since the Lost People fled Neverland?"

All three of my would-be captors stiffened as though they'd been slapped, their expressions ravaged by a grief so new and so raw that I knew I had my answer. My suspicions confirmed, I let out a long sigh.

"Not long, then. Ye have me condolences."

"Who are you?" James surged forward, grabbing me by my collar and angling his arm so the blade of his father's sword was perpendicular to my throat. "Tell me right now, or I will cut out your tongue. I swear I will."

He wouldn't, and we both knew it. But then, I had to admit he wasn't the one I was worried about; both Tiger Lily and Tinkerbell had proven themselves capable of mutilating someone they considered their enemy in the past, and I wasn't eager to lose my tongue.

After all, I was going to need it to do what I'd been sent here to do.

"I'm from the future," I replied, at last. "Sort of. And I t'ink I came here to pass along a message."

"You think?"

I shrugged. The truth was, I felt I was finally beginning to see a pattern to this madness—and I could see now it wasn't the Temples I had to blame, or at least not *only* the Temples. No, these trips through time and space were part of something else. Something bigger. Call it the inexplicability of fate, or perhaps the inexorable march of destiny, but either way it seemed I was being consistently manipulated into making sure what was *supposed* to happen *did* happen.

If so, it would explain why I'd been sent to signal Roland so that he might save his future protégé. Why I'd intervened to keep my younger self from crossing a powerful enchantress and gifted a young werewolf with the means to bind himself even tighter to his childhood friend. Why I'd helped Callie's parents and inadvertently bestowed upon her the nickname she would later go by—which was all very meta, by the way.

Of course, that didn't explain everything. It didn't explain my time with Starlight, for instance. Nor did it account for that boy at the Academy or the missing Chancery members. But then, perhaps this wasn't merely about preserving what was to come. Perhaps there was as much at stake here for the future as there was the present, only I didn't know it yet.

Either way, several important questions lingered, not the least of which was one that had been bothering me ever since I'd stumbled across that portentous note.

Why me?

"What is this message?" Tiger Lily asked, drawing me back into the moment at hand.

I cleared my throat. "That there's a group lookin' for ye to pick 'em up off the southern coast of Neverland. Or there will be, soon."

James frowned. "A group? In Neverland?"

"Aye. They should be there lookin' for the Lost People, for their help. They don't know what has happened to 'em. Not yet."

"And why would they be looking for our help?"

"Because Peter made one of 'em a promise, once. Hook, too. A promise it will be up to the three of ye to keep."

At the mention of Peter and Hook, the three Neverlanders fell silent. Regrettably, there was nothing I could do to ease their pain. Both men were already gone, and crying about it wasn't going to bring them back. Indeed, I found myself oddly unable to conjure up the remorse I'd felt upon first hearing the news; too much time had passed, and I'd suffered my own fair share of tragedies since.

"And why should we honor their promises?" James asked, his face wrenched with bitterness.

"Let's just say that it's in your best interests. Not to mention the best interests of what's left of Neverland."

"There *is* nothing left of Neverland."

"And what if I told ye that wasn't the case?"

The young man hesitated, looking uncharacteristically troubled.

"Who are they?" Tiger Lily placed a hand on his shoulder. "This group of yours. Are they all Manlings, like you?"

"I suppose ye might classify a couple of 'em that way, though not one of the bunch are what we might call Regulars. There should be six of 'em in total. For starters, there's Narcissus—"

"Like the flower?" Tiger Lily interjected.

"Like the flower."

The brave nodded. "The best people are named after flowers."

I scowled. How had I never made that connection? Oh well, it didn't matter, now. "Uh, right. Anyway, there's also Oberon. Ye probably know him by reputation. He's like a sort of sad, wannabe god here in Fae. Then there's Helen of Troy, who isn't really Helen at all but will use her powers of seduction to trick ye into believin' otherwise. Then Cathal. He's basically an enormous guard dog. Hard to miss. So is the talkin' tree, Eve. And finally there's Quinn MacKenna. She'll be the tall, fiery redhead. She's the one you'll want to listen to."

"Why her?" Tiger Lily asked.

"Because Pan and Hook owed her the favor. And because she is goin' to do her very best to help ye."

James perked up at this. "To help us restore Neverland, you mean? That is what you meant earlier, was it not? That it could be saved?"

I hesitated, unsure what to say to that. The fact of the matter was, the last time I'd been to Neverland was when I'd helped a sentient seed from the Tree of Knowledge uproot the entire landmass and turn it into a floating island—an island I hadn't laid eyes on since. Still, I supposed we *had* restored it, in so far as it was no longer the barren husk James had become accustomed to.

"She'll do her best," I replied, noncommittally.

The trio exchanged glances again.

Tiger Lily spoke next. "How do we know this is not some sort of elaborate trap?"

"Huh? What d'ye mean?"

"You know what I mean. What if this is all some sort of ploy to get us to return to Neverland?"

"To what end?" I let my gaze flit over each of my would-be captors in turn. "Your home is gone. What few Lost People remain are safely hidden away. Who's left who would want to do ye any harm?"

"Something has been bothering me," James interjected. "How is it you know so much?"

Ah, now this was the tricky part. While I wasn't entirely sure how all this worked, I'd seen enough movies to suspect that tipping off my younger self would send my life spiraling in an unfamiliar direction, leaving the current me in the lurch when and if I ever made it back to my own time. As such, I gave them the only answer I could, under the circumstances.

The one I'd been given.

"Because I have seen it," I replied. "Because I am a wizard who can move through time. Call me Merlin."

Tiger Lily grunted, her skepticism plain as day despite the death mask painted over her face. She turned to her companions and gestured for them to join her in a huddle, though when she spoke, it was plenty loud enough for me to hear.

"I say we cut off his toes, just to make sure he speaks the truth," she ventured.

"Oy! That isn't funny!"

"I agree we should make certain he isn't lying," James said, ignoring my outburst entirely. "But I would rather we not maim him."

Tiger Lily let out an exasperated sigh. "You never let me take their toes. How else am I going to finish making that necklace I have been working on?"

"Maybe you should consider using something else?"

Tiger Lily glanced sidelong at my crotch. "Are you saying what I think you are saying?"

"Probably not, no."

"We could always make him walk the plank," Tinkerbell chimed in brightly, her high-pitched voice ringing through the air.

Tiger Lily rapped the butt of her spear against the floorboards enthusiastically. "Yes! An excellent suggestion, especially for a no-good pixie."

"Bite me, Manling hands." Tinkerbell stuck her tongue out at her fellow Neverlander.

"I do not remember Peter complaining about my hands."

"Excuse me?!" Tinkerbell sputtered, her body strobing scarlet momentarily.

"Enough!" James snapped, cutting them both off before their exchange could escalate to blows. "Focus. Are you two sure having him walk the plank is a good idea?"

Tiger Lily glared at her diminutive companion but replied in a cool, detached voice. "I am sure. It is what the Captain would have wanted. He always did love a good splash."

"Pan, too!" Tinkerbell insisted.

"Very well, if you both are certain..."

"We are."

"Definitely."

"Oy!" I stomped my heels several times to get their attention. "Do

I not get a say in this? What if I can't swim, huh? D'ye ever t'ink of that?"

It was James who turned first, his expression so severe all of a sudden that it made me rethink my earlier estimation of the young man's scruples. Perhaps he *would* have cut out my tongue, after all. Or at the very least amputated a couple toes.

"I think a wizard who can move through time should be able to manage taking a little dip in the sea, don't you?" he asked.

Well, he had me there.

Dammit.

34

Less than a few minutes later, my normal-sized captors were dragging me up the stairs by the rope binding my arms. Tinkerbell, meanwhile, hovered a foot from my ear singing a bawdy pirate shanty about a lascivious nun in a voice that might have belonged to a creepy doll or an unhinged, prepubescent ghost.

"...and when she bared her breasts, they all confesseddddd, and that's why priests should be ladies!"

"Hold on, sorry. What the hell d'ye just say?" I nearly tripped over my own feet as I craned my neck to look back at the pixie.

Tinkerbell took one look at my face before she burst out laughing. She surged forward with a pulse of pinkish light, her gossamer wings leaving rosey motes drifting in their wake as she took off towards the deck. Up ahead and framed by the dark rim on the open doorway, I could see a cerulean sky riddled with long, slender clouds. A salty breeze drifted over us, bathing us in the fragrance of the sea.

"Stop stalling," Tiger Lily urged, tugging at my ropes as if I were a dog on a walk. "I have seen Manlings with stumps for feet move faster than you."

"Probably because they were tryin' to get away from ye."

Tiger Lily nodded. "Yes."

"Listen, I've been t'inkin'. About this whole walk the plank, prove I am what I say I am t'ing? Maybe we could have a little chat, instead. Like, maybe I could tell ye some stuff about yourselves that I shouldn't know? Or maybe we could do like some sort of test where ye ask me a question I shouldn't know the answer to, but it turns out that I do, because I'm from the future?"

"Hmm," James said. "Alright. When will I die?"

"Uh, well, I can't exactly give ye a precise date on that one, but—"

"Another one, then. Which of the Lost People will my sister marry?"

Damn, this really wasn't working out like I'd hoped. I shook my head, wishing I'd set some sort of parameters on this little Q&A. Like, you know, sports trivia or current events. Pop culture references. That sort of thing.

I cleared my throat. "So, when I said ask me somethin', what I meant was—"

James held up a hand. "I've heard enough."

"But—"

Tiger Lily yanked on my restraints again. "You are going to walk the plank. Accept it."

I groaned, wishing there was something I could say that might save me. Unfortunately, there wasn't much I could tell them that they'd believe, or even understand. Besides that, there was an inherent risk in revealing too much. What I needed from them—and by I, I meant the version of me destined to stand on that barren beach in desperate need of a ride—was to trust that what I'd told them was the truth. Otherwise, they might never show, which could very well rewrite history.

Only...so what if I did? After all, I *was* privy to a great many things that my younger self would have desperately liked to know. Secrets that never should have been kept from me and realities that might have made my life a whole lot easier. Like Frankenstein's true involvement, for example, or what awaited us all once we reached the Eighth Sea.

"Okay," I began, haltingly. "So, there might be a few more t'ings I left out if you'd be interest—"

"We have heard enough."

James emphasized his statement by lugging me up the few remaining steps and half-carrying, half-dragging me across the deck of his ship. When I tried to protest, one of Tiger Lily's surprisingly strong and calloused hands clamped over my mouth.

Eventually, I found myself standing at the base of a strip of wood about the length and breadth of an ironing board. Below it, dark blue waters stretched all the way to the horizon without a landmass in sight, suggesting we were awfully far out to sea. I warily eyed the waves that beat against the ship's hull, looking for signs of sharks circling, or maybe the silhouette of some prehistoric, mythical beast made entirely out of groping hands like a pervy puffer fish.

I mean, this *was* Fae, after all; anything was possible.

"This is it." James nudged Tiger Lily, who grudgingly removed her hand from my mouth. "Any last words?"

"Aye, I can t'ink of a few," I muttered.

"Then say them. But make it fast, wizard. This game of yours has gone on long enough."

I gritted my teeth as I realized there was only one way I was going to make them believe what I'd said was true: I had to perform a little magic. Unfortunately, as things stood I had one trick and one trick only at my disposal.

A disappearing act.

"Ye asked for it," I warned. Then I took a deep breath, turned my face to the sky, and screamed. "Oy, Veil! Get your ass over here right now and get me the hell out of here!"

Nothing happened.

"What kind of spell was that supposed to—"

I felt some invisible force grab me by my collar and tug before James could finish, causing both him and Tiger Lily to stumble backwards in surprise—an expression that I imagine became even more pronounced when I vanished right before their very eyes.

35

"Once, there may have been time to explain the purpose of this power and how to use it, but that time has passed."

36

I found myself in a brilliantly white world. The effect was almost blinding at first, like staring directly at a sun-drenched patch of pavement, but fortunately did not last long. Soon, discernible shapes became clear, their edges defined by the faint shadows they cast.

There was a couch beside me, for instance, as well as a pair of matching accent chairs on either side of a coffee table. A translucent vase full of bone-white sunflowers sat upon it, their stems submerged in what looked eerily like whole milk. Meanwhile, achromatic paintings adorned every wall but for the one occupied by a sizable bookshelf, its shelves cluttered with the spines of titleless books.

"Welcome to the Matrix," I muttered.

Frankly, I had to admit I wasn't too keen on the aesthetic; the total absence of color made it difficult to trust my eyes, not to mention the havoc it wrought on my spatial awareness. Indeed, this only got worse when I discovered the window behind me, outside which I spotted etiolated trees lining the edge of a chalk-colored cliff overlooking an ocean made of cream.

Feeling a little nauseous, I turned and put my back against the wall. And, when that didn't work, I shut my eyes. It was only then, with my newfound surroundings no longer assaulting my senses, that I realized not *everything* in the room had been white. I hastily opened my eyes and looked down, confirming that I was indeed wearing a long-sleeved evening dress and high-heeled shoes.

And both were *red*.

Like a bright, bright red.

"Who the fuck am I now, Jessica Rabbit?"

I sighed, stepped away from the wall, and turned a quick circle to be sure there were no other surprises. Unfortunately, it was then that I noticed a splotch of color where my back had been—a funky shape not unlike one of those Rorschach tests, albeit painted in red ink rather than blank. Worse, that wasn't the extent of the damage; bright red shoe prints marred the hardwood beneath my feet as though I'd stepped in a puddle of blood and started waltzing willy-nilly around the room, while a single set of handprints stained the windowsill where I'd leaned on it.

Except my palms were completely clean.

"Okay, Stephen King, ye can have your room back," I joked aloud, one hand cupped to my mouth to make myself heard by whomever happened to call this place home. When no one answered or immediately appeared, however, I decided it was up to me to investigate. And so I began scouring the room in search of whatever answers I could find.

In my experience, you could tell a lot about someone from what they chose to display in their home. For instance, the paintings on the walls—though lacking in color, the texture of the medium left an indelible mark on the canvases. So, good taste. Of course, that jived with the fine quality of the furniture and the tasteful floral arrangement.

Still, what I needed wasn't a personality profile, but a name. And to find *that*, I was going to have to stop skimming and start perusing —beginning with the bookshelf.

I wandered over and grabbed the nearest book, confident that I'd at least find an old watermark from a local library, or maybe even an inscription if I was lucky. I wasn't; the pages were utterly blank, the print too shallow to cast shadows. Annoyed, I set the book aside and retrieved a second. Same thing. Dammit. I fetched another, and then another, until I'd worked my way down two whole rows with nothing to show for it.

"Come on, ye stupid fuckin' t'ing," I cursed as I snatched the last book on that particular shelf.

Just as I was about to crack it open, however, a tremendous crash sounded from an adjoining hallway I hadn't noticed earlier.

"WHO DARES STEP FOOT IN MY HOUSE?!"

The words thundered throughout the room and were accompanied immediately by the clamor of footsteps. Heavy footsteps. I cringed and retreated from the source of that sound until my back was against the wall, acutely aware that I'd left behind a stack of books smeared red from my grubby touch and dozens of triangular smudges all over the floor. Shit.

Before I could decide whether to announce myself or simply start apologizing, however, a glowing white figure appeared around the corner, his blazing silhouette momentarily blinding me. I hastily shielded my face and tried to blink the spots out of my eyes, wary of an attack. Fortunately, none came. Instead, I lowered my arm to find a heavily muscled, shirtless man with a ginger mane and beard that jutted halfway down his chest glaring at me from the other side of the room.

"How did you get in here?!" he bellowed, spittle flying from his lips. His red-rimmed eyes danced with a peculiar sort of madness, a single vein bulging down the middle of his ruddy forehead.

"Okay, first of all, there's no need to shout," I replied, evenly. "This is a tiny livin' room, not an auditorium."

"Answer me!"

"I don't know, alright? I just sort of appeared. It was a shock to me, too."

"Liar!" he accused. "No one can enter without my permission. Not even...wait."

The red-haired brute took a halting step forward, studying me as though I were some sort of majestic bird moments from taking flight, or perhaps an exceedingly scrumptious cheeseburger about to hit the floor—he was a hard guy to read. I, meanwhile, did what any sane person would when she finds herself alone in a cage with a crazy person: I stayed very, very still.

"I know you," he said, squinting.

"Is that so?"

"Yes, yes. But from *where*?"

"Maybe we bumped into each other somewhere?" I suggested, wishing I had some way to find out whose face I happened to be wearing, this time. Not that this had done me any favors thus far.

"Impossible. It's been ages since I stepped foot out there." He waved his hand past his ear as if shooing away a fly. "And I don't have many visitors. Not after what happened last time."

"Wait, what happened last time?"

"Nothing that anyone can prove," he replied, distractedly. The madman rocked back on his heels and raised a finger to his lips in thought. Then, with a cry of comprehension, pointed directly at me. "I've got it! You are the spell made flesh, in the flesh!"

I experienced a twinge of recognition but managed to keep my expression blank as I replied. "Sorry, but I t'ink ye may have me mixed up with someone else."

"No, it *is* you. I can see it, clear as glass. You know, he always said he'd find a way, but after so many others tried and failed, I never imagined he'd succeed. Remarkable. Absolutely remarkable."

"Whoa, slow down." I held up a forestalling hand. "I'm not followin' anythin' you're sayin'. Maybe ye could start by tellin' me who the hell ye are? Or where in God's name I am?"

"Ah, yes. Introductions. You may call me Matthias. And this is my world. My own personal hell." Matthias threw his arms wide and performed a little twirl. "Lovely, isn't it?"

"Uh, aye. Very. I especially like all the, uh...white."

"It soothes me."

"That's...nice."

Matthias grunted and let his gaze flit from my dress to the various stains I'd left all over his living room—or his prison, as he'd dubbed it.

"Sorry about the mess," I said. "I was looking for answers."

"And did you find any?"

"Not really," I admitted.

"Then what's that in your hand?"

I frowned, realizing I still clutched the last book I'd taken from the shelf. I turned it over and saw the cover bore an embossed title which I could actually make out. I held the slender book up for Matthias to see.

"Ah," he said. "Foggerty's Fairy, W.S. Gilbert, 1874. How appropriate. What made you choose that one?"

"I didn't. It was the last book I picked up, that's all."

"Are you certain of that?"

"Of course. Why?"

Matthias shrugged. "It's a play with an interesting premise, that's all. The story is about a man who makes a deal with a fairy to change the past, thereby altering his present. As is so often the case, however, the outcome is not what he expected, and indeed his wish seems only to have made matters worse, at least at first. Funny how that so often happens, don't you think?"

"How often what happens?"

"Oh, you know. Someone tinkers with time, and everyone suffers for it."

"What's that supposed to mean?" I demanded.

"Just an observation. Anyway, the play itself was not particularly well-received, if memory serves. Too tedious. Still, its ambition should be applauded."

"Hold on. 'If memory serves?' Just how old are ye?"

"A better question," Matthias replied cagily, "is why you were sent here of all places? Unless..."

"Unless what?"

"Unless it was me you came to see. Yes, of course. It all makes sense, now." Matthias shook his head in disbelief. "And after all these centuries, to think *I* would be the Maker from the prophecy..."

"Sorry, d'ye just say 'Maker'? As in *the* Makers? I thought they were all gone."

Matthias barked a laugh. "Gone? No. Biding their time, perhaps. But nevermind that. Now that I know why you've come, we have far more pressing matters to attend to."

"Huh? Like what?"

"Like forging Masks."

37

No matter how hard I pressed Matthias for more information in the wake of his proclamation, the Maker didn't seem inclined to explain himself further. Instead, he urged me to join him for a tour of his prison—or at least that's how it came across, considering the fact he'd clearly done something to get himself locked up in what I had to assume was the equivalent of a padded room for all-powerful wizards.

"Look," I told him, "I'm not goin' anywhere with ye until ye tell me what the hell is goin' on. I mean it. First ye say that ye know me, and then ye start talkin' about travelin' through time and Makers and forgin' masks and whatever else. It's all too much."

Matthias cocked his head but said nothing.

"Well?" I asked.

"I was just waiting for you to ask an actual question."

I rolled my eyes. "Fine. Who is it ye t'ink I am?"

"Not who. What."

"What, then."

"I told you already. You are the spell made flesh."

"Aye, so ye keep sayin'. But what does it mean, and where are ye gettin' it from?"

Matthias sighed. "Do you really want to know?"

"I wouldn't be askin', otherwise."

The Maker nodded, closed his eyes, and began reciting something in a tone very much unlike his own—deeper somehow, with a great deal more gravitas, like an actor performing Shakespeare or a teenage boy trying to impress a girl.

"When the Dark Horse has been summoned and the Throne of Heaven sits empty...when the Watchers are no longer content to watch and the Pale Rider himself succumbs to Despair...when those below look up with Hope in their eyes and those above quake in fear...the Alpha and the Omega will be reforged in a furnace beneath the world. But first, the spell become flesh must be cast, a Maker must break his vow, and a child must be sacrificed. Otherwise, the rose will never bloom, the temple will crumble as though it never stood, and ashes shall become our sole birthright."

I shivered as he finished, the hairs on the back of my neck standing straight up for some inexplicable reason. Of course, I recognized the small passage from the note I'd found after being attacked in Dez's living room, but the rest of it was a jumbled mess of terms I'd only encountered in passing if at all.

The Dark Horse was the name of that spell that kept chasing me, or perhaps the person who'd cast it, I still wasn't clear on that bit. The Throne of Heaven was fairly self-explanatory, while the Watchers could have referred to the Grigori—one of whom I'd encountered years ago in a New York City subway station. The Pale Rider was another name for the Horseman of Death, though I wasn't sure what he'd have to be despaired about. The last I'd seen him he'd seemed in decent spirits, if a bit grumpy.

As for the rest, well, all I had was conjecture. The Alpha and the Omega reminded me of something Starlight had said, but much of that visit remained a blur to me. Of the spell, the Maker, and the mother, only the Maker seemed accounted for, and I was standing across from him. As for the rose and the temple, I could only assume it had to do with Callie and Nate, respectively—though I certainly didn't care for the way it ended.

"What's that from?" I asked.

"It's the Dark Horse prophecy," he replied, his manic grin slipping to reveal a grimace. "Passed down from before the time of Solomon, from before the Fall, if you can believe it. The prophecy that so many of my kind died trying to fulfill. And now here you are, proving it true with your very existence."

"Don't be ridiculous. What the hell do I have to do with any of that nonsense?"

Matthias grunted. "Everything. Can't you see? You were their contingency plan. Their insurance policy. You are the key."

"The key to what? And who're 'they'? I still don't—"

I was interrupted by a peal of thunder so cacophonous that it shook the suddenly much dimmer room. I wheeled to face the window, where I discovered a white world under siege; the ominous storm clouds were back, their sprawling mass lunging across the pure white sky even as bolt after bolt of scarlet lightning went arcing towards the ground. As I watched, a hooded rider with bright golden eyes emerged, a glowing green medallion dangling from his neck. I balked at the abrupt appearance of the terrifying apparition, struck by the sheer power it must have taken to summon such a specimen.

"My, my. It seems my descendant has truly come into his own."

I flinched to find Matthias standing beside me to peer out the window, his face scrunched up in thought.

"Your descendant?"

Matthias nodded. "That thing reeks of Elder magic, but I know Nate's work when I see it, even if it is beyond his current capabilities."

"Wait, are ye sayin' *Nate Temple* sent that after me? What the fuck for?"

"For a slight you've yet to commit, I'd imagine."

"Huh? That doesn't even make sense."

Mathias raised his half-lidded gaze to mine and a slow, eerie smile spread across his face. "Welcome to my world."

I shuddered. "Whatever. Look, it's been...well, I was goin' to say enlightenin', but honestly I have more questions now than when I arrived. But it's time I move on. I've been told on good authority that I can't let that storm catch up to me, and I don't intend to."

"Oh, there's no need to worry about that." Matthias patted my back, his meaty palm thumping like a freaking shovel against my skin. "It's like I told you. This is *my* world."

"Meanin' what?"

"Meaning I can do this."

The Maker snapped his fingers, and suddenly we stood in a completely different space. Gone were the paintings on the walls, the furniture, the stack of blood-stained books, and even the hardwood floors I'd ruined—supplanted instead by the dim confines of a large, puddle-ridden cave littered with glowing golden crystals. Indeed, the transition was so abrupt I wobbled and nearly fell, though I'll admit my inappropriate footwear didn't do me any favors. Matthias tried to help, but I waved him off.

"I'm fine," I snapped. "Just tell me where we are now."

"Still my home. I suppose you could call it my basement."

"Very funny."

Matthias shrugged. "My house has a lot of rooms. Though I must say this is one I never expected to visit again."

I frowned and took a moment to study the space, noticing for the first time an anvil the size of a dining room table some thirty feet away, its surface fashioned from the very same crystal that jutted from the walls. An impossibly large copper hammer leaned beside it, its exterior covered in a fine patina of mint green rust. There was also an enormous fire pit from which ghostly embers blazed, heating up the otherwise damp and chilly cavern.

"If that's true, why is there a fire?"

"Oh, that never goes out. Trust me, I've tried."

Finding it increasingly difficult to follow the twists and turns of this consistently baffling conversation, I simply shook my head. "But we're safe from the storm here, yes?"

Matthias snorted. "Of course. Not even that spell could track us down here."

Right. Of course, how silly of me.

"So, what now?"

The Maker held up a hand, his expression troubled as though

he'd caught wind of something foul. After a few tense moments, he relaxed, though only marginally. "We should hurry. Best not to be here when Hephaestus comes back."

"Wait, Hephaestus?" I gaped at the Maker. "As in the Greek god of the forge? Aphrodite's husband?"

"The very same."

"Hold on, I thought ye said this place was your basement? Why would he be usin' it?"

"I...may have lent it to him without his knowledge."

"Why would ye do that?"

"Because raw power does not come cheap, and I knew such power might one day be needed...even if I swore never to wield its like again. Delusion, I believe they call that."

"I don't understand."

"Nor do I expect you to." Matthias shook himself. "It's not important. Just know that for what comes next, mine is not the only power that will be called upon. A Maker may be able to bend reality to their will, but what we fashion here today will redefine reality, and only the power of a god can do that. Or a godkiller, in your case."

I opened my mouth to ask what the hell that was supposed to mean, but the Maker was apparently done talking; Matthias surged forward with his arms outstretched, drawing in a deep lungful of air —and with it, more power than I could have possibly fathomed.

38

For a moment, it was as if time folded in on itself, compressing incrementally until a day became an hour, an hour became a minute, and a second became an eternity. In that hushed space between one breath and another, I could see the light emitted by the crystals drifting outwards in lazy penumbra, the droplets of water hanging suspended in mid-air as they dribbled from the ceiling, the muscles of Matthias' naked back flexed and furrowed like one of Michaelangelo's anatomical studies.

Then, so abruptly it felt like being catapulted over the edge of an impossibly tall roller coaster, time reasserted itself, and I was struck by a wall of such sheer power that it left me quivering and unsteady. The experience was both enervating and electrifying—somewhere between acrobatic sex and an hour-long session of hot yoga. But then, I supposed that was the appealing thing about magic: it could do things for you that not even money could buy.

I was still recovering when I heard Matthias cry out in a language I didn't recognize. Latin, maybe? No, too guttural. This was something older—a tongue that had died out millennia ago. And yet, I understood it. Or at least I understood the intention behind the words. I could tell, for instance, that the Maker was beckoning to the raw power that permeated this place, pleading with it to align itself with him.

I could also tell when the cave responded; crackling energy began coiling about his outstretched hands, sending the occasional spark soaring towards the ceiling. The crystals began to flicker and strobe, leaving us in near impenetrable darkness one moment and almost blinding light the next. The air became thick with heat as that energy surrounded each of Matthias' hands to form gloves of shimmering, kaleidoscopic light. Then, with a sudden burst of power that made the floor tremble beneath my feet, Matthias fell to one knee and thrust his right arm into the ground up to his elbow.

He stayed like that for a long moment before withdrawing his arm from the rock, at which point I noticed a curved bit of rock cupped in the palm of his massive hand like a slender bowl—except it wasn't a bowl.

It was a mask.

A mask that, once removed from the bowels of the earth, radiated its own energy. I gasped to look at it, momentarily overwhelmed by sensations I couldn't explain, such as the weight of a cold iron shackle clamping tight around my throat, the stench of burning flesh and hair, and the perturbing sound of a lock latching shut.

Matthias set the first mask aside and delved into the earth again with his left arm, going even deeper and hesitating even longer this time. When at last he produced the second, I swore I could hear the collar around my throat snap above a cacophony of sighs and sobs, the taste of sweat and tears sitting heavy on my tongue as if I'd guzzled them down myself.

The Maker rose, albeit with the difficulty one might expect from a much older, much less fit specimen, drawing the power with him so that all I could do was stare as he plodded over to stand before a nearby wall. This time, the energy he collected was a frigid thing, leaving a layer of frost at his feet and turning my breath to fog. Matthias lunged without warning, driving a hand encased in power so deep into the wall his entire arm vanished within. Then, with a snarl, he drew back.

The third mask appeared, and what I'd described as frigidity became so much more—a cold so pervasive it hollowed out my bones and made from their empty husks a home. Grieving wails and tortured screams began wafting from the ceiling like the demented tracks played at a haunted house, only these were real. I don't know how I knew that, but I did.

Huddled, shivering, and covering my ears to block out those horrible sounds, I didn't even notice Matthias retrieve the final mask until it was already done. The screams quickly faded, supplanted by cheers and furtive whispers. The cold followed, its icy chill replaced by the borderline unpleasant sensation of sunlight beating down upon my skin—a sensation that got more and more unbearable the longer it went on.

I must have closed my eyes in the hopes of blunting the pain, because I didn't even hear Matthias approach until he called to me from a mere few feet away. I opened my eyes and flinched to find the cave far dimmer than before, the crystals faded to a dull amber. Matthias, meanwhile, was backlit by the masks he cradled—each of which burned with an internal glow.

"I have given them life," he said, his voice ragged with exhaustion. "Now it is up to you to give them a name."

"Up to me? But why—"

Matthias thrust the first mask at me so forcefully that I had no choice but to take it. I gritted my teeth, expecting the damned thing to burn my hands. Instead, I felt an absurdly heavy weight descend on me from above, pressing down as if someone had turned up the gravity in the room. I struggled to stay upright, determined not to fall to my knees no matter how badly I wanted to.

"Why...is it...so damned...heavy?" I managed to say between breaths.

"You tell me."

"What?"

"Tell me what you feel. The sensation. Name it."

It was only then that I realized I *did* feel something. Not just a steady assault of sensory information, though that was part of it, but an overwhelmingly tangible force. A force whose name I could actually visualize in my head.

"Justice," I whispered.

"Yes!"

Matthias snatched the mask from my grasp and passed me another. Unlike its predecessor, this one felt like I'd been tethered to an enormous balloon. It wasn't joy, and yet it wasn't *not* joy, either. It was something more cathartic than that. Something that could never be given freely, but could only be earned.

"Absolution."

"Good. Now, this one."

The instant I touched the third mask, a crushing sadness descended upon me like a tidal wave, squeezing me until I felt smothered by grief and sorrow. Struck by a nagging sense of familiarity and a great deal of personal torment, I only needed a few seconds before blurting out its name.

"Despair! That's despair. Please, just take it away."

Matthias did as I asked. "Here. The last."

I took the final mask with both hands like an offering, my nerves all but shot after experiencing so many visceral emotions over so short a span. Unlike its predecessors, however, the undercurrents particular to this mask had a subtlety to them that I had trouble deciphering. Moreover, I felt a sense of kinship with the damned thing— a recognition I couldn't rightly explain.

"What do you feel?" Matthias asked, stepping close. "Tell me."

"I feel..." I drifted off, unable to describe the emotion. There was a sort of bliss in it, but not the kind that stemmed from anything concrete. More the possibility of happiness, but so distant and so vulnerable it reminded me of a candle flame just waiting to be snuffed out.

Matthias leaned in. "What? What is it?"

"Hope. I feel...hope."

For some reason, this seemed to please the Maker; he snatched the Mask from my grasp and held all four aloft like precious jewels, all the while intoning in that dead language from before. I sagged in relief, assuming I'd fulfilled whatever role I'd been tasked with, only to experience a sudden lethargy so debilitating that I collapsed.

I dropped to all fours so fast that my dress tore, cracking both my knees against the cave floor and skinning my palms in the process. And yet, I hardly noticed. Instead, I found my attention drawn to the veins of power streaming down my arms.

I'd seen such veins before, back when I was channeling my inner goddess, but these were different, somehow: gold-tinged and coursing over my skin rather than pulsing beneath it, they spread down my forearms to my hands and finally to the floor where they began to spread, branching off like the limbs of a tree to pool at Matthias' feet.

The Maker knelt and reverently dipped just one of the masks into that golden puddle, dousing it as one might a slice of bread until it was sopping wet and shimmering with ichor. Then, with a curt gesture, all four masks vanished, the puddle dried up, and the crystals strobed to life once more.

39

Matthias fell back into his haunches with sweat pouring down his face, his breathing so labored he might as well have run a marathon. Surprisingly, I found myself in similar shape; my hair was drenched and rode the back of my neck like a wet mop, my skin was clammy and faintly feverish to the touch, and my heart wouldn't stop racing.

"What...the fuck...was that?" I demanded, breathlessly.

"Not sure what you mean," Matthias wheezed.

"Don't...give me that. What did...ye just do?"

The Maker rolled onto his side with a wince, a network of blue veins bulging beneath his pallid skin. "I broke a vow I never dreamed I'd break. What you see now is the price I must pay for that."

"What vow?"

"The Masks. Horsemen Masks, as yet unclaimed. I swore I'd never create another batch. Not after...well, that's not important."

While my mind was busy spinning with the implications of what Matthias had just said, the Maker gathered himself to stand. I snatched at his arm and felt a jolt of electricity surge up my own.

"Christ! What was that?!"

"The lingering effects of the spell we just cast. Although I wouldn't call it a spell, per se. More an act of creation, fueled by my power and yours. And of course the natural energies that permeate this place."

"Sorry, could ye run that by me again? *Whose* power?"

"Yours and mine. The power of a Maker and a godkiller. How else did you think Masks were forged?"

"I'd never really thought about it," I admitted. "But wait a minute, what does that have to do with that golden liquid? And where did it come from?"

"Ichor," he corrected. "The blood of a slain god, awarded to the vanquisher. In its raw state, it can be used to accomplish all manner of things."

I frowned as I considered this, reminded of my earlier boast to Callie's parents regarding the death of Chernobog—a particularly nasty deity I'd taken down during an exceptionally bloody battle against a coven of misguided witches. So, that explained where the so-called ichor had come from, at least.

"Then explain how ye knew I had it," I challenged him. "And how the hell d'ye make it come out of me like that?"

"Because otherwise you wouldn't have come. And that's easy. The power never rightfully belonged to you in the first place. All I did was siphon it from that absurd repository you are walking around with."

"What repository?"

Matthias waved me off. "Enough questions. It's time we leave."

I balled my fists, repressing the urge to scream at the ginger bastard for taking what he had from me. Frankly, the only reason I didn't was that he'd taken something I hadn't even known I possessed, which felt a little like mourning the death of a complete stranger: understandable, but not exactly rational. After all, while I may have ended up a little worse for wear, I wasn't injured in any visible way. The question was, what did we have to show for it?

"What d'ye do with the Masks?"

"Take my hand," Matthias insisted, ignoring my query. "I will take us somewhere safer."

"Safer? As in, not safe?"

"Nowhere is ever truly safe, and those who believe otherwise are fools."

I grunted at that. "I see you're a glass half-shattered kind of guy."

"I don't know what that means." Matthias swiped at his sweat-slick brow with his forearm, his lips curled in a sneer, his eyes haunted by what I could only assume was a particularly painful memory. "What I do know is that safety is a luxury only the ignorant can afford."

I had to admit he had a point, but that didn't mean I was inclined to let him derail the conversation. Not with so many of my questions left unanswered. For example, had we *really* just forged a bunch of Horsemen Masks? And what was with that whole naming ceremony thing?

In hindsight, I could've sworn I'd heard some of those titles before, and that they had something to do with Nate Temple—if only I could recall what. Unfortunately, since my impromptu platelet donation I was struggling to function, let alone think; my legs felt like jelly, my head was pounding, and my poor calves were killing me.

Stupid freaking heels.

"Before I even consider takin' your hand," I said after a moment's silence, "how about ye tell me why. Why d'ye do this? What was it all for?"

"We don't have time for this."

"Humor me."

"I could just leave you. I am certain Hephaestus would be pleased to find someone to blame for the siphoned power."

"If that's what ye want, then go. I have me own ride."

Or so I hoped.

The Maker grumbled something under his breath.

"What was that?"

"I said," he repeated himself in a much louder voice, "that you are as frustrating as he was. You know what? Fine. You want to know why this had to happen? Because lives are at stake. Or they will be, at any rate."

"Whose lives?"

Matthias snorted. "You'd know the answer to that better than I would. You've seen the results firsthand, or at the very least witnessed the fallout, or you wouldn't be here."

"I have no idea what you're talkin' about," I admitted, truthfully.

"Because you refuse to open your eyes!" Matthias snarled, his teeth bared like a wild animal. "It's all right there for you to put together, but you would rather be blind than face the truth."

I frowned, thoughtfully. Ordinarily, an outburst like that might have sent me into a rage of my own, but I found myself oddly calm in the face of the Maker's anger. Partially because I knew he was wrong; while it may have seemed obvious to Matthias what was going on, I was still very much floundering in the dark. That, and I was beginning to suspect Matthias was far less omniscient than I'd given him credit for initially. So much of what he said sounded like psychic mumbo-jumbo—nothing but broad, sweeping generalities that could mean anything...or nothing.

"Maybe ye could explain it to me," I replied, evenly. "Walk me through it. Let's start with the Horsemen Masks ye made."

Matthias shook his head in agitation. "They aren't finished, not yet. They've been given names, but they've yet to live up to them. That will be up to their owners."

"And who would those owners be?"

"Whoever the boy chooses."

"The boy?"

"My descendant."

So, Nate *was* involved. Which meant the Masks would very likely end up in his possession, assuming they hadn't already. I snapped my fingers in recollection. "The Horseman of Hope."

"Yes." Matthias grimaced, and I noticed he was trembling. When I asked him about it, he flinched. "It's nothing."

Except it wasn't nothing—I could tell. Indeed, if I didn't know better I'd have sworn Matthias had just seen a ghost. He'd gone even paler than before, and his eyes wouldn't stop flitting around the room. It was like someone had flipped a switch inside him, taking his self-assurance with it.

"What is it?" I asked, soothingly. "Ye can tell me."

"Too loud," he whispered. "It's all too loud. The colors, they won't stop screaming."

I experienced a brief surge of sympathy for the troubled Maker. Granted, he'd used me somehow, but—assuming he was telling the truth—he'd done it in the service of someone we both seemed to care for. If I couldn't forgive him for that, the least I could do was put it aside. After all, sometimes being the bigger person meant having the perspective necessary to offer a helping hand.

"This better not be a ploy to get me to leave before ye answer me questions," I teased.

"What?" Matthias turned a pair of dead eyes to me. "What were we doing? I...can't remember."

"That's alright." I held out my hand. "Ye we're goin' to take us somewhere safe, remember?"

"Somewhere safe?"

"Aye. Well, safer, at least."

"Safer." Matthias took a long look around before his eyes settled on my outstretched hand. "Yes. Of course."

And then, without warning, the Maker pushed me backwards into a different world.

40

I fell back into waist-high water and came up soaked and spluttering, my every sense heightened as a result of the sudden change in environment—not to mention the abrupt dip in temperature. As I blinked water out of my eyes and attempted to get my bearings, a cool, autumnal wind gusted over me, its cold caress only marginally offset by the warmth of the overhead sun.

Of Matthias, there was no sign. Indeed, I found myself all alone facing a rocky shore tucked between a pair of snow-capped mountains. Shocked and still recovering from the forging of the Masks as I was, it took me a moment to recognize the landscape as the beach I'd encountered before all this madness started. Of course, it wasn't entirely my fault; I was facing the opposite direction, and the season had clearly changed. Gone was the snow in the valley beyond, while green lichen and tufts of grass hugged the rocks further inland.

And yet, there was something beyond—a dusting of white that formed a solid layer on the horizon. Not snow, but something. A sheet of ice, maybe, or a cliff made of white stone?

"Why the fuck did he send me here?" I asked through chattering teeth. "Veil! Veil, where the hell am I? Get down here and tell me what's goin' on!"

To my great vexation but not necessarily my surprise, Veil neither appeared nor replied.

And so, with a grunt of annoyance, I tore off the red heels and waded forward until I reached the beach. Then, carefully so as not to cut my feet, I began making my way towards the valley—sensing, perhaps, that whatever answers I might find could only lie there.

As I got closer, however, I began to realize that what I'd mistaken for a naturally occurring phenomenon was in fact something else altogether; though large enough to be a cliff face, the object was rotund and had hundreds of articulated ridges, almost like...snakeskin.

Even as that thought crossed my mind, I saw all those ridges bunch and shift, its towering mass grinding the ground beneath like the plow of a tractor until the creature's monstrous head appeared. Easily the size of a jumbo airplane, it crested with a sinuous slowness to reveal a pair of fiery red eyes on either side of a serpent-like head crowned in spines not unlike those of a porcupine.

I froze, my nose picking up the beast's heady scent before my brain had time to process what I was seeing. Unfortunately, the creature registered my presence at the exact same moment; its tongue flicked out from between its lipless mouth and its nostrils flared.

"You ssshould not be here."

I could not have agreed more.

I began backpedaling without thinking, my every instinct urging me to run—not out of fear, but out of self-preservation. Just because I'd faced off against bigger, scarier monsters in my time didn't mean I wanted to go toe-to-scale against something that could swallow me whole. Especially not alone.

Except I wasn't alone.

Because it was at that moment that Veil at last deigned to appear, taking me into her arms like a nurturing mother even as the monster's thunderous voice boomed overhead.

"I will await your return, ssspellborn."

41

"...How do you expect selflessness to survive without repercussions?"

42

I jerked away from Veil's embrace, my every sense alerted to the possibility of being pursued by that horrifying monster. Only it appeared Veil had already vanished, as had the valley. Where once there had been blue skies and a blazing sun, now there were vaulted ceilings and hundreds, if not thousands, of metallic objects piled as high and far as my eye could see. And not merely metallic objects, either, but also elaborate period costumes, classical paintings I'd have expected to find hanging in the world's finest art museums, stacks of scrolls and leather-bound tomes, and a casual display of artifacts that would have fascinated many an archaeologist.

It was...glorious.

Glorious, and mind-boggling.

To be honest, I felt a little like a certain Disney princess when she first laid eyes on that breathtaking library—a scene which did it for just about every bibliophile with a pulse. Except this wasn't merely a compilation of literature, but perhaps the finest collection of material possessions anyone had ever dreamt of, let alone seen. The sort of place a retired black magic arms dealer like myself might call her Holy Grail...assuming the Holy Grail wasn't tucked away here somewhere, in which case I had no idea *what* to call it.

Heaven, maybe?

More astonishing still, this was only one room; I could make out dozens more just like it spaced along a seemingly infinite hallway.

Between starting off on the wrong foot with Matthias and very nearly getting swallowed whole by a giant, talking snake, however, I found myself reluctant to go snooping around. After all, surely a hoard such as this one was guarded by something—be it a guardian or some sort of trap, either of which could be triggered by my snooping. As such, I had to believe it might be best if I simply stayed put and touched nothing.

"Eh, fuck that," I muttered.

Ignoring my own instincts, I began creeping furtively from room to room like a mouse, if that mouse was a six-foot-tall ginger woman in a bright red dress that had seen better days.

Luckily, it seemed so long as I was content to look and not touch, I was free to wander as I pleased, giving me plenty of time to study the contents of each room. I did so with my head on a figurative swivel, my gaze flitting from shelves lined with charm necklaces and stoppered decanters to tables piled high with ancient weapons and random bits of armor. I even stumbled across a golden statue in the shape of a flattened hand sitting in a glass case with a sticky note attached that read "Reminder: Return to Midas."

Shaking my head in disbelief, I wandered back into the main hall in search of whomever or whatever I was meant to meet. Several fruitless minutes later, I came across a small, seemingly inconspicuous door tucked into the wall. Curious, I looked for a handle, only there wasn't one to be found—suggesting perhaps that whatever was on the other side of this door was somehow even more valuable. The real question was what that thing could possibly be...and how I could break in and find out.

"This all feels like a dream," I muttered, awestruck.

"That depends. How do your dreams usually end?"

Startled and expecting to be impaled at any moment, I flinched and spun to face the speaker only to find myself standing mere inches from a short, stunning young woman with large almond-shaped eyes, smooth, sun-kissed skin, and a bright, flirtatious smile. She wore a sheer, practically transparent, toga that barely covered her heaving bosom while simultaneously clinging to the curves of her impractically tiny waist and girthy hips.

"Um..." I cleared my throat, nervously.

"Don't worry," she whispered conspiratorially, "you can tell me. I'm sworn to secrecy."

"Sworn to whom? Wait, sorry. I'm gettin' ahead of meself. Who are ye, and where am I?"

The young woman smiled. "Some people call me Hope. But you can call me Pandora. And this is the Armory. Welcome. I've been expecting you."

43

Pandora directed me to take the seat across from her after having led us to a room occupied by a single, solitary table surrounded by high-backed chairs. And no, before you ask, the table wasn't of the Round variety. Disappointing, I know.

In the gentle candlelight cast by the squat candelabra centerpiece, my companion's flawless skin was the color of melted caramel, her hair so soft and dark it gleamed. The look in her eyes, however, was far less inviting; the Armory's guardian studied me with the unblinking intensity usually reserved for misbehaved children or small-time crooks.

"So..." I began, "Pandora was it? Were your parents hippies, or are ye really meant to be her?"

The corner of Pandora's mouth twitched. "You tell me."

I hesitated, though more to gather my thoughts than to give credence to the question. Frankly, one look was enough to confirm her identity; while the woman before me may not have had the overwhelming presence of a god, she could most certainly have been created by one—or so the legend went, anyway. Indeed, if the myths were to be believed, she'd been fashioned by none other than

Hephaestus himself...the very same Olympian whose forge we'd used to fashion those Horsemen Masks.

Coincidence? Maybe.

Too bad I didn't believe in them.

"I t'ink you're her," I replied at last. "The real Pandora. I reckon I've met enough of ye Greeks to know an imposter when I see one. What I don't know is how ye knew to expect me. Not to mention how this so-called Armory of yours even exists, or how come I've never heard of it."

"Perhaps you weren't meant to until now, or perhaps you have and you simply don't remember."

"Hah. As if I'd forget a place like this."

"As if, indeed." Pandora shrugged and smiled enigmatically. "Please allow me to apologize again for the lack of refreshments, by the way. I'm not used to receiving visitors on short notice, especially not without a chaperone."

"It's fine. But wait, I thought ye said ye knew I was comin'?"

"I did. Just not when."

"Right," I drawled, rubbing at the bridge of my nose to stave off the budding migraine I knew was coming. "So then, how'd ye know it was me and not some random intruder?"

"Oh, there was never any danger of that. Our security measures keep unwelcome visitors out. Plus, I was forewarned."

"Forewarned by whom?"

She waved that away. "It's not important."

"Why not let me decide that for meself?"

"If I thought it would help, I would. But I can tell from looking at you that you are not yet prepared for the answers you seek. Soon, perhaps, but not now."

"Ye sound like Veil," I muttered.

"Veil?" Pandora cocked her head. "I take it you're referring to that thing hiding in your shadow?"

"That what hidin' in me what?"

Pandora pointed. "Right there."

"Where?" I got up out of my chair and hurriedly scanned the floor for my shadow. As soon as I saw it, I knew at once what Pandora was referring to: several shades darker than it should have been and bulging conspicuously, my shadow resembled not so much a silhouette of a person as an oil stain.

"Oy, Veil, ye better come out this instant!" I demanded. "This is a total breach of me privacy!"

To be honest, I wasn't sure if that made logistical sense, but I was beyond caring; I was sick and tired of Veil appearing only when it suited her. Besides, the longer this madness went on, the more questions I had—questions I felt I deserved the answers to, whether I was ready to hear them or not.

Veil let out a long suffering sigh as she made her presence known, her corporeal form emerging from my cast shadow like a specter from the floorboards of a haunted house. I shuddered, realizing she must have been spying on me this *entire* time. And that was to say nothing of the depraved angle she'd chosen to do it from.

"Not cool, Veil," I chastised. "Way not cool."

"I wasn't hiding there until recently," she countered, though I could tell from her slumped posture that she felt guilty, nonetheless. "I didn't have to. But after what just happened back there, I thought it best to stay as close as possible. I couldn't risk losing track of you again."

"You're tellin' me poppin' in to see that monster wasn't on our itinerary?"

"Not at all."

"So you're sayin' I *can* get off this crazy ride. I just have to find someone willin' and able to throw me off the platform."

"No! I mean, no. You wouldn't want to do that. The consequences would be catastrophic. At best."

"Likely story. Pervert."

"I am not a—"

"Please. Save it for the jury."

"Jury? What jury?"

I turned to Pandora. "Ye don't happen to have a courtroom tucked away somewhere in this place, do ye?"

The Greek bit her lip to keep from laughing and shook her head. "Afraid not."

"Damn."

"We do have a few guillotines laying around, though."

"Ooh, really?"

"Look, I get it," Veil growled through gritted teeth. "I'm sorry I used your shadow without your permission. There. Are you happy?"

"Ye mean existentially? Because to tell the truth I've had better days. Or has it been weeks? See, I've sort of lost track of time what with ye *chuckin' me through time and space on a freakin' whim*."

"Ah. So, that's what this is about."

"Of course that's what this is about!" I snapped. "Ye t'ink I really give a shite that ye were lookin' up me skirt for the past hour and change?"

"...don't you?"

"Well, obviously! But that's besides the point."

"Excuse me," Pandora interjected, glibly, "but would it be possible for the two of you to have this conversation some other time? It's just that we have other, more pressing matters to discuss."

I frowned. "Other matters like what?"

"Like what brought you here in the first place."

I stared blankly at her.

"The armor," she went on coaxingly, as though I should know what she was talking about. "The very first set of Valkyrie armor forged by the dwarves of Svartalfheim, gifted to Brunhilde by Odin himself, marked with the sigil of Hope."

"What about it?"

"You're here to add it to our collection."

44

"The hell I am!"

Pandora's eyes widened at my sudden outburst. "You make it sound like this is the first you're hearing about it."

"That's because it is. What in the world makes ye t'ink I'd just hand over Nevermore?"

"Nevermore?"

"Me armor. That's what I call her."

"Her?"

I pursed my lips. "It. Whatever."

Pandora swung a hopeful gaze over to my shadowy companion as if looking for some support, but Veil could only shrug. Pandora sighed. "Ah. Well, I suppose that at least explains why you arrived so much later than expected."

"Actually," Veil cut in, "that was my fault. I didn't expect the Maker to interfere the way he did. It...complicated things."

I frowned, wondering what Veil meant by that. Judging from what she'd said earlier, I could only speculate that Matthias had thrown me off course with his little stunt. The question was, why? And what was up with Veil's reaction when I'd mentioned jumping ship? Surely it didn't matter whether I wanted off or not, under the circumstances.

Unless...

"I see." Pandora began idly playing with a lock of her hair. "That is a shame. The armor might have proven far more valuable to us had it come into our possession sooner. Naturally, however, the terms of the deal still stand."

"What deal?" I demanded.

With deliberate slowness, Pandora reached into her cleavage and retrieved a glass vial no larger than my pinky finger, inside which sat a single amber nugget roughly the size of a rear molar. She placed the vial on the table, at which point the rock within began shifting colors —first gold, then steely grey, then aquamarine, then carmine, and so on.

"A philosopher's stone," Pandora said. "In exchange for the armor."

"Oh please," I scoffed. "The philosopher's stone is a myth. Ye don't really expect me to believe..."

I drifted off as Pandora's expression hardened, sensing I'd offended her. Still, what I was saying was true: there *was* no such thing as a philosopher's stone. I knew that for a fact after years spent both receiving and denying requests from various buyers, not to mention the dozens of rumored sightings that had never panned out.

Though, if the stone really did exist, I had to admit this was precisely the sort of place I'd have expected to find it. The trouble was, the philosopher's stone was a talisman of mythical proportions, capable of turning lead into gold when it wasn't being used to grant immortality or bring the dead back to life. Indeed, the very notion that such a thing *might* exist had driven thousands to their deaths in search of its elusive properties—not to mention those wealthy saps who'd sponsored their alchemical research.

Which begged the question: how had Pandora come by it?

"This is the philosopher's stone," she insisted. "Or a piece of it, at least. I was told the original had been shattered long ago, and its shards divided amongst several prominent families."

"Then how d'ye come by it?"

Pandora smiled. "By conventional means, I assure you. The

Armory is home to many such relics, though few as illustrious. Or as powerful."

"Okay, okay." I held up a hand. "Let's say I believe ye. What makes ye t'ink I'd be willin' to trade Brunhilde's armor for any price, let alone a tiny fragment of the philosopher's stone? I mean, what would I even use it for?"

"What you do with it is your business. This shard may only be a small piece of a much larger whole, but it contains enough latent power to make you rich beyond your wildest dreams, or even grant everlasting life to someone you love. Surely that must appeal to you."

I hesitated. Frankly, limitless wealth was certainly appealing—especially for someone who'd found herself completely penniless not that long ago. With access to that much money, I could get back my apartment, my things, and my life. So too was the idea of handing out immortality, a commodity that was fast becoming a prerequisite for anyone in my life. After all, I really didn't want to end up burying my loved ones like that poor Scottish bastard in *Highlander*.

Wait...burying my loved ones.

"Could it..." I began, haltingly. "What if I wanted to revive someone? A dead someone. Could the shard do that?"

"Provided you knew where their body had been laid to rest and where their soul was being kept, yes."

"And how would I find out the second part? Where someone's soul ended up, I mean."

Pandora pursed her lips in thought. "There are a few beings out there capable of tracking down souls. For a price, of course. I am afraid I don't know anyone, personally. But perhaps your friend here—"

Veil coughed into a gloved fist. "Sorry, no."

Pandora shrugged. "Well, in any event, the answer to your question is yes. It is possible."

I nodded, doing my best to hide my disappointment. Still, Pandora's offer was an intriguing one; while my bond with Nevermore had served me better than I could have ever imagined, no suit of armor could ever grant me the one wish I so desperately craved.

To make my only family whole again.

I cleared my throat. "So...how do we do this?"

45

As it turned out, the answer was relatively simple.

All I had to do was get naked. Well, momentarily, at least. Pandora had been kind enough to offer me a change of clothes in light of the situation, and I was pleased to learn they wouldn't come from her own wardrobe; I didn't want to compare curves and develop a complex.

According to Veil, the red dress I wore was merely a powerful illusion, no different than the various outfits and appearances I'd taken on to this point. To what end, of course, she'd declined to explain. Still, it meant all I had to do was break the illusion and remove Nevermore piece by painstaking piece.

To my relief, the former was accomplished with a snap of Veil's fingers. The latter, however, proved itself far more taxing; the absurd difficulty of removing an entire set of heavy armor aside, it actually upset me a great deal to see Brunhilde's armor laid out on the table like a sacrificial offering.

Once, the sheer sight of her had moved me to recite poetry. Now all I felt was regret and a vague sense of loss. It wasn't merely the armor's superior quality and capabilities I mourned, either, but everything we'd survived together. The mists of Niflheim. The frigid wastelands of Helheim. The mean streets of Boston. Even the freaking Ozarks. And that was to say nothing of how Freya was bound to react when she found out I'd traded away a piece of her people's history for my own personal gain.

Still, it was too late to back out now.

As I paused to assess the fit of my new clothes, however, I noticed something odd: rather than reflecting candlelight as I'd originally assumed, it appeared Brunhilde's armor was actively glowing with power.

And I wasn't the only one who noticed.

"These marks," Pandora said, sounding awed as she leaned over the gleaming breastplate. "Who...no, *how* was this done?"

I craned my neck to see what Pandora meant and found her fingers tracing a quartet of symbols carved into the metal to form the rough shape of a diamond. The first was an hourglass turned sideways that I recognized as the rune of hope—a sigil that had already been there when the armor came into my possession. The other three, however, were completely unfamiliar.

Sitting below and therefore opposite hope was a symbol that reminded me of a flag at half-mast, while the other two resembled an arrow pointed upwards and a pair of right angles stacked diagonally.

"I've never seen those before in me life," I swore.

"*Dagaz. Thurisaz. Tiwaz. Jera.*" Pandora shook her head. "They are all here. Not just Hope, but Despair, Justice, and Absolution. Each of the runes, and in this pattern. The Dreaded Sign, symbol of the Dread Four."

"Oh, right. Like the Masks." I tugged at the scratchy cloak I'd been given, which made it even worse. It was only after scratching at my collar, however, that I noticed Pandora staring at me with her mouth agape. "What?"

"You said the name Matthias, earlier. And your companion mentioned the Maker. Did he...touch you?"

I cringed. "I mean, technically. But not in the 'show me on the doll' sort of way."

"The what?"

"Nevermind." I waved her off. "Anyway, yes. The answer is yes."

Pandora nodded. "Then that explains it. Though what he could have been thinking I hesitate to even imagine."

"I'm not followin'. How about ye, Veil? Any idea what she's talkin' about?"

"Nope."

"This rune," Pandora explained, jabbing with a perfectly manicured finger. "*Dagaz*. It was meant to denote *possession*."

I frowned. "As in ownership?"

"Yes, exactly! Except now there are four where there should be only one. Do you have any idea what that means?"

"Totally."

"Oh." Pandora, having clearly expected a different answer, straightened in surprise. "Really?"

"It means you're about to get the point. *Hope*fully."

Pandora narrowed her eyes at me. "It *means* this armor was originally earmarked for the Daughter of Hope. Now, any of their offspring could claim it. The Daughter of Justice, for example. Or perhaps even the child of Hope and Despair."

"Umm, are we talkin' biological offspring, or...?"

"Regardless," she went on as though I hadn't spoken, "to entrust a single owner with so much untapped potential...whoever inherits this suit will be granted untold power. Enough to turn the tide, or perhaps to tip the scales."

"Ye don't sound too thrilled about that."

"On the contrary, it is in my nature to welcome the unknown."

"So does that mean the deal is still on?"

Pandora hesitated. "I am afraid not. Thanks to the Maker's interference, the terms are lopsided in our favor. Which means, if you want the deal to go through, you must negotiate for a better price."

For a second there, I couldn't believe my ears. Had she said *I* needed to negotiate a better price? As in *she* owed *me*? If so...holy shit.

Feeling a bit like a grandmother in a gift shop, I began making a mental list of all the objects I'd laid eyes on since my arrival, ranking them in order of sheer epicness. Then, realizing I'd only gotten a good look at a half-dozen rooms, I decided to go ahead and push my luck.

"I want the Holy Grail."

Pandora snickered. "Not here. And even if it was, you'd be in my debt."

"Hmm. Okay, then. A map to the Fountain of Youth."

"If you want. But fair warning, it dried up six years ago."

"Seriously? Only six?"

Pandora shrugged. "Climate change. What can you do?"

Swearing under my breath, I started naming randomly awesome and otherwise unobtainable goodies.

"Zeus' thunderbolt."

"Also not here."

"The Shroud of Turin."

"Worthless bit of cloth, magically speaking."

"No shite, really? Okay. Um...the Book of Thoth."

"Already on loan, I'm afraid."

"Dammit. Excalibur."

"Sorry, that would be Alex's."

"Who the fuck is Alex?"

"Oh, that's right. You won't have met." Pandora gave me the sort of lingering once-over I'd have expected from a lecherous old man. "If you ever find yourself back here, remind me and I'll introduce you. Incidentally, where do you stand on casual nudity? And would you say you're pro-bath, or...?"

"Excuse me?"

Pandora giggled. "Relax. I'm only teasing. Though I suppose you *could* always ask for a night of unbridled passion. If you were so inclined."

"I'm...uh, good. T'anks."

"Your loss."

After taking a moment to recover from the Greek's playful advances, I decided to plop down and give my situation some serious thought. From what I could gather, it appeared I wouldn't be walking away with some all-powerful weapon or mindblowing relic in addition to the philosopher's stone—not that I'd expected as much. Still, that left a few intriguing possibilities. Perhaps I'd have better luck asking for a less conspicuous item with considerable utility.

Indeed, I even had one in mind.

"I don't suppose ye have a genuine skeleton key lyin' around here, somewhere?" I ventured. "Ye know, a magic key that can open any door?"

Pandora hesitated. "We...do. Yes."

"What's the matter? Is that not a fair trade?"

"No, it is. I merely wonder what you intend to do with such a thing."

I shrugged. "Break into places, probably. Or out of 'em. I can't tell ye how many times havin' one would've saved me arse."

This was true; with a skeleton key at my disposal, I might have broken out of any number of unpleasant locations—a list of which included a clandestine Russian gaol, an underwater prison cell, an Otherworld slave camp, a torture chamber in Hel, and a dungeon in Massachusetts. Which, in hindsight, was a rather distressing compilation. Ironically, though, that had nothing to do with why I wanted one.

"I guess that's as valid a reason as any," Pandora replied. "Very well. A skeleton key and a philosopher's stone in exchange for the armor. Do we have a deal?"

Knowing how crucial the next few minutes would be, I slipped out of my chair and held out a hand for the goods. "Aye. We have a deal."

Pandora passed me the vial, then reached down her toga a second time to produce a remarkably unremarkable object—nothing more than a thin sliver of black metal in the vague shape of a key.

"Fuck me, how much d'ye keep in there?"

Pandora handed over the skeleton key with a smirk. "I'd encourage you to come over here and find out, but you passed on that option, remember?"

"Aye, that I did. Guess I deserved that. Anyway." I turned to Veil. "I take it that means we're movin' on?"

Veil dipped her head. "Whenever you are ready."

I cast one last, long look at Brunhilde's armor. Then, without so much as a word of warning, I pocketed both artifacts, grabbed my chair, and swung it at Veil with everything I had.

46

V eil went down hard, surrounded by the shattered remnants of the chair. Meanwhile, I bolted for the door, chased by the sound of Pandora's outraged shouts. Once I made it to the hallway, it was a matter of seconds before I reached my intended destination: the handleless door. Snatching the skeleton key from my pocket, I pressed its blunt tip against the wood and waited.

Nothing.

"Goddammit," I muttered anxiously, "don't tell me there was some sort of magic word, or—"

I was interrupted by a slight pulse against my fingers and a sudden flare of power that rustled like a breeze across my skin. Then, the invisible latch clicked, and the door creaked open.

I was in.

To my surprise, what lay on the other side appeared to be nothing more than an ordinary hallway of a ritzy office building. Fortunately, that suited me just fine; while I hadn't known what to expect, the whole point of this crazy scheme of mine was to get away from Veil— something I hadn't known was possible until she'd let it slip. Hence my need for a skeleton key and the subsequent assault.

And so, desperate to make my escape and knowing Veil was

bound to be on my heels any minute now—not to mention whatever Pandora had planned for me after I broke one of her chairs—I lunged through the open doorway and hastily slammed the door shut behind me.

Breathing heavily, I peeled away from the door and watched it, praying that the handleless door would prove impassable, even for Veil. When no one appeared, I let out a sigh of relief.

"Now, where the hell am I?" I asked, turning to inspect my surroundings.

The hallway was, as I'd mentioned, of the corporate variety: nothing but marble floors and partitioned walls made of glass and steel, beyond which sat empty conference tables and high-backed leather chairs. While certainly chic in a minimalist sort of way, I had to admit the effect was a little soulless. A splash of color to liven the place up would be nice, for instance. Maybe some plants or a few demotivational posters for shits and giggles, like "Overconfidence" featuring a cat stalking an eagle, or "Procrastination" with an empty frame.

Now that my adrenaline levels had settled somewhat, I abandoned the door and started roaming the halls, keeping my eyes peeled for anything that might tell me where and when I was. After peeking into a few empty rooms, I finally found a cubicle with a desk and computer. Unfortunately, the latter required a username and password that I didn't have. The former, however, was unlocked. Rifling through the various drawers, I stumbled across a couple notepads, a stack of manila folders, and a corporate calendar from the current year. A calendar riddled with pictures of notable St. Louis landmarks underscored by inspirational if esoteric quotes, the cover of which read two words.

Grimm Tech.

"Well, I'll be damned."

47

Grimm Tech, formerly Temple Industries, was a company owned by Nate Temple but run by none other than my very dear friend and hacker extraordinaire, Othello. Though "very dear" might be overselling it a bit, after I totally left her in the lurch by going gallivanting across the realms without so much as a phone call. In fact, if I were her I would definitely have a few choice words for yours truly.

Oh well, I guess that meant we were due for a reunion.

Besides, if anyone could help me stave off a spectral shadow-dweller intent on leapfrogging me from one place and time to the next, it was Othello. The Russian woman had a knack for problem-solving that often included rampant violence—a trait I'd really come to cherish in my friends.

With every intention of finding Othello's office and begging for sanctuary, I dumped everything I'd found in a single drawer and prepared to leave. Sadly, it seemed I hadn't managed to be quite as circumspect as I'd hoped while snooping around, because the instant I turned around I found myself face to face with an attractive older woman wearing too much makeup and too little clothes.

"Excuse me, can I help you?" she asked.

"Uh, yes. Actually. I was lookin' for Othello's office. D'ye know by chance where I might find it, or really just her? We have some business to discuss."

The woman pursed her lips as she looked me up and down, no doubt curious as to why I looked like I'd wandered off the set of *The Bachelor: Witches be Trippin.*

"It's a long story," I explained, gesturing to my outfit.

"Does that story include the reason why you aren't wearing a badge?"

The woman held up a badge attached to a lanyard around her neck. Delisa Pennell, Grimm Tech Accounting. The picture on her ID wasn't exactly flattering, but then she'd obviously lost some weight and dyed her hair a brighter shade of blonde since it was taken.

I nodded. "Aye, that it most certainly does."

"Good, because unless you can prove to me in the next five seconds that you are actually supposed to be here, which by the way I very much doubt, I am going to call this number and alert security." Delisa held up her phone for me to see, her thumb poised over the call button. "Five. Four. Three."

"Alright, alright. But first, seriously...since when did countdowns become a t'ing people do?"

Delisa sighed and hit the call button.

"Oy! I thought ye were goin' to give me a chance to explain?"

"I lied."

"But—"

She pressed the phone to her ear and held up a finger. "Hello, security? I'd like to report a break in. Yes, the 69th floor. A woman. Very large. No, not fat, you idiot. Tall. She's wearing, well, I don't know what you'd call it, honestly. A cloak? Whatever homeless people wear. No, I didn't say she's homeless. I said she looks homeless." Delisa pulled the phone from her ear. "You aren't homeless, are you?"

I shook my head, dumbly.

"No, not homeless. But possibly violent. She says she wants to see Ms. Othello. Yes, I realize that. What? How am I supposed to know if she's armed? No, she hasn't threatened me. But she was going through an employee's desk when I found her, so I'd be prepared for anything. She's probably a spy who's pretending to be homeless."

"I'm not a—"

"Hold on, she's saying something. Yes, what is it?"

I took a deep, calming breath. "I am *not* a spy. I'm a friend of Othello's who misplaced her guest pass, or whatever. Just call and ask her and she'll vouch for me, I swear."

Delisa stared right into my eyes as she returned the phone to her ear. "Hey, yeah, so I think she may also be on drugs. Best you send up all the boys, just to be safe. And maybe the dogs, too."

"Dogs?!" I spluttered. "Why the hell would ye need to bring in dogs?"

"Wow. She *really* didn't like the sound of that. She must have the drugs on her person. You should hurry and get up here before she flushes them. Oh, you've already sent someone up? Great. And what about the alarm? Yes, I do think it would be a good idea. No, I'm not kidding. What if she's not alone? No, of course I'm not telling you how to do your job. What I'm telling you is how to do it better."

And, with that, Delisa hung up the phone.

"What an odious shithead," she swore, shaking her head. "Thinks that just because he signs us in every day that he's got actual law enforcement experience. Idiot. Now the security team they keep on the payroll, well, let's just say those boys know exactly what they're doing. I swear, you couldn't find that many six packs at a gas station. For fuck's sake, I'd set myself on fire just to have them put me out with their bodies."

"Okay, question. Are ye totally insane?!"

"Oh, look," she said, pointing to the fluorescent panels on the ceiling, which had begun pulsing alternately red and blue like the lights of a cop car. "That means the alarms are about to go. You should probably make yourself scarce before they get here. I'll wait here."

"Seriously? Why would I run? I haven't done anythin'."

"You mean you weren't just poking around in the desk of an employee who works in a building known to contain some of the world's most innovative and therefore coveted intellectual property? A building, I might add, with a security team on payroll whose only purpose is to deal with threats like unwanted intruders."

Well, shit.

When she put it like that.

"Look, I wasn't tryin' to—"

"Shhhh." Delisa waved me off even as she began reapplying her lipstick using a vanity mirror she'd retrieved from the clutch she wore on her hip. "I'll have you know this is almost exactly how I met my last husband, Sam. What a man. Now, I won't have you ruining my chances of convincing one of those boys to take me out for a stiff drink to calm my poor nerves. So, get."

A sudden blare of ear-shattering alarms interrupted whatever retort I might have come up with, leaving me no choice but to flee the scene as Delisa had suggested—though not before wrenching her stupid vanity mirror from her hand and chucking it down the hall.

"That's it, honey!" she called after me with an encouraging wave. "Give them a good chase!"

I swore and took off down the hall, hoping I could outrun my pursuers and make it to the executive offices on the top floor—assuming that's where they were kept. In any case, from there I figured I could, hopefully, find Othello and clear up this misunderstanding before I ended up in jail facing charges of corporate espionage. Or worse, shot by a bunch of trigger-happy Regulars working for Nate Temple.

"What a story that would make," I grumbled to myself, huffing as I booked it down the hallway in search of a stairwell. "Hi, Nate, remember me? I'm the girl ye sicced a freakin' spell on. Oh and yes, your corporate goon squad *did* find me runnin' around your offices, but only because for some unknown fuckin' reason it was connected to a goddamned Armory guarded by Pan-fuckin'-dora!"

Having fully expected to stumble across at least one stairwell by the end of my tirade, I was disappointed when I reached the end of the hallway with nothing to show for it besides a stitch in my side and distressingly ragged breathing—something that was going to take some getting used to now that I could no longer rely on Nevermore's substantial stamina reserves to keep me upright.

"Is that the alarm? Shouldn't we be leaving?"

"What? No, no. I'm sure it's just one of those stupid vigilance drills those idiots downstairs keep running. Let's just ignore it and get another slice of cake. I'm sure it'll be over soon."

I frowned to hear voices over the sound of the alarm. I ducked down and peered around the corner only to discover a conference room full of Grimm Tech employees wearing cheap, plastic birthday hats and enjoying what looked to have been a rather sizable cake in the shape of a baseball bat...or a penis. From where I hid it was tough to tell.

"Are you sure?" the woman standing nearest to the door asked. "What if they do a floor sweep?"

"Then we'll offer them some cake, too," replied her male companion. "Come on, Paige, loosen up. It's Friday. Plus it's Helen's birthday."

"About that. Isn't her birthday next month?"

"Well, it's not like she'll be here on her *actual* birthday. That's what PTO is for. I hear she's going on a cruise."

"Wha—I asked for PTO for my birthday six months ago and you said no!"

"That doesn't sound like me. Did you file the request on the online system?"

"The online system was down!"

"Really?"

"Yes, really! I work in IT, Malcolm. I think I would know."

"Well...then I wouldn't have been able to give you the time off, anyway. Not with the system down."

The woman groaned, and I had to wonder what kept her from decking her supervisor in his smug little face—probably why I'd never thrive working an office job. That, and the dogged insistence on sobriety. Whatever she was going to do or say, however, it appeared I wouldn't have a chance to find out; the instant I pulled away from the door, I could hear the din of thumping boots, clinking metal, and panting dogs above the racket of the alarms.

Guess they'd found me.

Crap.

48

What Delisa had described as a security team was apparently more of a professional hit squad: dressed in all black, sporting military grade assault rifles, and liberally covered in Kevlar, the would-be mercenaries were clearing each room with remarkable efficiency. Even though I knew it was only a matter of time before I was discovered, I went ahead and ducked behind a pair of potted ferns—a ruse I expected would save me five or ten minutes, at most.

"Well, unhygienic Midwest prison, here I come."

"Not necessarily," came a reply to my right.

"Jesus Christ!" I swore as I spun around, very nearly knocking over one of the ferns and getting myself caught right then and there.

Veil peeled herself off the hallway wall like an ink stain come to life, her cloaked silhouette not unlike what you might expect from an Angel of Death. "Of course, that depends. Are you going to keep hitting me with furniture and running off? Because, if so, I'll be happy to leave you here."

I cringed. "Look, I'm sorry about that, but—"

"But you thought you might get rid of me and find your own way back home? Even though I made it pretty clear that doing so would have some serious consequences." Veil gestured first to the strobing lights and then to the crew of men in black working their way from room to room with their guns drawn. "You know, like this."

I shook my head. "And what, I was just supposed to take your word for it? Besides, you've got it all wrong. This was a simple misunderstandin', that's all.

"Is that right? So, it didn't have anything to do with you wandering into someplace you didn't belong without a proper disguise? Oh, and let me guess, trying to make direct contact with someone you weren't supposed to talk to?"

"What?" I cleared my throat, guiltily. "No. Of course not."

"Liar."

"Okay, fine, so what? Ye keep sayin' ye have no idea where and when I'll end up next, and ye still refuse to tell me who or what is behind all this, so why should I trust a single damned t'ing ye have to say?"

Veil sighed. "You want the truth?"

"I swear to God, if ye tell me I can't handle the truth..."

"The truth is it's not just my job to make sure you get where you're meant to be. It's also my job to keep you safe. Which means I'm not the bad guy. Or girl, in this case."

"And so I ask again, why on earth should I believe ye?"

"Because it's the truth. And because you have no choice."

"Which is the point! Why shouldn't I take me chances and run? Hell, even if I end up in jail, at least I'll be safe from whatever this scheme of yours is."

Veil shook her head. "You're acting like a selfish child. Can't you see how much good you've already done? Why would you want to stop now?"

"Ye t'ink I'm bein' selfish?" I balled my hands into fists at my sides. "I'm bein' *practical*. Ye don't know the long term consequences of any of this any more than I do. How could ye?"

"You're right."

"I know I'm...wait, what?"

"It's true, I have no idea what will happen. What I do know is that the choices you make, no matter what those choices are, *must* be made for the present to exist. And you have to trust me on that."

"Ye really want me to trust ye?" I asked, scoffing, "Then tell me who the hell ye are."

"I don't know who I am!"

I froze, startled as much by Veil's unexpected outburst as the words themselves. "Sorry, what?"

"I...have memories. Of the places you've visited. Even of some of those individuals you've met. But nothing of my own. I couldn't give you my name, because I don't know it. All I know is that I am here to help you, even if that means pushing you."

I frowned, trying to reconcile her admission with our situation. I supposed I should have felt sympathy for the poor specter. After all, I'd lost myself before—more than once, in fact. Unfortunately, I couldn't muster the emotion, not after everything I'd seen. After everything I'd been asked to do.

"I only have one question," I said, at last. "How does all this end? And don't tell me ye don't know, because I won't believe ye."

Veil turned to study the hall, where the security team was fast closing in. "It ends with one final choice. A choice you've already started to make. A trade, you might say. The life of someone you love, or the power to stop what's coming."

"You're talkin' about Dez," I said, realization dawning. "Does that mean there's really a chance that it could work? That I could bring her back?"

"I'm afraid the answer to that question will not present itself until your journey is concluded. And to do that, we must move on. Preferably sooner rather than later."

I followed Veil's gaze and saw several of the armed men headed in our general direction with their weapons raised. Still, I hesitated, all too aware that Veil had just dangled the juiciest carrot I could think of right in front of me—a classic manipulation tactic almost guaranteed to get me to go along with her. And yet...could I afford not to take the chance? The answer, of course, was obvious.

I held out my hand.

"Fine, ye win. Let's get this over with."

49

"...If we abolish their prison, we force the good to host the bad."

50

I loathed the smell of brimstone in the morning. Unfortunately, that was the very first thing I encountered in the wake of our abrupt departure from Grimm Tech. That, and the hiss of steam erupting from a crack in the ground some ten feet to my left. I grimaced as I sat up, my skin already clammy from the sudden humidity.

"Where the hell did I end up this time?" I groaned.

"Got it in one."

Startled to hear her voice, I looked up and found Veil looming over me like a damned gargoyle with a claw outstretched.

"Don't give me that look," she said. "I just saved your ass. The least you could do is show a little gratitude."

I swatted her hand away. "Ye can't take credit for savin' somethin' ye put at risk in the first place. And I can stand on me own, t'anks."

Veil sighed but made no further effort to help me up.

"Where are we?" I asked again, feeling slightly nauseated as I climbed to my feet. Perhaps it was the stench of rotten eggs permeating the air, or perhaps the faint miasma that swirled above our heads; grey and oppressive, the mere sight of the fumes made me sick to my stomach. Beyond it I could just make out a cavernous, stalactite-laden ceiling from which acid sporadically dripped, forming smoldering pits in the stone floor around us.

"We've been over this," Veil replied. "We're in Hell. Or a pocket of it, anyway."

"Of course we are." I rubbed the bridge of my nose. "Great. And what are we here for, exactly?"

"Presumably to talk to him."

Veil pointed, and I turned to find a charcoal smudge in the shape of a man staring at us from behind bars made of ice and fire. As I looked on, the blurred figure surged forward with almost inhuman speed to thrust its smear of a face between those bars, head tilted like an animal trying to decide whether we were something to play with or something to eat.

"Wow, that's not creepy. And who, or should I say what, the fuck is that?"

"That," Veil replied, "would be Mordred."

"Mordred?" I swung my attention back to my companion in confusion. "Shouldn't he be free?"

"Not yet. Soon, I think."

Ah. So, we were back in the past, presumably sometime before I graced the law offices of *Hansel, Hansel, & Gretel* with my presence for the first time. Interesting.

"Wait," I said, struck by a rather distressing notion. "Ye don't expect me to break him out, do ye? Because that's definitely not somethin' I would do of me own free will."

Veil grunted a laugh. "No, that's not why we're here. Frankly, you don't have the means. That task will fall to someone else."

I sighed in relief. "Okay, so what, I'm just supposed to waltz right over there and talk to him?"

"If you like. Personally, I'd walk. But then I'm not much of a dancer."

"Hah hah."

"A word of warning, if I may?" Veil held up a solitary finger. "Be on your guard, and don't get too close. I cannot say how, but I knew this man well, assuming what humanity he had has survived this place. Mordred was devious and cold and always planned several steps ahead, often to the detriment of his enemies. Avoid making deals, and do not let him get under your skin."

I frowned. "If he's so dangerous, how'd he end up locked up down here?"

"That I do not know," Veil confessed, hesitantly. "Though if I had to speculate, I imagine his ruthless practicality was to blame. If Mordred has one weakness, it's that he expects everyone to behave in their own best interests. People who act irrationally are by their very nature unpredictable, but even more so to a schemer like him."

"So ye t'ink he miscalculated, somehow? Misjudged someone, I mean?"

Veil inclined her head. "We all make mistakes."

"Aye, I suppose we do. Anyway, I appreciate the advice. Alright, I'm off to see what the convict has to say for himself. Wish me luck."

"Luck."

Taking Veil at her word, I approached Mordred's cell with excess caution—even going so far as to halt a good five paces away. The cell's occupant didn't so much as twitch throughout, though I could sense Mordred's unwavering attention the same way I would have any predator's. Once it was clear I wasn't planning to close the distance between us, however, the blurred bastard did something even more disconcerting.

He spoke.

"I was wondering how long it would take before you came to gloat," Mordred said, his voice so raspy it was like listening to fallen leaves skittering across a sidewalk.

"I'm sorry?"

"You should be. You and those friends of yours, locking me down here for eternity. And for what crime? A little insurrection? A little patricide? Please. Of the two of us, who has more blood on his hands?"

"Okay, first of all," I replied, holding up a forestalling hand, "not a he. Secondly, while this all sounds very cathartic, I am a hundred percent sure ye have me confused for someone else."

Mordred leaned incrementally forward until the light emanating from the bars of his cell reflected off his smudge of a face. "You really aren't him, are you?"

"Aren't whom?"

"The man whose face you're wearing. The Archwizard."

There it was again, that mention of an Archwizard—the very same I'd heard from Morgan le Fay and a handful of others along my journey. Of course, it was only now, standing across from a man intimately tied to Arthurian legend—a man with only a few notable adversaries—that I made the connection. And it was a connection I should have made much, much sooner.

"Merlin. Merlin is the Archwizard."

"Dogs can't look up."

"Huh?"

"Oh, forgive me, were we not stating obvious facts?"

I shook my head, not at Mordred's sarcasm, but at my own foolishness. Of *course* this was all tied to my father. It should have occured to me when I'd felt compelled to use his name with the Neverlanders, but then I supposed I hadn't had much time to consider the possibility, what with the whole walk the plank debacle, not to mention meeting the Maker.

I glanced back over my shoulder at Veil, wondering yet again just how much she knew, or at the very least how much she suspected. But my spectral chauffeur was too busy meandering about the cavern to notice—almost as if she were trying extra hard to keep her distance after the shadow-rape incident.

"So," Mordred went on, "I take it this means you are either an enemy bold enough to wear his face, or a friend in disguise. Which is it?"

"Neither. I'm his daughter."

"Don't be ridiculous," Mordred scoffed. "Merlin could not bear children. That was the price he paid, amongst other things, for what he became."

"And yet, here I am."

"Which makes you delusional, not right."

I shrugged.

"Very well," he said. "For the sake of argument, who was your mother?"

I hesitated, wondering whether or not I should share that particular detail. After all, while Mordred appeared to be safely caged away for now, that didn't change the fact that he would one day be let loose on the world once more. As such, especially after weighing everything Veil had told me, it seemed prudent to steer the conversation elsewhere.

"That's me business, not yours. Now, about Merlin—"

"Ah, so you don't know."

"Nice try," I replied, refusing to be baited. "But I'm not here to talk about me."

"Why are you here, then?"

Truthfully, I had no idea. That said, now that we'd exchanged a few words, I found myself curious. Had my father really imprisoned him here? If so, why? And what about Mordred's claim that he had blood on his hands?

"I...I want to ask ye about him. Merlin. Ye knew him, obviously. I want to know what he was like."

"You really want to know?"

I nodded.

"Then tell me who your mother is."

"Was," I corrected. "And we've been over this."

Mordred began pacing back and forth, though his attention never wavered from me for so much as an instant. "I will make you a deal. You tell me her name, and I will answer any question you have. Not just about Merlin, but any question your heart desires."

The offer was tempting. More than tempting, in fact. At this point in my life I could count on one hand the things I knew about my father, and most of those had been passed along via my mother's ghost—a sliver of her consciousness left behind to guide and eventually groom me into a vessel capable of containing her power. A process, by the way, which was very much still in flux.

"Questions," I amended. "Plural."

Mordred barked a laugh. "Good catch. Very well. Her name for my answers."

I hesitated, Veil's warnings echoing in my head. In the end, however, I simply couldn't pass up the opportunity—not for so straightforward a price. "We have a deal."

"Well? I'm waiting."

"Nemain. Her name was Nemain."

For an instant, the charcoal smudge blurring Mordred's face and body wavered to reveal a tall, athletic man with long, dark hair and green eyes so pale they reminded me of mint ice cream. Mordred's hair hung in lank ringlets around his shoulders and his bulging jaw was covered in a thick layer of scruff. A jaw, I should mention, that had come unhinged with shock.

"Impossible," was all he said.

"I do not t'ink that word means what ye t'ink it means," I replied, evenly. "For that matter, I'm startin' to worry about how reliable a source ye are."

Mordred ignored me and resumed pacing, his entire body blurred out once more. "That fool!" he hissed under his breath. "That brilliant fool! He actually managed to fulfill that ridiculous prophecy. Which means *their* time must be near at hand. The Catalysts. With even one of them on my side, the things we could achieve...but that can wait. First, I'll have to find Avalon. Then I'll retrieve the suits and occupy whatever's left of Camelot."

"Oy!" I interjected forcefully. "What in the world are ye babblin' on about? We had a deal. I have questions, and ye promised me answers."

"And to think," Mordred went on as though I hadn't spoken. "That he would actually call you his daughter...and here I thought I could be cruel."

"Huh? Okay, seriously, what the hell are ye talkin' about?" I demanded, angrily.

Without warning, Mordred surged forward, wrapping both his hands around the bars of his cell with a death grip that sent sparks and chips of ice flying. A low keen began to emanate overhead, its irritating whine audible over the sound of Mordred's ragged tenor as he spoke.

"I am talking about the Omega War, you foolish thing. The final battle that will decide who rules not only the world of men, but every conceivable world in existence."

"A war to end all wars, that's what all this crazy is about?" I indicated him with a wax-on motion. "Bit dramatic, don't ye t'ink?"

"Oh, it will happen. The Archwizard has all but ensured it, or you wouldn't be here. But mark my words, I will be the one who stands victorious this time around. You think I've heard nothing of the outside world while I was down here? That I've been sitting idle? No. This time will be different. And you know why?"

"I assume that's a rhetorical—"

"Because—"

"There it is."

"Because," Mordred reiterated, "I've discovered the secret to freeing the Vanquished. I know the location of all Four Treasures, which means I hold the keys to shattering that realm once and for all. And, once that is done, I can assure you they'll bind themselves willingly to my cause, making me more than a king. More than a legend. I will become more powerful than any god, because I will represent the hand that tips the scales."

"That's nice," I said, evenly. "Now, about Merlin—"

Before I could continue, however, I heard Veil shout a warning as a dozen figures began emerging from the smoldering pits in the ground like zombies from the grave. Sporting black turtlenecks and combat pants, they were unremarkable in every respect except one: Mexican sugar skulls sat where their heads should have been. Painted in a wide variety of patterns and colors, I had to admit the *calavera* made for a surprisingly terrifying alternative to a face.

"Candy Skulls," I murmured, recalling the curious appellation I'd heard uttered years and years ago. Who'd said it and why, unfortunately, I could no longer remember. And yet, I knew instinctively that these strange creatures were not to be trifled with.

Within seconds, dozens more had risen from the ground, until the entire cavern was swarming with toothy grins and empty sockets. All of which, I was sorry to say, were fixated on yours truly.

"We have to go!" Veil called as she rushed to my side, the Candy Skulls leering at us like a pride of lions staring down a pair of gangly gazelles.

"But I had questions—"

"There's no time. I think those are his jailers, which probably means whatever you two talked about has them riled up."

"We didn't talk about anythin'! It was all this asshole runnin' his mouth like a lunatic."

"Then what are they doing here? Or, better yet, why are they *getting closer?*"

I could see she was right. With a frustrated groan, I whirled to face Mordred and demand he do something. Except this time I found myself looking not at a blurry figure, but the man I'd caught a glimpse of before—if that man had taken a hefty dose of PCP.

"I hope we meet again," Mordred said as he nuzzled the bars of his cell like a cat, his skin sizzling where it came into contact with that elemental substance. "I really, really do."

I shuddered, sensing in that moment that Mordred's vaguely ecstatic expression would haunt me until the day I died—and probably longer, with my luck. Thankfully, I didn't have very long to look at it before Veil snatched me by my arm and yanked the hell out of me.

Or was that yanked the me out of Hell?

Either way, we were moving on.

51

"Death will call to you soon enough without you seeking him out."

52

I sagged and nearly fell backwards, my balance thrown by the weight of the armor I found myself wearing in the aftermath of my lopsided conversation with Mordred. While inwardly cursing the thoroughness of the illusion responsible for altering my appearance, I was pleased to find myself supported by a concerned companion—a companion I assumed was Veil.

Only it turned out I was wrong.

"Are you alright, Róta?" asked the goddess who caught me, her eyes searching my face.

"Freya?"

With a figure just past maidenhood and the manner of a queen, Odin's wife appeared almost precisely as she had the day we met— the only difference being her choice of attire. Rather than a dark cloak made of feathers, she wore a yellow sundress with a modest neckline beneath a cream-colored cardigan. The result was more elementary school teacher than de facto ruler of the Vanir, but I wasn't fooled. After all, I'd experienced her displeasure firsthand.

"Have you finally dispensed with that silly title?" The Norse goddess cocked an eyebrow. "You don't look well, Róta. Did you train on an empty stomach and skip breakfast again?"

I nodded, numbly, which seemed to appease her. The goddess released my arm and patted my shoulder with a great deal more affection than she'd ever shown me in the past. Then again, I supposed I hadn't given her much cause.

"I do wish they'd hurry up," Freya said after a moment's silence. "My lifespan may be infinite, but my patience is not."

I could tell she meant this as a joke, and that I was expected to say something in return. Unfortunately, I had to believe I'd be found out the instant I opened my mouth; Freya was not the type to overlook strange behavior. Fortunately, a trio of newcomers arrived before my silence dragged on too long, emerging out of thin air and throwing me for yet another loop.

"What are they doin' here?" I muttered softly under my breath.

The here was actually not that noteworthy; unlike some of my more exotic landing spots, the five of us stood in what appeared to be an abandoned warehouse sitting on the docks alongside a murky, sluggish river. The odor of gutted fish stunk up the place, and I swore I could see an old school riverboat chugging against the current several miles off. Indeed, only the graffiti spray painted on the nearest wall suggested a more modern era.

The what, meanwhile, was far more fascinating. Especially since it involved at least three people I knew, not counting the body I inhabited—a Valkyrie under Freya's command who went by the name Róta. Those individuals included Freya herself, my friend Othello, and her longterm romantic partner, Hemingway, otherwise known as the Horseman of Death.

The former appeared a tad younger than the Othello I was acquainted with, though not by much. She was still the trim-waisted, heavy-busted woman I had come to know and love, though I wasn't used to seeing her without that trademark, shit-eating grin of hers. Instead, she appeared anxious, perhaps even pained.

The latter, on the other hand, appeared not as I'd seen him first as a child in my dining room or even last as an old man in the valleys of Fólkvangr, but as I'd come to know him best: a jaded, hollow-eyed youth. And yet, I had to believe whatever was happening here was taking place before Hemingway and I had been introduced, as it appeared whatever chemistry the Horseman and his beloved shared in my time was nowhere to be found.

In fact, Hemingway seemed much more besotted with the fifth and final member of our group; he had his arm slung possessively around the shoulders of a mousy young woman with a nest of curly brown hair and comically large glasses—a woman who struck me as familiar even though I knew for a fact I'd never laid eyes on her before.

"Is this her?" asked Freya of Hemingway as she gestured to Othello, who seemed to pale beneath the goddess' scrutiny. That, or she was simply under the weather. She certainly had that look about her.

"It is," Hemingway replied. "And I'm afraid she doesn't have long, so we'll have to hurry."

"Yes, I can see that. The Temple boy's magic is literally eating her from the inside out. I take it you found what you were after?"

Hemingway allowed his arm to slip from the mousy woman's shoulders as he produced what appeared to be some sort of amulet from his jacket pocket. He held it up. "This shard should take care of the memories. They've already been...what was the word you two used?"

"Uploaded," replied the two women in unison.

Hemingway grunted. "Uploaded. That's right. And what about you? Were you able to find a suitable vessel?"

"Róta did, yes. Róta? Remove the sheet."

I frowned and turned to look where Freya was indicating and discovered a plastic sheet covering what looked to be a body. With a grimace, I did as she asked, exposing the nude form of a very attractive, albeit very dead, woman. Except she wasn't really dead—more like comatose, her breathing coming slow and steady. Stranger still, it was a body I recognized.

Kára.

What the hell was going on here?

"A body without a soul," Freya went on once Kára had been

revealed. "I have already fortified her flesh, as you asked. All that's needed now is the oath, and she will rise as a Valkyrie in my service, per our agreement. I trust you gave her the words?"

Hemingway nodded. "I have, yes. She's as prepared as anyone could be."

"And what about this one?" Freya asked, turning to the mousy woman. "Will she be able to do her part and fool the others?"

"I trust Anichka with my life," Othello interjected, speaking up for the first time. Except...it wasn't Othello's voice; Othello had a thick Russian accent to rival my own motley brogue, whereas this woman spoke the clear, uninflected English of the Midwest.

"I hope you mean that literally. After all, she *will* be taking over your life. Your friends will become her friends, your family her family. Your body hers to cherish or abuse. Your dreams and wants hers to fulfill or deny. Anything less and those you wish to deceive will see her coming a mile away."

Othello spared Hemingway a glance. "I've been assured it's the only way. But yes, I meant what I said. Anichka is at least as capable as I am, and she has good reason to want a fresh start, not to mention a good heart. She'll do fine."

"Plus I will be there to guide her," the Horseman of Death added. "As promised."

"I see." Freya turned back to Anichka with a pensive frown. "I trust they've told you what a soul swap entails? I am afraid it won't be pleasant."

Anichka thrust her glasses further up her nose. "Where I come from, pain is part of daily routine. It does not scare me. Besides, when Othello tells me what is at stake, how could I say no? I owe her too much. Also, what she says is true. I have my own reasons for choosing this."

I noticed Anichka's eyes lingered on Hemingway as she said that last bit. Moreover, I recognized the accent she spoke with— Othello's accent. My Othello's accent, but in an unfamiliar tone of voice. Which begged the question yet again: what the hell was going on?

Freya, meanwhile, shrugged as if to say that was good enough for her. "Very well. Then shall we begin?"

The trio exchanged looks.

"We're ready," Othello declared.

While I weighed the potential consequences of speaking up or keeping silent, the foursome got to work clearing a space around Kára's body. Hemingway escorted the two women to their respective spots like the director of a stage play while Freya began reciting an incantation in a language I couldn't comprehend. His job done, the Horseman ambled over to stand casually beside me.

I opened my mouth to ask him to explain more about what was going on, then thought better of it. Whatever was happening here, it was clear everyone involved was on board. Which meant intervening now would not only get me in trouble, but possibly derail the whole thing—an eventuality I'd have been a lot more comfortable with if only I had more than a vague idea what was happening.

I shook my head as Freya's voice grew progressively louder, and with it a shift in the air currents. Within seconds, gusts of wind began tearing through the warehouse, whipping about scraps of grimy old newspaper and other such detritus.

"Anichka!" Othello called to her companion over the roar of the wind. "Before I go, I need you to do something for me! It's about Nate...look, I don't know what we were, or what we might have been if we'd had more time, but I need to know you'll do everything you can to keep him safe."

Anichka jerked a nod. "Of course, my friend! And do not worry. If he is half the man you say he is, then I am sure it will be my pleasure."

"I hope she's right," Hemingway muttered under his breath.

I shot him a puzzled glance.

The Horseman sighed. "I've known toddlers who were more predictable than Nate Temple, and that was before we decided to remove the soul of the woman he gave up his magic for. I know your Lady believes he'll be grateful when the time comes, but I have it on good authority that he hates being lied to, no matter the reason."

I frowned as I tried to puzzle out what Hemingway had just told me. Othello was having her soul removed? No, not removed, I realized. Replaced. That's what Anichka was here for. That was why Freya had talked about taking over Othello's life. But then that meant...no, it couldn't be, could it?

Was Anichka *my* Othello?

It certainly explained the accent discrepancy, not to mention the nagging sense of familiarity. Plus there was that name. Anichka. *Rasputin's* Anichka! That's where I'd heard it before! Not only that, but I could finally see the strong resemblance between the mousy Russian woman and her cousin, Vitaly—a resemblance that I'd falsely attributed to Othello. All of which suggested the Othello I knew was somehow separate from the Othello everyone else was familiar with.

Was it possible she'd concealed her true self from them? That she'd been faking it for her friend's sake? But why?

And what about the real Othello? Was Nate's magic seriously killing her? Was that why they'd all agreed to this? Except that still didn't explain what Kára had to do with any of it. Unless...was it possible she was meant to be the new vessel for Othello's soul? If true, it would make the Kára I knew and this Othello one and the same.

But then what about her memory?

Before I could voice even one of the dozens of questions racing through my mind, however, Freya's chanting ceased—replaced instead by a low keening sound from both Othello and Anichka as they crumpled to their knees. Light began to play under their skin, illuminating bones and muscles and veins with strobe-like bursts of lightning behind a veil of storm clouds.

Freya began drawing symbols in the air, her fingertips trailing fire that left patterns of smoke loitering above our heads. I recognized some as Nordic runes, though not all. In fact, I could have sworn I saw some Greek letters tucked away in there, as well—the symbol for Alpha and Omega bookending a vast array of characters.

The wind picked up once more, this time swirling around us with such violence that I had to shield my face with my arm and blink past tears. And so it was I felt rather than saw Hemingway step forward, his body wrapped in a pitch black cloak with his hood raised, leaning on the monstrous scythe he clutched in his right hand.

The wind stopped.

Othello collapsed a moment later, her eyes open and unseeing. Anichka was next, her body flopping to the floor like a rag doll next to Kára's so that all three women lay side by side, still as the grave. Those of us left standing looked on in silence, and I began to wonder whether I'd made a terrible mistake, whether my silence had cost these women their lives.

And then Othello arched her back and screamed.

Hemingway, having reverted back to his previous form without my noticing, rushed to her side and hastily clasped that strange amulet around her neck. Expecting it to improve her condition, I was taken aback when Othello started convulsing instead, her eyes rolling so far in the back of her head I could see nothing but white.

"It will pass," Hemingway kept repeating in a voice one might use to soothe a child, hugging her close as she thrashed, seemingly oblivious to the many blows he took in the process.

"Róta," Freya said, tapping me on the shoulder. The goddess looked fatigued, if not downright exhausted. Still, when she spoke she did so without a hint of weariness. "I am going to take our new recruit on ahead. We don't want her waking up to this. Her mind will be muddled enough as it is. Come find us once everything has settled down here."

Not knowing what else to do or say, I simply nodded and watched as Freya lifted Kára's body, cradling it as though the Valkyrie weighed nothing. The two of them vanished a moment later, leaving the limp body of Anichka behind like discarded trash.

"You can go," Hemingway told me. "I've got things under control here."

I opened my mouth to argue, but I could see from the loving way he held the woman in his arms that he was telling the truth; whatever he and the newly reborn Anichka intended to do next was none of my concern. After all, it was clear my role here was merely to observe, and the show was obviously over.

As such, I left the warehouse, stepping out onto a broken sidewalk where Veil was waiting for me with open arms. Literally.

53

"...You two were destined to find each other..."

54

I awoke bundled and warm beneath silk sheets, my head buried in the crook of a man's muscular shoulder. I snuggled in to lay my cheek against his bare chest without thinking, my body responding instinctively to the comfort of being held. I couldn't be sure how long I stayed like that, relishing the press of someone else's skin to mine—a sensation I'd denied myself for far too long. What I could be sure of, however, was how quickly the moment was ruined once a third person crawled onto the bed.

Startled by the unexpected dip in the otherwise firm mattress, I sat up, taking the covers with me and exposing my slumbering companion to the elements. Groaning, he hastily rolled over and buried his face in the pillows, exposing a remarkably toned and completely nude backside in the process.

"Apologies, I did not mean to wake you," said the newcomer, a natural blonde with the face and body of a supermodel, if super-models were notorious for having tapered ears and ageless skin. In other words, an elf. And a buck naked elf, at that.

"Don't worry, I was already up," I replied groggily, inwardly cursing at Veil for putting me in yet another compromising situation, if not the *most* compromising situation I could think of, short of a jilted lover bursting in to blow us all away.

And even then, at least I wouldn't have to be embarrassed for very long.

I'd be dead, after all.

With a sigh, I wrapped the sheet around myself and scooted backwards until I was propped up against the headboard. Then, in a voice that sounded far calmer than I felt, I asked the elven girl where we were.

"You do not know?" she asked, eyebrow arched.

I shook my head.

"What a shame." A naughty smile tugged at her rosebud lips. "It was a night I will never forget."

"I...uh..."

"Relax, I am only teasing. This is Lord Oberon's bedchamber. Quite the place, isn't it?"

Her tone was glib as she turned from me to study the windowless, candlelit room. I followed her gaze, noting in particular a pair of matte black chandeliers hanging from the ceiling and thick fur rugs displayed along the walls, not to mention the clothes strewn haphazardly across the floor.

"It sure is," I replied with a grimace. I began massaging my temples with the hand not keeping what little dignity I had left intact, my mind buzzing with the implications of being discovered and carted before the Goblin King—a ruthless Faeling lord whose tendency to stab first and ask questions later was well known.

"Is something wrong?" the elven girl asked.

I shook my head. "Could ye maybe tell me how we ended up here, though?"

"You truly do not remember? You were the one who insisted we sneak in and sample our lord's wine collection while he was away. Though what happened next was all thanks to this one." The elven girl playfully spanked our dozing companion on his right buttock. "Not that we ever stood a chance. After all, Riann can be quite convincing when he puts his body to it."

I froze, too startled to speak. The elf, meanwhile, turned to leer at the naked man in bed beside me. A man who wasn't a man at all, but a Faeling, not to mention a very dear friend of mine.

A friend I thought I'd lost forever.

"Sorry, but d'ye say Riann? As in Riann O'Rye?"

"Oh, come now. Surely you did not drink so much wine that you forgot our names, as well?"

"I'm sorry, I wish I could remember," I lied. "I'm sure it'll all come back to me. But, in the meantime...that *is* Riann O'Rye, isn't it?"

"I am not sure. He told me his name was Riann, that is all I know. He serves as a castle guard. We met in the gardens where I work. I am Elvin, by the way."

"Like the chipmunk?"

"What?"

"Nothin', nevermind," I waved her off, distractedly, too busy trying to organize my jumbled thoughts to mock her parents for naming their daughter the human equivalent of "person."

"Well, anyway," the elf went on, stifling a yawn with one perfectly manicured hand. "It seems we wore the poor guard out. A pity. I would have liked to pick up where we left off. Unless perhaps you might be interested in a little—"

"No! I mean, no t'anks. I actually have somewhere to be. Totally overslept, ye know how it is. Anyway, ye should try to lay down and get some rest."

"Oh I intend to. I could use it after everything the three of us did to one another last night. With our mouths."

"Well, then—"

"And our hands."

"I—"

"And our feet."

"Jesus, okay." I cleared my throat awkwardly. "Right, well, sweet dreams I guess."

"Mmm. I prefer my dreams salty."

Realizing the nymphomaniacal elf could keep this innuendo going all day, I ignored the comment and instead slipped out from beneath the covers to fetch a robe I'd noticed laying discarded beside the bed. As I was throwing it on, I took a quick peek and saw that I too wore the flesh of an elf. Indeed, toned and almost impossibly slim through the hips and shoulders, I could have worn any off the rack outfit my heart desired—a dream every woman has at least once in her life.

Unfortunately, I wasn't able to relish the moment as much as I'd have liked, not with Riann's—or rather Ryan's—naked body on display.

I could remember vividly the last time I'd seen him. His skin had been blue, then, his heart a clockwork device fashioned from a cyclops' eye, his body providing refuge for a malevolent soul. I could still remember his last words to me, and the terrible sorrow that had accompanied them.

I'll be closer than you think.

Looking down now at his pale, unmarked flesh, I felt a desperate urge to wake the Faeling up. To warn him of the terrible fate he was destined to suffer not only at the hands of his foes, but also his friends. Me, especially. Not that I expected him to believe me; under the circumstances, whatever I told him would no doubt come off as the paranoid ramblings of some drunken elven strumpet.

But what if I *could* convince him? What if I could somehow alter his future? Maybe if I cautioned him not to accept the Winter Queen's offer to become the new Jack Frost, or if I told him not to return to Fae with Cassandra all those years ago, or—

"Open up this door!" demanded a booming voice, each word punctuated by a heavy pounding on the bedchamber door. "We know you are in there! Come out now in the name of Lord Oberon, or we will break down the doors and drag you before the court by your entrails!"

55

Elvin and I exchanged startled looks as the relentless pounding on the door continued, each knock followed by a series of increasingly less imaginative threats. Ryan, meanwhile, stirred just long enough to snarl and cover his ears with a pillow.

Typical.

Fortunately, it seemed the door was made of sturdier stuff than our friends outside had accounted for. That, or they were simply loath to break down their king's bedchamber door.

My money was on the latter.

"Who the hell is that?" I hissed.

"It sounds like the royal guard," Elvin replied in a trembling voice, her eyes wide as dinner plates. "Someone must have seen us."

"Ye t'ink?" I sighed. "I don't suppose there's any chance they'll let us off easy when they finally decide to force their way in here?"

"Us? Maybe. But Riann...he was supposed to be on duty this morning. If they find out he missed his watch, he will be punished."

"Punished how?"

Elvin grimaced. "The royal guard are mostly goblins, handpicked by Lord Oberon for their...ruthlessness. If they discover one of the castle guards has shirked his duties..."

The elf drifted off rather than list the possibilities, though I could imagine they all would involve some form of torture. Given the less than ideal circumstances, I put whatever thoughts I had of altering the future on the back burner and instead began formulating a plan.

"Thieves!" barked the royal guard outside, distracting me. "Return what you have taken and perhaps our lord will show mercy!"

Thieves? I frowned. Was he talking about the wine? No, that couldn't be; unless the Fae had perfected a method of distilling alcoholic beverages from bile, they wouldn't be seeing any of those vintages again. But then what else could they mean?

"What is he talkin' about?" I asked Elvin, who looked as perplexed as I did.

"I have no idea."

"Whatever. It doesn't matter. We have more important t'ings to worry about, like findin' another way out of here. I don't suppose ye know of one?"

Elvin gulped and nodded. "There is a servant's entrance that leads to the downstairs kitchens, but it will not take them long to overtake us once they come through the door. Only the brownies use it, which means we would have to crouch the whole time. Plus, we will be spotted long before we reach the lower floors."

"Worry about all that later. For now, get him up and start makin' your way down. I'll stay behind and keep 'em distracted."

"Distracted how?"

"With me mouth."

Elvin gaped at me.

"Not like that! I meant talkin', ye pervert. Now go on, before they knock down that door and find all three of us in here. Oh, but do me a favor won't ye? Give that dumbass a hug for me when this is all over."

"A hug? Why?"

I wished I had time to explain, but deep down I knew I had to ensure his escape—even if that meant condemning him to what some might consider a far worse fate. Instead, I told her the truth.

"Because I'm goin' to miss him."

Elvin shot me a curious look before fashioning a toga out of the covers and slipping out of bed. Then she did as I asked, shoving at Ryan until he was coherent enough to be lured out of bed by her cajoling—or at least her cleavage. Even with his sleep tousled hair and half-lidded eyes, the Faeling was as handsome as ever, the sight of his familiar face hitting me like a punch to the gut.

"What is going on?" he asked of his elven companion, huskily.

"We are making our escape. Now, move."

"Escaping from what?"

"The royal guards." Elvin snatched one of the pelts off the wall and tossed it at him. "Hurry and put that on."

"Were you this bossy last night? Because I seem to remember... wait, what about her? Is she coming?"

Ryan turned to stare at me with those gentle, uncomprehending eyes, and for a moment I considered telling him everything. So what if he didn't believe me? If there was even a chance it could change the future, shouldn't I at least try? But then I heard the heavy thunk of an axe head burying itself in the door, and I knew we were all out of time.

"Go!" I hissed.

Elvin snatched at Ryan like she might a wayward toddler, and together the pair disappeared behind a curtain obscuring a small door sitting flush with the wall, their footsteps receding until all I could hear was the crunch of splintered wood and the shouts of angry goblins.

"I'll be seein' ye, Ryan O'Rye," I whispered to no one in particular, a heavy weight pressing on my heart.

And then I got to work.

56

Once I was alone, I set about piecing together a serviceable outfit from the clothes strewn across the floor of Oberon's bedchamber, though the real challenge proved getting dressed while goblins literally beat down the door as it turned out that looking like an elf and moving like one were two very different things.

Still, I managed to find a pelt to hide behind with time to spare; contrary to what you may have learned from Jack Nicholson's riveting performance in *The Shining*, chopping through a door with an axe is a pretty time consuming affair. Especially if said door happens to be made of solid oak.

Not knowing how many royal guards to expect and having no weapons beyond a few improvised instruments, my plan was to lie in wait until the goblins came pouring into the room, then try to sneak out behind them and make a break for it. Assuming that failed, which I had to admit was a very strong possibility, I'd channel my inner Karen and demand an audience with their manager, AKA Oberon himself, with as much imperiousness as I could muster.

Just as I was preparing myself for the impending breach, however, the assault on the door stopped as the royal guards outside began shouting, their startled cries soon supplanted by squeals of pain and cacophonous thuds. I poked my head out from my hiding place and saw a kaleidoscope of light flashing through the forearm-sized hole in the door—first blue, then green, then silver, and finally red. Then, as suddenly as the ruckus had begun, all was silent.

That was until a pair of eerily familiar voices sounded just outside the door.

"Well, I'd say we made a mess of that," said the first, belonging to a man.

"You mean *you* made a mess of that," snapped the second, a woman. "I said we needed to go up one level and cut across the rooftops if we wanted to avoid running into guards. Now they'll all be after us."

"And I already told *you* we'd be better off facing them down here than risk alerting their sentries on the roof. Do you have any idea how many Fae have wings? I'll give you a hint, it's about as many as have sharp teeth and claws. Besides, not all of us are masters of wind magic, and I for one have a very rational fear of falling to my death from the ramparts of a castle!"

"Give me a break. Are all you Temples such babies? I hope not, or stealing back these stupid ashes was a colossal waste of time."

"They aren't stupid, and we are *not* babies. We are the last scions of the ancient bloodline, destined to inherit—"

"Destined to inherit the will of the gods and reforge the hearts of humankind, blah, blah, blah. So you keep saying. Though that still doesn't explain why you needed someone like me to help you pull off this little caper, or why you're still talking when we should be escaping."

"...I really don't like you."

"Well, that's a relief. I'd hate for our relationship to be one-sided. Now, can we get going already? Or does the great Calvin Temple need a minute to collect himself? Hmm?"

Before her companion could reply, however, a distant shout sounded, followed by a tremendous explosion and the snarl of fire.

"Makayla, lookout!"

My initial suspicions confirmed, I rushed to the door and pressed my face to the hole, desperate to see what was happening to Nate's parents out in the hall. Regrettably, I was too late; all I saw were flashes of color as two dozen armed goblins raced past, each dancing nimbly over the forms of their fallen comrades as they pursued their elusive quarry.

Once I was sure they were all long gone, I removed the bar blocking the door and slipped out into the hallway, wary of any unexpected movement. All I found, however, was a deserted corridor littered with smoldering goblins, their armor alternatively scorched, gouged, melted, and crushed. Indeed, if I didn't know any better, I'd have guessed they were taken out by a tornado made of fire and knives.

Upon closer inspection, I discovered a fresh bloodstain splattered across a blown out section of wall—a crimson trail that continued in the direction the guards had gone. I strolled over, wondering which of the two wizards had been hurt and whether they'd survive long enough to escape the castle.

But then, of course they would; if they hadn't, I'd never have met them in the future. Wasn't that sort of the point of all this? Either way, the unexpected presence of Calvin and Makayla did raise a host of fascinating questions, including what they were doing here in the first place, or why they'd gone out of their way to take out these guards. Wait...were they the thieves the royal guards had been after? But then, why target Oberon's bedchambers?

Oh yeah, and since when were Calvin and Makayla so acrimonious?

While I attempted to puzzle out at least a few of these questions, I spotted something left behind among the rubble—a stone object almost indistinguishable from the debris that surrounded it but for the slight difference in color. Making sure I was still alone, I began clearing the site of the explosion to reveal an hourglass fashioned from some sort of composite. Granite, maybe? I picked the hourglass up and held it aloft, unsure whether the trinket had belonged to the Temples or had simply been dropped by a careless guard.

"What are ye doin' here?" I asked if the hourglass, bewildered.

"Waiting for you, I expect."

I whirled around and nearly clocked Veil in the process, my heart hammering so hard I thought I might faint. "Jesus Christ! Would ye please stop sneakin' up on me?!"

"But why, when it's so much fun? Anyway, it's time to go. Another wave of guards will be here soon with your friends in tow."

"Wait, which ones? Calvin and Makayla? Or Ryan and the elf?"

"The latter."

"Seriously? How'd they get caught? The royal guards are all here."

"It wasn't the royal guards. It seems your friend Ryan was meant to be guarding the castle vaults this morning. Which, as I'm sure you've realized by now, just so happened to have been hit by none other than Calvin and Makayla Temple."

"Wait, that was *today*?!" I exclaimed, realizing too late that I already knew this story. Indeed, Ryan had been the one to tell it to me, ages ago. How the Temples had snuck into Lord Oberon's castle, drugged him, and stolen a powerful artifact of some kind—resulting in his exile from Fae. "But Ryan said they drugged him! Not that he was sleepin' off a drunken threesome in his boss' bed."

Veil tried to cover a laugh with a cough. "How very politically savvy of him."

When she put it like that, I supposed I could see her point; admitting to the truth in this case would be tantamount to walking into Oberon's throne room and taking a piss on his chair while he was still in it.

Basically, a death sentence.

"Fine," I said, "but shouldn't we be stickin' around, then? To make sure the Temples escape, or that Ryan isn't executed? I mean, why else am I here? I've done nothing but hide behind a door, and the two people I tried to cover for got caught, anyway."

"I wouldn't say that. You kept your friend from being discovered and summarily spitroasted, and you stumbled across a remarkably powerful object that may come in handy sooner than you think."

"Ye say that like ye know where we're goin'," I noted, suspiciously.

"I thought ye said our destinations are as much a mystery to ye as they are to me."

Veil shook her head. "I am starting to see a pattern form, that's all. Call it a ripple of cause and effect, visible only to someone on the outside looking in."

"Well? Care to share?"

"And ruin the surprise? Absolutely not."

I rolled my eyes. "Which means you're basically still as much in the dark as I am."

Veil shrugged nonchalantly, and for a moment I considered pushing back at her suggestion that we leave. After all, there had to be something I could do for Ryan, even if it had ultimately been his own dumbass fault for screwing up so badly in the first place. Sadly, I wasn't sure what that something could be; without access to proper armor and weapons and with my godlike powers either on the fritz or locked up behind some crazy metaphysical door like a wild animal, I was essentially nothing more than a casual bystander.

"Fine," I said, eventually. "But this time, can we make sure I'm wearin' clothes, please?"

"I mean..."

I sighed. "Just do it."

57

"You see, if their gods tell them what to do, we take away their ability to decide for themselves."

58

I woke to the clink of ice as several cubes settled to the bottom of the empty rocks glass in front of me, my right eye covered by some sort of bandage or patch. I reached for it instinctively, probing at the unfamiliar accessory with my fingertips while muted country music played in the background, its twangy tones mingling with the rustle of fabric, the slurping of booze, and the din of conversation.

"Is everything alright, Allfather?"

I froze, forgetting all about my impairment for the moment as a woman slid into the booth across from mine, the leather groaning as if in protest. Of course, I couldn't blame the poor thing; the booth's occupant was a densely muscular blonde who no doubt weighed more than her athletic frame suggested.

"Hilde?" I said, surprised. "What are ye doin' here?"

The Valkyrie cocked an eyebrow. "Responding to your invitation. It was you who asked me here, wasn't it?"

"Um..." I leaned back, trying to make sense of the situation, and just happened to catch sight of my reflection in the grimy mirror behind the bar. I appeared as a distinguished older man with a bushy, iron grey beard and a mane of silver hair, dressed like a retired musician in acid wash jeans and a brown leather jacket. Oh, and I wore an eye patch. Which, when coupled with the appellation Hilde had used upon arrival, suggested one very disturbing possibility: Hilde thought I was the Allfather, otherwise known as Odin, lord and ruler of the Aesir.

"I see," Hilde said, misinterpreting my silence for denial. "I did wonder when I'd discovered you still haven't reached out to Lady Freya, who is very concerned about you, by the way."

"Well, I—"

Hilde held up a hand. "It's alright. The Allfather can do as he wishes. If that means disappearing on us all, then so be it. I won't even ask where you've been. And don't worry, I won't tell anyone where to find you. Just know that, if you didn't send for me, then someone else has."

Having absolutely no idea what Hilde was going on about, I opted instead to keep my trap shut and wait her out. With her sentiments delivered and no response from me, however, it seemed the conversation had run its course.

"Well then, I'm off," the Valkyrie said. "Actually, would you mind pointing me in the direction of the bathrooms? I have a long trip back to Fólkvangr ahead of me."

Spotting a water closet sign hanging at the opposite side of the room, I gestured. Hilde thanked me, got up, and navigated the crowded restaurant, her stunning Nordic features and remarkably taut body drawing stares from every table she passed. Including, as it turned out, the two men seated at the bar some ten feet to my left.

Two men, coincidentally, whom I recognized.

The first was a younger, more disheveled Special Agent Leo Jeffries dressed in a crumpled suit with the jacket thrown over the back of his stool. The second, a blonde giant whose jeans and t-shirt threatened to burst at the seams, was Gunnar Randulf. And let me just say, *somebody* had eaten all their vegetables.

As I stared at the two men, struggling to process the sheer fuckery that seemed to be going on, the music that had been playing over the speakers faded and eventually died off altogether.

"I'm sorry," Gunnar said, his gravelly voice audible in the sudden quiet. "I know it was my idea, but we both know I can't come back to work for the FBI. Not with everything else I have going on."

"You mean Temple," Leo replied.

Gunnar took a sip from the large pint in his right hand before nodding. "He's my best friend, and he needs me. After what happened to Calvin and Makayla...and after that whole dragon cabal thing we uncovered...something is happening in St. Louis. I can't say what, yet, but I know Nate will end up involved. He can't help himself."

"Sounds like he isn't the only one."

Gunnar grunted. "I'd argue, but we both know I'd be lying."

Leo chuckled. "Please, I wouldn't even need to read you. You're a terrible liar, especially for a cop."

"Good thing I'm not a cop anymore, then."

"I wouldn't go that far. Your idea, recruiting Freaks to do the job? I still think it's a good one. It's like you said, there are monsters and then there are *monsters*. If we can't find a way to get both kinds off the streets, then why even bother?"

"Yeah. Sounds pretty damn obvious, doesn't it? Too bad it'll never happen."

"I wouldn't be so sure about that."

Gunnar paused to consider the man beside him. "There'll be pushback, you know. Agency politics to contend with. I take it you have a backer?"

Leo nodded. "A senator. His daughter got attacked by one of your kind a few years back. Holds himself responsible."

"What happened to the girl?" Gunnar asked, his shoulders practically vibrating with tension.

"She's alright. Runs with a pack in upstate New York these days. They're estranged. Anyway, it turns out he and a few of his buddies are uncommonly sympathetic to our cause. Not sure if it'll last, but I think they'd support us long enough to form an under-the-radar unit."

"That's...wow, Leo. That's great, really."

Leo nodded. "I don't suppose that changes your mind on coming back?"

Gunnar hesitated.

"I mean, just think of all the good we could do," Leo went on, passionately. "An independent unit, responding to threats across the country. Everyone we could help. We—"

"I can't, Leo. I'm sorry, but I've made up my mind."

"Right. Yeah, okay. I hope you don't blame me for asking."

"Of course not. I'd be insulted if you didn't. But Leo, promise me you won't do this until you've got the right team, alright? If you really want to come after us Freaks, you'll need more ammunition than being able to tell if someone's yanking your chain. Trust me."

"I don't suppose you have any recommendations?"

Gunnar barked a laugh. "I can think of a few, but to be honest I wouldn't trust them to fall in line. Plus most of them are criminals."

"What kind of criminals?" Leo asked, suspiciously.

"The reformed kind, or so they say. Don't worry, if any of them turn out to be bad apples, I'll make sure they're dealt with."

"Even if that includes Nate Temple?"

"It won't." Gunnar took a long pull of his drink, finishing it in a single gulp. "Pass something on to the rest of the Bureau for me, would you? Steer clear of St. Louis for a while. Focus on the rest of the country. I have a gut feeling things are going to get a lot uglier around here."

"I'll see what I can do."

The blonde giant nodded and slipped from his chair. He reached for the wallet tucked in the back pocket of his painted-on jeans, but Leo waved him off.

"I've got it. I'm going to stick around and have another one. I'm off duty, remember?"

"Right. Well, take care. I mean it."

Leo toasted him and took a sip. "See you around, wolfman."

59

"Allfather? Did you hear what I said?"

I turned towards the sound of Hilde's voice, blinking owlishly. Gunnar had stepped out a few minutes ago by this point, while Leo had polished off his first beer and ordered a second, leaving me to ponder over everything I'd heard. It hadn't taken me long to decipher the context of their conversation, most of which had revolved around the formation of what would one day become the SICCO squad. What had taken me a while to figure out, however, was the reason I'd been privy to it in the first place—and while wearing Odin's face, no less.

"I said I'm off," Hilde continued. "Unless there's something else you needed?"

"Actually, there is. Take a seat. D'ye see that man over there?"

Hilde frowned and swung her attention to the bar, where Leo sat nursing his pint, seemingly oblivious to the various sports programs on display overhead. Somewhere, some bar patron decided to put on another song. Not country this time, but a classic 90s ballad.

"What about him?" Hilde asked as she sat down, her expression perplexed.

"His name is Special Agent Leo Jeffries. I want ye to work for him."

"What? Why?"

"Because I've foreseen how much good you'll do together." I tapped my eye patch, recalling tales of Odin's prophetic knowledge. "And because he'll never accomplish what he aims to without help. Your help, specifically."

The Valkyrie scowled. "And what is it he aims to do, exactly?

"Good. But I'll leave the details to him. All I need is for ye to go over there and say I sent ye. If he has any questions, tell him I approve of his plans and trust his intent. He'll know you're tellin' the truth."

"Allfather...you know I don't work for you, strictly speaking. Unless Lady Freya—"

"She knows," I lied.

"But—"

"I told ye," I interrupted. "I have *seen* this. It's your destiny to meet this man."

Hilde straightened perceptively. "As it was my mother's destiny to meet my father?"

I shook my head, realizing too late that I may have unintentionally struck a nerve. After all, it had been Odin who condemned Hilde's mother, Brunhilde, to an eternal sleep behind a wall of fire—a sleep disturbed by the hero Sigurd, Hilde's father. Had it been a classic Disney princess story, perhaps that might have been the end of it. Unfortunately, a host of intrigues and betrayals followed, culminating in Sigurd's murder and Brunhilde's suicide.

"On the contrary," I replied, projecting a confidence I didn't feel, "their tragedy began the moment your mother chose to ignore my wishes. Had she listened to me, all their pain might have been avoided."

Of course, this was all a lie. Or at the very least, conjecture. However, I alone knew what fate had in store for Leo and Hilde—a fate rife with trials and tribulations, certainly, but also love. Genuine, powerful love. And if it meant lying to preserve that future, I knew I wouldn't lose a wink of sleep.

Besides, what I'd said before was true: they were destined to help people. Without Hilde at his side, Leo might never make his dream a reality and form the unit responsible for solving so many supernatural crimes, not to mention what that all might mean for me, personally.

"But this is *Midgard*," Hilde finally said, her shoulders slumped in defeat. "You really expect me to live among these people? For how long?"

"As long as it takes. Trust me, in a few years' time, it'll be almost impossible to convince ye to leave."

"I can't imagine that," she admitted. "But if the Allfather says it's true, then it must be so. And you're certain Lady Freya is alright with this?"

"Why would I lie?" I asked, hedging the truth as best I could and praying the guilt I felt didn't show on my face. After all, I knew for a fact Freya was anything *but* fine with it; Hilde's sudden and mysterious disappearance would trouble the Norse goddess for years until I arrived to confirm the Valkyrie's whereabouts. But then, what other choice did I have?

Hilde sighed. "Very well."

The Valkyrie swung her legs out from under the table, rose, stretched, and bid me a terse farewell before joining Leo at the bar. I watched them for a moment, noting with some amusement the instant attraction that flared between the two, before scooting out of my own seat and heading for the door beyond which I suspected I'd find Veil waiting. Moreover, I did so feeling pretty damn good about what had just happened, regardless of my deceit.

You know, maybe this wouldn't be so bad, after all.

60

" ... The Road of Bones is not a place. It is a realm unto itself. Many, many years ago a war was fought there, a war between the Tiny Gods. The Makers. Those who had the will to shape the world as they saw fit. It was a terrible war which threatened every living creature. In the final days, a Maker sacrificed herself to seal it—and the powers which remain there—away from the rest of the world. The path you walk, what they call the Road of Bones, was paved by her blood and carved from her flesh."

61

A bloodcurdling shriek startled me awake, its shrill cry followed almost immediately by a bestial roar that sent the hairs on the back of my neck standing straight up. I rolled onto my side to find the air thick with foul smelling smoke, surrounded by the clash of steel and the screams of the dying.

Heart hammering against my chest, I staggered awkwardly to my feet, the ankle-deep snow on the ground crunching beneath the soles of my fur-lined boots, its once-pristine surface stained pink with spilled blood. It wasn't until the smoke cleared that I saw the reason why; bodies, so many I could hardly believe my eyes, surrounded me on all sides as though I stood at the epicenter of a crop circle made of corpses.

Several had already frozen over, their bloodless flesh caked in a thin layer of frost. Most lay curled around their pain, their grievous wounds unattended, their whimpering either unheard or unacknowledged until it was too late.

I recognized some of the fallen from their features: the green-skinned goblins and long-tusked ogres, for instance. Or the elves with their fair skin and pointed ears. Others I had never seen before in my life: great antlered beasts with cloven hooves, humanoids made entirely of light, and armored knights with the faces of lizards. Of other survivors, however, I saw no sign. Indeed, it wasn't until I turned my attention elsewhere that I spotted another living soul.

And, consequently, discovered where I was.

The ravine known as the Road of Bones wove between a pair of towering cliffs made entirely of ice before widening into a snow-covered valley. Dozens of frozen pillars jutted from those otherwise sheer walls, forming impromptu bridges that spanned the gap. Of course, when last I'd laid eyes upon this particular place, those walk-ways had stood unoccupied and the ravine had been riddled with permafrosted corpses.

Now, however, I could make out dozens of figures warring for supremacy atop those pillars, while hundreds more warred within the narrow confines of the ravine—some the size of trolls, others no bigger than sprites. I stood some thirty yards from the worst of it, watching carrion birds the size of dogs circling against the muted backdrop of a dull grey sky and trying to figure out what atrocities I'd committed in my past life to deserve being chucked into the middle of a freaking war zone.

"Brigid! You're alright! Thank goodness. Here, come and take Lugh's feet!"

I turned to find a pair of individuals laboring to carry an absurdly well-proportioned, half-naked man caked in equal parts blood and golden ichor between them. The speaker, a freckle-faced woman in a chainmail coif and medieval tabard with a sword strapped to her hip, was utterly unfamiliar to me. Her grizzled companion, however, was someone I very much recognized, while I would've put money on the fact that I'd once cuddled up next to the injured party in a boat set adrift in the waters of a crimson sea.

"Manannan mac Lir?!" I called back, hardly able to believe my eyes at the sight of a Tuatha de Danann here of all places. "What are ye doin' here?"

"What does it look like?" snapped the sea god. "Now stop yappin' and do what the Maker says, girl! Lugh is in a bad way."

Though not exactly charmed by the tone he'd chosen to take with me, I did as the god asked and rushed over to help share the load—even though that meant stepping over a disturbing number of corpses. When I got there, however, the so-called Maker appeared to have changed her mind; instead of having me take his legs, she instructed me to help them settle the legendary warrior against a propped-up shield. Afterwards, she unbelted her sword and passed it over to me, sheath and all, though only after fiddling with the pommel.

"Here," she insisted. "Take this. Manannan, give her the spear."

"Huh? What for?"

"Safekeeping. You didn't see Lugh go down. I did. He pushed the devourer too far, and it shattered in his face. He's fortunate to have survived, but I doubt very much he'll recover in time to rejoin the battle."

Manannan balked at this. "But we've already lost several of the Mabinogi, not to mention Cliodhna and her banshees. If Gwyp ap Nudd were to withdraw to Annwn, and without Lugh to rally our forces..."

The Maker cringed. "I know. We cannot win."

"I didn't say that."

"No, but we were both thinking it. And you're right. We were outmatched from the moment we arrived."

"We shouldn't have been." The sea god's eyes darkened visibly with rage. "If the Morrígna had answered our call, we might have put 'em on their heels. And the Dagda! Had he stood with us, they would have surrendered right away."

"Perhaps, perhaps not. We can never know. It's also possible we simply fooled ourselves into believing we could preempt the prophecy, and that this was always to be our fate."

"Not that blasted prophecy, again! I told ye, no one knows who spewed that nonsense, or why. For all we know, it was *them*."

"You may be right." The Maker cast her gaze over the battlefield. "Still, we have failed, and now it is up to us to salvage what we can."

Manannan looked as though he wanted to argue but couldn't. Instead, he grumbled under his breath, produced a spear from the ether, and tossed it at me. I struggled at first to hold both weapons, and only in that moment realized I'd seen them before.

The first I recognized as Joyeuse, also known as Charlemagne's singing sword—a magically enhanced blade with glittering gold bands wound around the hilt to end in a nest of open prongs. The second was Areadbhar as I'd first laid eyes on her—a smoldering crater at the heart of her Damascus steel blade where the bejeweled heart of a dead Jotunn, otherwise known as a devourer, was supposed to sit.

"Where d'ye get—" I began.

"There's no time," the Maker interrupted. "Just promise to take good care of them."

"Very good care," Manannan seconded.

I nodded, not trusting myself to speak, yet with so many questions running through my mind. Like why were the Tuatha de Danann here of all places, and who was it were they fighting? And, for that matter, who the hell was this Maker woman they appeared to have allied themselves with?

"As for you," she said, turning to Manannan, "I hope I can count on you to sound the retreat."

"What? Don't be ridiculous. I've got plenty of fight left in me."

"Which is why I am asking you. With Lugh wounded, your kind will look to you for guidance. They will listen to you."

"And I'm supposed to tell them what? To give up, after everythin' we sacrificed to get here?"

"No. You're going to tell them to live and fight another day. Then you're going to gather as many who will listen as you can and lead them to Tír na Nóg."

"But that's—"

"The only choice you have, unless you'd rather see your entire people wiped out here and now."

"Better that than lose ourselves to that place! Tír na Nóg is as much a prison as a refuge, ye know that."

"Of course I do. I helped make it." The Maker bestowed a sad, knowing smile upon her companion. "But this is not about how you feel, or even ensuring the survival of the Tuatha de Danann who remain. It's about saving those who worship you. Those who follow you. Don't they deserve to be happy, even if that happiness stems from ignorance?"

Manannan looked away. "And what will ye be doin', then, while we're runnin' away with our tails tucked between our legs?"

"I'll be here," she replied, matter-of-factly. "Sealing this place away before this thing we started bleeds over into the mortal realm."

The sea god turned, his expression aghast. "Ye can't be serious."

"Someone has to pay the price for our hubris, my friend. My kind cannot be allowed to reign free as they have these past centuries. For the age of men to begin, the age of Tiny Gods must end."

"Surely there must be another way."

"If there is, I have not yet thought of it." The Maker reached out to squeeze the sea god's meaty bicep. "Know that I will always cherish our time together and appreciate the sanctuary your people offered us. Now, take Lugh and go, while there's still time."

The Maker snapped her fingers, and the shield Lugh was slumped against reknit itself, the wood warping as though it was made of taffy to become a boat big enough to cradle the legendary warrior. Manannan took hold of the prow with one hand and pawed at his face with the other, tear tracks staining his grizzled, soot-stained face.

"As you command, Lady Ambrosius."

"Oh, come now," she replied, swatting at him. "As if I would ever give you an order. Besides, you know how I hate that name."

"You're right." The sea god managed a slight smile. "Fair winds, Verity Temple."

"Farewell, Manannan mac Lir."

62

I stood rooted next to the woman called Verity Temple as Manannan returned to the battlefield with Lugh in tow, bellowing orders as he went. To say I was shocked would have been a massive understatement. I mean, what were the odds that I would stumble across yet another one of Nate's ancestors on top of everything else? And another Maker, at that.

"You should go, too," Verity said to me once Manannan was well out of ear shot. "Whoever you are."

I straightened in surprise. "Sorry, what?"

"There is no need to pretend. I knew you weren't Brigid from the first moment I saw you. The girl was never much of a runner. Far too clumsy."

I must admit I did briefly consider lying, if only out of sheer reflex. Sadly, I could tell that was never going to work; the Maker clearly knew I wasn't who my face said I was, and no amount of dissembling was going to change that fact.

"Right," I said. "So, about that..."

"Relax," she went on, cooly. "I do not mean you any harm. Whatever my son's reasons for sending you in particular to collect the spoils, I must admit I am relieved to know they will serve a greater purpose. Though perhaps I could ask you a small favor in return? Would you pass on a message for me? Tell him he was right, after all, and that I only wish I'd listened."

"I'm sorry, I'm not sure I follow. Who are we talkin' about?"

"The wizard whose magic you reek of. Merlin. My son."

The moment she spoke the words, it suddenly felt as if every limb in my body belonged to someone else—my own skin somehow alien and unwelcome—and in the end it was all I could manage to stand there gaping at her like an idiot. I mean, *this* was Merlin's mother? A freaking *Temple*? But then, that would make her my...and it would make me a...

No way.

No fucking way.

"That can't be—"

"I am sorry to interrupt, child, but we are out of time. Go after Manannan now, while you still can, or you will end up like the rest."

"Wait, no, I need to tell ye—"

Verity cut off what I'd been about to say with a mere flick of her wrist, the gesture accompanied by a wave of power that sent me skidding backwards and pinwheeling my arms like a kid on an ice rink. I ended up on one knee some several yards away with both Joyeuse and Areadbhar jutting from a nearby snowdrift.

It took me less than a minute to recover, and yet by that point, Verity had already begun her spell—if that's what it was. Either way, as I staggered to my feet, I saw the Maker encased in a revolving spiral of ice and rock and snow that spun faster and faster until I had trouble making out her silhouette, let alone her face.

And it was at that moment that I felt rather than saw Veil's hand settle onto my shoulder.

"No!" I snarled, shaking her off. "Don't ye dare!"

"There is nothing more for you to do here," she countered, though I swore I could hear pity in her voice.

"The hell there isn't! Ye heard her! That's Merlin's mother behind all that. Me grandmother, for Christ's sakes! I'm not leavin' until I get a chance to talk to her. To tell her who I am."

"And if I thought that was possible, I would let you. But I am afraid it's too late for that."

"Too late, how? She's right there!"

Veil looked away.

"Whatever," I snapped, turning back. "I'll just drag her out, meself."

"Don't be a fool!" Veil grabbed me by the arm. "Don't tell me you've forgotten what happens to this place? What it becomes? *She* is the one! The Tiny God who turned against her own kind, sealing away so much of their power, and this is when it happens. Don't you get it? She's already dead."

I wrenched my arm free. "You'd say anythin' to get me to leave with ye, wouldn't ye?"

"Look for yourself!"

"I will!"

After hastily snatching up the sword and spear, I strode towards the vortex, determined to prove Veil wrong. She *had* to be wrong. My grandmother was alive, and she was going to tell me everything I wanted to know about my father, and she was going to love me, because that's what grandmothers were supposed to do. Veil would see.

Except Veil wasn't wrong.

Standing as close as I dared without actually getting caught up in its current, I was able to see past the funnel of debris and make out the shriveled figure within—wizened and rent apart by fissures that oozed power in the form of an infernal blue light, the Maker resembled not so much a person as a doll plucked from a fireplace.

"She was gone the moment she swallowed the devourer she stole from that sword," Veil explained as she approached from behind, her voice soft once more. "By doing so, she saved countless lives, including many whom your mother considered family. If that's any consolation."

It wasn't.

Because my grandmother was dead.

And she hadn't even known my name.

"Get me out of here," I whispered.

63

"Long ago, when we put Lugh to rest, we entrusted the spear to a man, a wizard we thought we could trust."

64

Momentarily blinded by the searing light of a noonday sun, I cursed and shielded my eyes. Once I'd confirmed my retinas hadn't in fact shriveled up and died, however, I cautiously lowered my arm and discovered myself standing on a small bluff perched some twenty feet into the ocean, surrounded by a sheer cliff face on one side and a pristine, white sand beach on the other.

It was significantly warmer here. Perhaps too warm, if not for the refreshing breeze rolling off the water. On it, I could smell the brine of the ocean. That, and something else, I realized—something fetid and musky.

The nose-rankling odor of death.

Scenting the air, I began turning a slow circle only to discover an unexpected weight dragging at my hip where Joyeuse had been strapped, while a lifeless Areadbhar leaned against a nearby boulder. Not knowing what else to do, I took the spear in hand and used her to navigate the uneven footing while I tracked the smell to its source.

It didn't take long; the foul odor grew stronger as I reached the beach, and stronger still the farther west I traveled. Of Veil there was no sign, which was a relief. After what I'd just been through, I wasn't in the mood to talk to anyone, let alone the one person who might have warned me what to expect. I mean, what a thing to spring on someone: oh, by the way, your grandmother was a Temple, not to mention an exceptionally powerful Maker who made a habit of hanging out with gods.

Like, what the fuck, right?

Engrossed in thoughts like these, it took me a minute to spot the body of a satyr laying facedown in the surf. The tide washed over the poor creature in waves, drenching his lower half and leaving wet fur and dripping hooves in its wake as I raced to his side. Upon closer inspection, I noticed all manner of cuts and abrasions marring the creature's naked back with liquid gold welling from the wounds. He was also missing a horn.

Thinking quickly, I tossed Areadbhar well beyond the tide's reach and promptly gathered the satyr's arms. He was ridiculously heavy, and yet I managed to drag him far enough inland to keep the waves from taking him. Then, with substantial effort, I turned the poor bastard over.

I grunted, surprised to find I vaguely recognized the face—as if from a dream, or perhaps a premonition.

"Pan?" I asked, the name tickling a memory of a ferocious battle fought on a cliff's edge. A battle that had ended in heartache.

The god's eyes snapped open.

I nearly jumped out of my skin as Pan drew in a massive, shuddering breath. Quickly, I gripped the hilt of my sword, afraid I might have to finish what the fall had started should the Greek deity turn violent. In the end, however, I need not have bothered; he was far too weak to present any kind of threat. Indeed, the god's breathing was horribly labored, his eyes glazed over with pain, and ichor dribbled from his mouth.

Still, he saw me.

"You," he said, then smiled.

Not knowing how to respond to that, I instead tried to encourage the satyr—insisting he would recover despite all evidence to the contrary. I wished I could have told him help was coming, but the truth was I wasn't even sure where we were, let alone what it would take to heal a god.

Pan chuckled. "There is no need for that, old friend. I have nothing left to do. The boy...he..." The god coughed, his face a grimace of pain. "He has learned all he can from me. You were right, by the way. He was...worthy."

I frowned, wondering if the dying god was merely hallucinating, or if he was somehow familiar with whatever guise I happened to be wearing. Probably the latter, I decided, given the circumstances. Not that this clarified anything—especially the bit about the boy.

"Will you call him for me?" Pan asked, grabbing my free hand and drawing it to his chest with a desperation that wrenched my heart.

"Call whom?"

"The boatman. We had a bet...him and I..."

Seeing the god was fast losing consciousness, I gave him a little shake. "Pan? Pan! Wake up."

Pan's eyes fluttered, and he cracked yet another smile. "He is going to be so *mad*..."

With his final breath, the god cackled a ragged laugh. Then, with the abruptness of a flame being extinguished, Pan's face went slack and the hand holding mine fell limp into the sand. I was surprised to find tears trickling down my face as I sat back. After all, we hadn't exactly known each other that well. Perhaps it was as simple as being vulnerable in the face of death, or perhaps it was the sheer waste and futility of it all. Either way, I felt so wretched that it took me a solid minute to realize the god had placed something in my hand before he died.

Several somethings, in fact.

All four coins were worn and obviously ancient, their once golden luster now a muddy brown. Still, I knew at once what they were for, and why Pan had given them to me—though why he'd given me two sets as opposed to one, I couldn't be sure. Regardless, it was clear Pan meant for me to fulfill his dying wish.

And so, I judiciously placed a single coin on each of the dead god's eyes and waited for an old acquaintance to come and collect his due.

65

Charon appeared much the same as last I'd seen him: swaddled in a burlap robe riddled with stains, the boatman's ebony eyes sat like gaping holes against the stark contrast of his bloodless face, his poor mouth sewn shut with a knotted leather cord.

Strangely enough, he did seem less corporeal than I remembered, as if the sun's rays were somehow able to pass through him—a side effect, perhaps, of leaving his usual domain behind. Not that this prevented the world's most infamous ferryman from hopping out and dragging his unwieldy craft onto the shore.

Once he'd managed to beach the vessel, Charon turned and began slogging towards us, his bony feet crunching against sand, his tattered robe dragging along behind him to the tune of hissing snakes. If it surprised the boatman to find me looming over the body of a dead god, he gave no sign. Indeed, he said nothing at all until he, too, stood over Pan's corpse.

"Well, fuck."

I gaped at him in surprise.

"He owed me money," Charon explained in that chilling, ventriloquist voice of his. He sighed, bent down, and collected the archaic coins with a single flick of his knobby wrist. "Poker night just won't be the same without him."

I frowned. "Wait, I don't understand. Why d'ye say that like he's gone forever?"

"Hmm?"

"I mean, ye hangout with dead people all the time, right? Won't he, I don't know, join ye in the afterlife or whatever?"

"Are you high?" The boatman wheezed a laugh. "Don't be an idiot. The afterlife is for mortals, not gods, otherwise what would be the point of immortality? It's simple. You play by different rules, you can expect different rewards."

I supposed that made sense, though I had to admit I'd never really given it much thought until now. "So, that means he's..."

"Gone. For good. Yeah."

"Ah, I see. Sorry."

Charon shook his head. "Don't be. That smug look on his face tells me he probably died doing what he loved."

"Which was what, exactly?"

"Driving someone mad." Charon straightened and beckoned me forward. "Anyway, come on and help me get him into the boat before he starts to smell worse than he already does."

I considered making a comment about the boatman's own distinct lack of hygiene but ultimately decided it wasn't worth the trouble. Instead, the two of us half-carried, half-dragged the fallen god to the tide's edge. Then, with a fair amount of coordinated effort, we slung Pan's body into the waiting boat and adjusted him into what could have been a sleeping position.

The ghoulish boatman offered humorous anecdotes about the satyr as we worked, his sandpapery voice occasionally drowned out by the sound of the waves crashing against the shore.

"...and that's when I knew I was never going to see my little toe again," he finished with a snicker. "What a birthday that was."

"So ye two were friends, I take it?"

Charon cocked his head. "Close enough. We shared a common

interest, I guess you'd say. We still do, in a way. But then you'd know that already if you were who your face says you are."

I hesitated, both surprised and intrigued to learn the boatman had seen through my current illusion. "And who would that be, exactly?"

"You mean you don't know?" Charon snorted. "Well I'm certainly not going to be the one to tell you."

"Right. But say I really wanted to know..."

"I'd tell you to invest in a mirror."

"What if I offered to pay?" I held out my hand, displaying the second set of coins I'd been given for Charon's perusal. "In exchange for these, maybe ye could answer some questions?"

Rather than accept my offer, however, Charon reached out and firmly closed my hand into a fist around the coins, his disapproval plain.

"Those are not for you to barter away."

"But—"

"I said no."

Cursing under my breath, I pocketed the coins and let my gaze wander along the shoreline as Charon began the laborious process of dragging his boat back out to sea, wondering when Veil was planning to appear and whisk me away to yet another location. After all, hadn't I already done what I'd come here to do? Or was there something more?

"Wait, Charon!" I called. "Was there somethin' else i was supposed to give ye?"

"Like what?"

An instinct I couldn't ignore nagged at me as the boatman reached the water—a sense that I'd left something profoundly important undone. When I ultimately couldn't figure out what that might have been, however, the boatman went ahead and clambered into his boat, where he retrieved a can of beer from a decidedly out-of-place cooler.

Charon cracked the tab and proceeded to thoroughly douse himself with the sudsy liquid, though I could've sworn he was watching me the entire time—almost as if he were trying to tell me something. Unfortunately, I was too busy being grossed out to notice; I cringed to watch all that beer spill down Charon's front, imagining how it would feel to have alcohol distilled from the River Styx soaking my top.

And that's when it hit me.

The River Styx.

Realization dawning, I hurriedly unbelted Joyeuse and rushed back to collect Areadbhar. Then, just as Charon was preparing to push the boat out into the water with his oar, I raced after him with both weapons in hand.

"Hold on!" I yelled. "Ye have to take these and drop 'em in the Lethe!"

"I don't have to do anything," Charon replied, though he stopped what he was doing long enough for me to close the gap and even indicated I should drop them in the boat next to Pan once I arrived.

As such, it was obvious the boatman meant to wind me up; he'd clearly anticipated me handing over both weapons, though I wasn't sure how considering I hadn't even made the connection until it was almost too late.

It was the memory of our little drinking contest that had done it —reminding me of not only our brief tenure together in Charon's boat, but of the waterways we'd traveled. The first had been the River Styx, while the second had been the Lethe. Moreover, it was beneath the Lethe that Ryan and I stumbled across the tools we needed to recover our memories in a land that time forgot.

Only...what if we hadn't?

Too late, I paused to consider the alternatives. Would Ryan and I still be there, calling each other by our respective nicknames, each of us blissfully ignorant of our pasts or our futures? Somehow, the very notion of that filled me with an overwhelming sense of longing.

"Actually," I said, reaching for the weapons, "maybe I should stop and t'ink about—"

Charon swatted at me with his oar like I was a child with her hand in a cookie jar. "No takesies-backsies."

"What the shite, dude?" I drew back with a hiss, my hand throbbing like hell. "That hurt!"

"Oh, stop whining," he replied, tossing me a battered metal flask that he must have retrieved from somewhere on his person. "Here. If it still hurts in an hour, take a sip of that. You'll forget any of this ever happened. But be careful. That shit is potent. Too much of it and you may not remember your own name."

I eyed the flask, reminded suspiciously of the shooter he'd given me as a prize for surviving his drinking contest. Still, considering how much that particular item had come in handy at the time, I went ahead and slipped the flask into a back pocket, no questions asked. Sadly, that still left me with several dozen unrelated questions that needed answered.

Charon thrust his oar into the sand and pushed off before I could say anything more, however, his boat bobbing along as he wheeled it round to face the horizon. To my chagrin, the ferryman didn't even bother looking back, let alone offer a wave goodbye—almost as if he was only too glad to be rid of me. Indeed, the grotesque figure had already faded from sight completely by the time Veil appeared at my arm to ask if I was ready to leave.

I was.

66

"I think you underestimate the power of prophecy."

67

A child's laugh brought me around this time—an unexpectedly uplifting sound after everything I'd had to endure of late. Gone was the deserted beach and the relentless drone of the ocean, replaced by an untamed forest rife with the tiny chittering of woodland creatures and the rustle of wind through the boughs. Dappled sunlight drifted through the canopy overhead, the trees garlanded with flowered vines and hanging moss.

Well, most of the trees, anyway.

There was one, taller and far more ancient than all the rest, which towered high above the rest. The Hangman's Tree, as it was known, stood like a primordial reminder of what a tree could be when given an eternity to grow—its very name evoking childhood memories of Dez perched beside my bed, reading stories to me of Peter Pan and his Lost Boys. Tales of wild adventures highlighted by pirates, abductions, and fairy dust.

I'd seen this particular tree before, sometimes in my dreams, and at least twice in real life. In my dreams, it had appeared much as it did now: so vibrant with life it seemed almost animate, if not sentient. In real life, the tree had fallen into various states of decay—wizened and rotting in one instance, and all but dead in the other.

"Which still doesn't tell me what I'm doin' here," I mumbled under my breath.

As if in answer, the laughter resumed, this time emerging from one of the burls high up in the tree's enormous trunk—a burl which swung open before my very eyes, allowing a gaggle of feral children to come tumbling out. I gasped, expecting them to plummet, only to watch the lot of them go soaring heavenward like a flock of startled birds.

"Oh, to be a child again."

Veil, standing some ten feet off to my left, stared after the parade of children with a wistfulness I wouldn't have expected from her.

"You've made yourself scarce lately," I noted. "What gives?"

"You mean why did I leave you to deal with things on your own at the Road of Bones?"

"And the beach, aye."

Veil shrugged. "I wasn't needed. Besides, my presence would have raised questions neither of us could answer."

"But you're here, now."

"Yes."

"Which implies ye will be needed for whatever this is," I supplied, showcasing the forest. "Care to explain why?"

"Let's talk about this inside."

Veil turned and began walking without waiting for my approval, heading directly for the base of the Hangman Tree's trunk. Sensing I didn't have much choice in the matter, I muttered a curse and followed after her, catching up just as she reached the roots.

To my surprise, Veil managed to find a hidden entrance beyond a curtain of vines with very little difficulty. When I asked how she'd known it was there, however, she claimed not to remember.

"It's like being able to tie your own shoelaces," she explained. "It's easier if I don't think too hard about it. Now come on, we are shorter on time here than other places."

"Huh? Why?"

"Because we're trespassing, for one thing. And because that damned spell has caught our scent, again."

Right. Nate's spell. I'd frankly forgotten about it after everything that had happened recently. As for the trespassing comment, well, I couldn't argue with that either; we were a pair of adults about to wander into the sanctuary of armed children who would no doubt return in due time. Best not to linger.

Still, I found myself progressing slowly once we stepped inside, fascinated by the differences between my last visit and this one. Back then, an older, wiser Peter Pan had been my guide. He'd led me from chamber to chamber, many of which were littered by a smattering of discarded toys covered in dust and cobwebs. Overhead, hanging from knotted twine like beaded curtains from a bygone era, were the wooden swords of fallen Lost Boys.

The swords remained, though there were far fewer in my estimation. Of the toys, however, there were dozens more, and all of them recently used. More importantly, the entire vibe of the place had changed—the depressing pall from my previous trip supplanted by a warm, inviting energy. No longer a mausoleum, but a cherished home.

"I can't tell ye how weird it is bein' back here," I said aloud.

"How do you think I feel?" she replied, distractedly.

"Sorry, what was that?"

"Shhh." Veil halted as we reached the main living area, her arm outstretched. "Keep your voice down, or you'll wake the baby."

"Baby? What baby?"

Veil pointed, and I saw a pair of adults sprawled across two sofas from completely different eras, a swaddled infant lying between them in a modest wicker basket. I bypassed Veil's arm and took a cautious step forward, my eyes still adjusting to the dimness of the tree's interior. Not satisfied, I took another, and then another, until at last I stood not ten feet from the slumbering trio.

I squatted down to study all three faces, though it was the baby's which intrigued me most.

"Hello, baby Nate," I whispered.

68

Veil drew me away from the charmingly domestic scene with a gloved finger pressed to her lips as though I were about to start crowing like Rufio and wake the lot of them. Truth be told, I *had* considered doing something similar—if only to get my hands on baby Nate's chubby little cheeks. In the end, however, I decided it wasn't worth the trouble. After all, I'd seen what the two of them could do to a gang of unsuspecting goblins; I wasn't interested in finding out what they'd do to the stranger who woke their baby.

And so the two of us tiptoed past, weaving between furniture and avoiding tripping over toys until we stood before a winding staircase carved from the tree itself, its narrow steps spiraling so high that it disappeared into the inky darkness high above our heads. Of the knotted ropes I had expected to find hanging from the top of the tree, there was no sign.

"After you," Veil whispered, gesturing to the stairs.

"Ye can't be serious."

"Do I look like I'm joking?"

"No, ye look like you're about to go to a leper's funeral. And ye know that wasn't what I was gettin' at. I meant, what the hell makes ye t'ink I'm goin' up all those stairs? Use your stupid spatial magic, or whatever it is."

"It doesn't work like that."

"Well then ye better t'ink of another way, because I'm not doin' it."

"Even if the fate of the whole world was at stake?"

"...is it?"

"Probably."

I glared at my companion for a good twenty seconds before letting out a sigh and marching up the first few steps. "Where are we headed, anyway?"

"I'll let you know when we get there."

I won't bore you with the details of the miserable trek that followed. Suffice it to say, my legs had started cramping by the time Veil tapped my shoulder. She, of course, had managed the whole ascent without uttering so much as a single sound.

"There," she insisted, pointing.

I took a moment to wipe the sweat from my eyes before turning to look, recognizing at once the landing Peter had led me to all those years ago. Back then there had hung a makeshift curtain obscuring a small recess, beyond which had resided...something. I frowned, unable to recall just what it was the most famous Neverlander had gone so far out of his way to show me.

Taking my cue from the patiently waiting Veil, I crept forward and perused the space, only to discover a glass cylinder set in the heart of the wood, almost as if the tree had grown up around it. Within the cylinder was a grain of something so small I had to squint to make it out.

"I...is that a grain of sand?" I asked. "I feel like I should know, but...there's somethin'...."

Veil moved to stand at my side. "Blocking your memory. Yes. That's why we're here. To set things right."

"I don't understand."

"I know, and that's the problem. Do you recall what Peter said about this place when he first brought you here?"

"Somethin' about the Temples?" I ventured, my memory of the conversation murky at best. "He said they put it here. That it...wait, I t'ink I remember now. He said *they* were the reason time came to Neverland."

"And what about Eve? Do you remember your conversation with her about it?"

Did I? I grimaced as a sudden headache started pounding against my skull. Still, I tried to answer Veil's question as best I could. "She... said the Temples took it. That they did it to stop what was happenin' to everyone on the island. But that can't be right, can it? I mean, it's right here. And how could they have put it here *and* taken it?"

"What else did she tell you?"

I hesitated. "Hmm. There was somethin' about Neverland bein' a seed. I t'ink she said it was Merlin who planted it. That's why we thought there might be a bond between us. One we could exploit. But, in the end, it was Eve who..."

Sacrificed herself, I finished silently.

The moment I thought it, I realized I could feel Neverland's attention fixated on us. More than that, I was reminded of our unprecedented melding—a soul-searing experience that should have left a far more lasting impact on me than it had. Though, in my defense, my life had become one formative experience after another shortly after that. Indeed, you might say it was a miracle I'd made it this far in one piece.

Assuming I had.

Veil placed a hand on my shoulder. "Did she tell you anything about the grain itself? About what it was meant to do?"

"Only that Merlin was responsible for it, too. She never said why, though, I don't t'ink. Maybe somethin' to do with holdin' back time? That is what it does, isn't it?"

Veil shook her head. "Not exactly. That's simply what Peter was told when he first stumbled across it as an adult. An unwitting falsehood he passed on to Neverland, who then fed it to Eve. In fact, what you see there isn't even a grain of sand at all, but a speck of bone dust."

"Um, gross."

Veil grunted an acknowledgment. "Anyway, that lie and the illusion it came with is the reason your mind contains two contradictory realities. One in which the speck remains in place, unnoticed for centuries by all except the Temples, who can do nothing to prevent it and indeed will be blamed for its existence once it is discovered. And a second in which the speck is mysteriously absent, for which the Temples will also be deemed responsible."

"Hold on, what illusion?"

"The one you saw through when Peter brought you here, even if your mind couldn't process it at the time."

"Okay...but who would cast an illusion like that? And why?"

"To discredit the Temple name, perhaps? Or to poison their relationship with this place and the Beast it contained? I can only speculate. All I am sure of is that change would never have come to Neverland unless the speck was first removed."

"Okay, but removed by whom? Assumin' Calvin and Makayla had nothin' to do with it, like ye say."

Rather than answer my question, Veil asked me another. "Do you remember the first thing I told you about the choices you would face on this journey?"

"That they'd suck?" I replied, sarcastically.

"That they wouldn't be choices, at all. That you'd instinctively know what to do when the time came. But this, here, now...this is where that stops. Because this is when you realize you're the one who has to condemn them."

"Condemn whom? What are ye talkin' about?"

Veil raised a forestalling hand. "'Sorry, I'm getting ahead of myself. Firstly, you should know the speck does not hold back time. It holds back *change*. That's why Peter Pan never grew up. Why he and Hook engaged each other time and time again. Why the games never ended. Only, it was never meant for them. The speck was the lock on a cage designed to imprison an exceptionally powerful Beast."

"Neverland," I supplied.

"Yes."

"Sorry, I'm still not followin'. I mean, what you're sayin' makes sense, but what does any of it have to do with me?"

"Well, you *are* the one with the key."

I frowned, confused. What key? Too late, it came to me: the skeleton key I'd bartered off Pandora. A key capable of unlocking any door. With a growing sense of trepidation, I began rifling through my pockets, feeling past the assorted objects I'd collected throughout my travels until I found the right one and withdrew it.

"I don't get it," I admitted. "You're sayin' I'm supposed to use this to what, set her free? But then that would mean..."

"That you were the one. The reason Neverland fades and its people die. The reason all this senseless violence ends."

"No way," I whispered, staring in horror at the skeleton key. "That can't be true. It just can't."

"Why not?"

"Because I didn't ask for this!" I shouted, accidentally dropping the key to the ground where it went skittering against the wall. I left it there. "Don't ye get it? I don't have the right to make that decision. No one does."

"Oh no?" Veil cocked her head. "And how is this any different than the choice you made back in the ruins of Avalon? Because at the time you sure seemed happy to embrace the certainty of your future over the uncertainty of theirs."

"It's different because I know what happens to these people!" I snapped. "Not suspect. I *know*."

As I spoke, I couldn't help but picture the grief-riddled faces of the trio I'd encountered aboard the *Jolly Roger* as I spoke the words. James, with his father's sword strapped awkwardly to his hip. Tiger Lily, so fiercely protective of the one piece of Peter she had left. And of course Tinkerbell, who'd called Neverland home longer than any of them.

"What happens if I refuse?" I asked in a much more subdued voice.

"Then the future will change. Or perhaps not. It's impossible to know. But you have to understand that by leaving the speck where it is, you may very well doom this place to a cycle of violence that will go on for an untold number of years. More children will come, and more children will die. Peter Pan will never grow up, and Hook will never grow old. James and Wendy will never be born, Eve will never find a home, and it's possible you may never survive your first trip to Fae."

I grimaced, my stomach lurching at the possibility that she was right. "So you're sayin' how I feel doesn't matter. That I have to do this."

"How you feel *does* matter. But you have to see that stopping time in its tracks is not and will never be natural. A tale without end is not a story. It's a lecture."

Rather than continue what was fast becoming a circuitous argument, I opted instead to close my eyes and focus on my breathing. Granted, I knew what Veil was saying: without the capacity to change, existence itself lost all meaning. Without it, we became static caricatures, repeating the same mistakes for all eternity—earning nicknames like The Boy Who Would Not Grow Up instead of becoming who we were truly meant to be.

"How would we do it?" I asked through gritted teeth. "Remove the speck, I mean."

"It's already done."

I opened my eyes to find a slump-shouldered Veil holding both the skeleton key and the glass container. The trunk of the tree lay conspicuously empty like a gaping eye socket or a missing tooth, and I swore I could feel the island itself vibrating in satisfaction beneath my feet.

"But I thought ye said..."

"It doesn't matter which of us did the deed," she replied, sounding oddly taxed. "Only that you accepted the necessity of it. Now, here. Take these and let's go."

69

"At times, I wonder still if the Temples were gods themselves, or at least blessed with a vision of the future that was far clearer than even your mother's..."

70

I came to parked on a bench in the middle of a snow-covered cemetery wearing a heavy rain jacket and clutching an open umbrella. A fine mist descended from a grim, cloud-strewn sky —too light to be called rain, but enough to cast a faint sheen on the walking path that cut across the sprawling graveyard, its paved surface winding like a silver ribbon beyond the curve of a frozen lake some miles off.

Behind me towered a silver maple tree, its skeletal boughs straining towards the heavens, while directly in front—nestled in a natural depression and set well away from the rest of the cemetery— stood a private plot devoted to an extraordinarily wealthy family. A truth made evident not only by the monolithic mausoleum that occupied it, but also by the name chiseled into its opulent facade.

Temple.

A study in contradictions, the architectural marvel was plainly influenced by an astoundingly extravagant blend of cultures and aesthetics, ranging anywhere from the Corinthian columns supporting its marble slab of a roof to the alabaster effigies that occupied its many alcoves. Of the latter, I recognized a few as soldiers from various periods of antiquity, while others took on the appearance of robed scholars, scepter-wielding aristocrats, and even the occasional exhibitionist.

Personally, I thought they could have reined it in a little, but then what did a middle-class plebe like me know?

"What a rice cake tastes like," I said, bitterly. "And how much is too much to pay for parkin'."

As if I'd somehow willed it into existence, a black sedan appeared at the far end of the road, its headlights backlighting one dead tree after another as it crept forward and eventually parked in front of the Temple mausoleum. Once it became clear no one was getting out of the car, I turned my attention to the entrance of that enormous edifice, waiting for someone self-important to emerge.

The first individual to do so, however, was a relatively unimpressive, seemingly ordinary man carrying a metal pail loaded with various cleaning supplies. Stoutly built and coated in so much coarse, iron-grey hair he reminded me vaguely of a Brillo pad with legs, he wore the modest uniform of a janitor and seemed completely uninterested in the presence of the idling vehicle as he went about his business.

The second to exit, however, was exactly the type of person I'd expected to see: impeccably dressed in a black suit and tie, with his hair perfectly coiffed and a severe expression written across his face that said in no uncertain terms *I am very busy and important, so don't you dare get in my way* Nate Temple appeared every bit the tragic billionaire I'd first laid eyes on all those years ago.

But then, I supposed that description wasn't exactly charitable; the wizard *had* been visiting his family crypt, after all.

As I watched, Nate jogged over to the sedan and practically threw himself into the backseat. The driver took off a moment later, nearly hydroplaning in his eagerness to leave the cemetery behind.

"Someone's in a hurry," I mumbled, thoughtfully.

"Aye, the lad has a few pressing things on his mind. Not that I or anyone else could blame 'im."

I turned, surprised to find the janitor from before leaning against the maple tree with a newspaper propped atop his head to fend off the drizzle. Up close, I realized he looked somewhat familiar—though not enough for me to place him. I scowled, trying to place his brogueish accent.

"Scottish?"

"Aye. Yeh 'ave a good ear, lass. Anyway, if you're here to pay your respects, now's the time. I'll 'ave to shut her down for visitors, soon."

"Sorry, but who would I be payin' me respects to, exactly?"

"Why, Calvin and Makayla Temple, of course. T'was their funeral today. Ended a few hours ago, in fact."

71

The news of Calvin and Makayla's passing hit me harder than I would have expected. After all, it was only an hour ago for me that I'd laid eyes on the couple as they slept, their entire adult lives ahead of them. Obviously, I should have expected it; they'd been dead for at least a couple years before I ever met their son, which was to say nothing of our meet-and-greet in Hell. And yet still I was caught unprepared. Indeed, I was so taken aback that I didn't realize the mausoleum's caretaker had said something until I caught him waving his newspaper at me.

"Crap, I'm sorry," I said. "What was that ye were sayin'?"

"I said you'd better hurry. Yeh never know when the weather might take a turn for the worst. I 'ave a feeling there's a proper storm on the way. And I've got a knack for such things."

I frowned, aware of a wry glimmer in the caretaker's eye as he mentioned the likelihood of a storm. Was it possible the old man knew more than he was letting on? And why was he encouraging me to visit the Temple family crypt? Had he confused me for an estranged family member, perhaps? Or was it possible I wore the face of a relative he recognized?

Regardless of the reason, I decided I would take him up on his offer. One, because I wanted to see if the mausoleum's interior matched its gauche exterior. And two, because I felt I owed it to Calvin and Makayla.

"Is the door open?" I asked, gesturing. "Like can I just walk in?"

"Aye, though I would'ne take your sweet time, yeh ken? Storm or no, I'll be back at dusk to close the place down, and yeh would'ne want to end up stuck overnight in a place like that."

"Oh, right. T'anks. I appreciate it. Oh, and sorry, but I didn't catch your name..."

"Mallory." The caretaker doffed his newspaper as though it were a bowler hat, flashed me a grin, and stepped away from the tree. "I'm off, for now. Take care, lass."

Suspicious by nature, I waited until the mysterious caretaker had disappeared beyond the nearby tree line before I made my way down to the mausoleum grounds. I took the steps slowly upon reaching the mausoleum proper, wary of slipping on a patch of black ice and cracking my skull open in the process.

"How ironic that would be," I muttered as I went. "Right, Veil?"

Veil didn't reply, which told me either she wasn't lurking nearby, or she wasn't in a chatty mood. Honestly, I couldn't have cared which; I was beginning to suspect she was fast becoming as fed up with all this as I was. That, or these little trips of ours were taking something out of her.

In any event, I passed through the mausoleum doors, greeted by the eerie silence common to all final resting places—a contemplative hush that only those too young to fear their own mortality would dare disturb. Which was too bad, really; if I were a ghost chained for eternity to a crypt, I'd definitely have preferred eavesdropping on some good gossip every now and again to watching people wander around staring like they were at some sort of fancy art gallery.

And yet, that's precisely what I did.

Mouth hanging open in awe, I shuffled down a central walkway lined with alcoves occupied by life-sized statues of the deceased, as well as elaborate benches, marble pedestals, and leather-bound books cradled within glass cases. As I progressed, the names displayed on the spine of those books began to sound increasingly modern, though there were several that repeated themselves from one generation to the next.

Eventually, I reached a domed nave wreathed in stained-glass windows, their vibrant colors dulled only by the dimness of the light outside. A relatively tasteful fountain gurgled against the far wall of the antechamber, backed by an absurdly intricate mosaic that formed what appeared to be a family tree focused on roots as opposed to branches.

As I got closer, I noticed blue sapphires lodged beside the name of each woman, while it seemed rubies had been reserved for the men. Some names I even recognized, though I'll admit they took me a painstakingly long time to find. Matthias Temple, father of Ichabod. Calvin and Makayla Temple. Nathin Laurent Temple.

And then, after so long I had almost given up, there it was, so high up I had to squint to be sure: Verity Temple. Descending from her was a single root, a solitary ruby, and a name that had been worn too smooth to make out. Of further descendants, however, there was no sign.

"Figures," I said with a sigh.

Deciding I'd wasted enough time hunting for clues I was probably never going to find anyway, I turned on my heel and continued along until I stumbled across a padded leather divan and a pair of startlingly familiar faces set in stone.

Calvin and Makayla Temple stared at me with cool, lifeless eyes, their expressions far more serene than their colorful personalities would have suggested. They'd been turned outwards ever so slightly, allowing their marble flesh to meet at the hip and shoulder even as they welcomed their visitors with extended hands.

Still, they appeared unfinished, somehow—as if the sculptor had left some aspect of their creation undone. It was the hands, I realized; palm up and yet strangely flexed, they appeared empty in a way that spoke volumes.

I tried to picture Nate standing in my place, curious about whether or not he'd felt the same way. Whether he'd stared at his parent's empty hands and wished they had something more tangible to offer him than a whole lot of unanswered questions. After all, I knew for a fact they'd intended to leave things behind, to pass on the tools their only son would need to survive.

Tools like...

Wait.

Struck by a sudden flash of inspiration, I began rummaging through the pockets of my raincoat, ignoring the texture of cold metal and smooth glass in favor of rough stone. Moments later, I held out two objects. The first I'd expected to find, while the second I'd retrieved by accident. Still, the moment I saw what they were, I knew where they both belonged.

A few seconds later, I stepped back to admire my handiwork.

The stone pyramid I'd been instructed by his parents to give Nate sat cupped in Makayla's hand, while in Calvin's sat the hourglass I'd stumbled across outside Oberon's bedchamber. Both objects looked perfectly natural in their new setting, almost as though they were meant to be there all along.

"Not too shabby, if I do say so meself," I said, shooting a pair of finger guns for good measure.

"Not at all," replied Veil, who sat on the fountain's edge, watching me. "You're doing very well, in fact."

"That's it," I said, scowling. "The next bell I see, I'm hangin' it around your neck."

"Good luck with that."

"I take it this was what I was meant to do?" I jerked my chin towards the statues. "To leave these here for Nate to find? It was, wasn't it?"

Veil rose creakily without replying, brushed at her clothes, and gestured me forward with a sigh. "Come on, this place has always given me the creeps."

"... **F**ate can be a weapon. It can also be a shield. Knowing one's future can mean salvation, or damnation, depending on the path we take."

I awoke slumped over a desk in a dark room, the sounds of a battle in the background as if from a radio far away, the air stale with the scent of mothballs and dust. Sensing I wasn't in any immediate danger, I remained there for a moment and allowed my eyes to adjust, only to discover the dimness had less to do with ambience than aesthetic as everything, from the floors to the walls to the furniture, had been painted black.

Not surprisingly, I was reminded instantly of the room's antithesis —specifically the pure white realm Matthias Temple called home. And yet, the room itself reminded me of somewhere else: Calvin's office in Chateau Falco. Indeed, it was identical in nearly every respect. There was the cabinet of leather-bound books to my right, the chaise lounge flush against the wall, and even a box of cigars on the desk sitting next to a sheet of pitch black paper.

Indeed, the only difference I could see was the presence of a conspicuously large man peering out one of the bay windows behind me.

"Matthias? Is that ye?"

The man flinched as though I'd struck him and yanked the curtain closed, making it that much more difficult to see his face as he backed away. Still, I'd gotten a good enough look to know I'd guessed correctly—and that something terrible had happened to the poor Maker.

"Matthias," I called again, rising from my seat. "It's me! The girl who helped ye forge the Masks. The one in the red dress, remember?"

"The girl in the red dress?"

The question came as a garbled whisper from the farthest corner of the room where I could see the Maker had slid to the ground and huddled into a ball, rocking back and forth like a child.

"Aye, that's me." I glanced down at myself and saw I no longer wore the raincoat or the dress or indeed any of my past outfits, but instead a skintight leather number under a heavy trench. "Or was me, I guess. Anyway, that doesn't matter. Look, where am I? And what happened to your face?"

Matthias looked up, his expression hard to decipher in the gloom, and yet I could make out clearly the dark stain upon his swollen lips and down his beard. Blood. The Maker had been coughing up blood.

"You shouldn't be here," he replied, revealing a mouth full of missing teeth and bleeding gums. "The Reverie is not for you. You should go now, before he finishes with the Elders and comes back."

"I'm not goin' anywhere until ye talk to me. Who is 'he'? And 'the Elders'? Who are they?"

"See for yourself." Matthias shuddered and glanced at the window he'd been staring out a moment ago. In his eyes, I saw not the madness I had become accustomed to, but fear. No, not fear, I decided. Terror. Abject terror.

Curious as to what could have possibly terrified the once imposing Maker, I wandered over to the window and pulled back the curtain. At first, all I saw was a dilapidated courtyard, its cobblestones scorched and even shattered in some places. A few fires blazed here and there, permeating the air with black, wispy smoke. When I swung my attention to the right, however, I discovered a far more gruesome scene waiting for me.

"What the hell?" I pressed my face against the glass, squinting to make out the details of the massacre happening below.

There, a small cohort of heavily armored knights were busy mowing down albino lizard men and women armed with bone clubs and spears, cutting through them by the dozen as though they were no more than children armed with sticks. Their reptilian corpses had already begun to litter the ground, and I swore I could see the elderly and barely grown children amongst them.

Still, the lizard people fought on like demons, lashing out with inhuman reflexes while singing strange, wordless songs that had the hair on the back of my neck standing straight up. And yet the knights continued to fend them off with ease. Indeed, the largest of the armored knights at the center of the fighting—presumably their leader—had yet to draw a single weapon. Instead, he strode forward with his arms outstretched, and from the scaled flesh of those his hands touched, there erupted fonts of blood and viscera.

"Fuck me," I said, disbelieving. "What's goin' on out there?"

"The Elders have come to the Citadel to seek revenge against the invaders."

"The Elders, they're the lizards?"

"They shouldn't have come," Matthias went on in a strained whisper, ignoring me. "They are doomed. The boy cares nothing for them. He cares nothing for anyone or anything. Well, almost no one."

"Hold on, you've lost me. What boy?"

"Aiden. I...thought I could make him happy. That's why I made the things he pleaded for. Why I said nothing when he and his men wiped out Elder village after Elder village. I even told him where to find Death and the lies he would have to tell. And still, he wasn't satisfied. No, never satisfied. Just...angry. Especially whenever I mentioned *him*..."

I hesitated, head cocked. Aiden...hadn't that been the name of the troubled boy I'd encountered at the Academy? Was he out there, tearing through hapless lizard folk? Somehow, I couldn't reconcile the possibility; whatever had happened to the poor kid between then and now, it seemed impossible he'd have gotten involved in an all-out genocide.

"Wait, him who?" I asked, picking up on the Maker's emphasis of the word.

"His brother. The wizard responsible for my son's death. The Dark Horse. Nate Temple."

Christ, that was a lot to unpack.

"Wait, that's why you're here, isn't it?" Matthias shouted suddenly, his voice taking on a sudden fervency. He crawled forward and grasped my hands in his, clutching at them as if I were a life preserver and he a man about to go under. "You can help him! He will come. Aiden has most certainly ensured it. But he must not come alone. I've deciphered most of it, you see. The prophecy. I know the players. All of them."

"The Dark Horse Prophecy," I supplied.

"Yes! Yes. The child who must be sacrificed, I know who she is! More importantly, I know what she is meant to do. Without her at his side, Nate will surely fail. Or worse, he will succeed, and the Dark Horse will trample over us all."

"Listen," I began as I tried lifting the rambling Maker to his feet, "we can talk about all this, later. Why don't ye let me get ye out of here, first? We'll get that mouth looked at, and—"

Matthias shook me off. "No! It's too late for that. Besides, he would never let me go. You have no idea what he is like. I thought I was mad, but him...he would see us all burn and dance in our ashes."

"Okay, okay. Calm down."

"No, you have to do this for me," the Maker insisted. He fumbled with something hanging about his neck and pressed a small leather pouch into my hand. "Use this if you must to keep them calm. You'll find the girl and her mother will be found in the shadows where the dead lie. You must lead them to the staircase beneath the roots and send them down. She'll be safe there."

"I don't—"

"It's her destiny, you understand?" he interjected. "Only the Dark Horse can save her from what's to come, and only she can tame him."

"Look, I—"

Matthias surged to his feet and grabbed me firmly by the shoulders, tears pouring down his cheeks. "If you see Nate, ask him why he never wrote back to me. Now, go!"

He thrust me backwards, and I fell into what felt like an endless abyss.

74

"...You must discover what you are capable of. What you will be asked to do. And that time draws near."

75

I crash landed flat on my back staring up at a grey sky drizzled with dark smoke, the air driven so hard from my lungs that for a moment I feared I would never breathe again. Fortunately, that fear soon proved unfounded. Blinking through tears and coughing vigorously into my sleeve, I managed to roll onto my side a few seconds later, hoping to get my bearings.

Which was when I saw that I'd somehow ended up back in the sprawling cemetery that housed the Temple mausoleum.

Of course, a few things had changed since my last visit. The weather was different, for one thing. The sky was overcast and snow fell in droves. There were also a couple more gravestones than I remembered standing between me and the Temple family plot, while the paved road that wound along the grounds appeared slightly worse for wear with faint bulges and ugly cracks marring its once smooth surface.

Oh yeah, and there was a freaking *battle* going on.

All around me and leading up to the steps of the mausoleum, I discovered men and women and monsters engaged in some sort of demented battle royale that would have looked ridiculous were it not for the rampant violence on display. Indeed, as I watched, cloaked wizards sent balls of fire and blocks of ice soaring towards Faelings of all shapes and sizes huddled behind shields and gravestones, while armed einherjar launched themselves manically into the fray at every opportunity.

"What the fu—"

Something barreled into me from behind before I could finish my sentence, knocking me face first to the ground. I swore and reached for my nose as the Norse son of a bitch who'd run me over flung himself at a club-wielding ogre twice his size. Abruptly aware or how exposed I was lying down in the middle of the battle field, I ignored my throbbing appendage and instead leapt to my feet just in time to avoid the rag doll remains of the einherjar as the ogre sent him skipping across the earth like a ground ball.

"You!" cried the ogre, pointing at me like a major league ball player calling his next shot. "You're mine!"

"Sorry, I'm taken!" I called back with a wave. "But good luck out there!"

I turned and ran before the ogre could reply, or—more importantly—take a swing at yours truly. Unfortunately, I'd only made it thirty or so feet before an errant bolt of lightning clipped my shoulder and sent me spinning like Julie Andrews in *The Sound of Music*.

I collapsed to one knee, my right arm hanging limp and useless at my side, and scoured the landscape for a place to hide. Sadly, there was only so much cover to be found in a graveyard, and most of it was already being used. Just as I was about to give up and simply make a run for it, however, I saw a winged figure soaring overhead.

"Kára!" I shouted up to the Valkyrie, who either couldn't hear me or was too busy to take notice as she sped across the sky towards the front steps of the mausoleum. Of course, if that was where she was headed, it meant there might be others present who I could turn to for help.

The question was, how was I going to survive long enough to get there? Since giving up my armor and my weapons, not to mention the mysterious absence of all that divine power supposedly coursing through my veins, I was basically a sitting duck surrounded by hungry hellhounds. Indeed, from where I crouched, it seemed I had no choice but to race at full speed across the clearing and pray to perhaps the only God I hadn't met.

"Quinn! There you are."

I yelped and spun to find Veil standing practically on top of me, her formless silhouette obscuring my view of the sky beyond. I rose to my full height and thrust an accusatory finger in her face.

"What did I tell ye about sneakin' up on people?!" Then, before she could reply, I snatched her up in a full-on bear hug. "I never thought I'd say this, but I am genuinely happy to see ye."

76

"Okay, that's enough of that," I said, letting go of the spectral figure and patting her arm awkwardly. "Now, get us the hell out of here."

Veil, however, was already shaking her head. "I'm afraid I can't do that. The Maker may have been premature by sending you here, but this was always where you were meant to be."

"Of course it was," I muttered, eyeing the increasingly chaotic battlefield. "And I don't suppose ye could tell me what I'm meant to do, besides get caught in the crossfire and die?"

"Don't be ridiculous. You aren't going to die—"

That was as far as Veil got before a flaming tornado ripped past us to slam into a four-door, late model sedan parked alongside the road. The impact sent the vehicle tumbling across the lawn to collide with a tree, where both it and the car burst into flames. The fighting died down for a moment in the wake of the pyrotechnics, then immediately resumed with a goblin kicking the wizard who'd fired off the shot in the groin.

Veil cleared her throat. "Okay, so maybe we shouldn't be standing out in the open, like this."

"No shite. Any suggestions? I saw a friend of mine go into the mausoleum over there, but there are practically three whole armies standing between us and it."

"There is a way. But you won't like it."

"Look, if it gets us from here to there without havin' our heads caved in or our limbs blown off, I'm all ears."

Veil nodded. "Remember when I hid in your shadow?"

"Like a total creep, aye."

"Well, this would sort of be the opposite of that."

"What, ye want me to crawl into your shadow? How would that even work?"

"I'm not entirely sure I can explain it. Honestly, it would be far easier just to show you."

I hesitated, wondering whether the risk of what she was proposing would prove worth the reward—or what the risks were at all, really. Unfortunately, we didn't have time to consider other alternatives. If Veil said she knew a way, I would have to take her at her word.

"Do it."

As if prepared for that exact response, Veil immediately pounced on me, pinning my arms to the ground with a strength I hadn't known she possessed. Then, with almost painstaking slowness, she lowered herself until not even a centimeter of space remained between us. Frankly, it should have felt sexual, or even simply unpleasant, but it didn't. Instead, it felt almost like I was being given back something that had been taken from me—a sense of wholeness I hadn't known I lacked.

Just as I was about to demand to know what was happening, Veil's weight disappeared. Indeed, Veil herself vanished in the blink of an eye, leaving behind nothing but the faint odor of soft leather and the rustle of velvet.

More than a little baffled, I sat up to find the world had gone a little gray, as if someone had dialed back the saturation and muted all the colors. Stranger still, a smoky miasma had enveloped my entire body like a shawl.

"Consider us even," came a disembodied voice so close to my ear I nearly screamed when I heard it. "I lived in your shadow for a time, now you will see what it is like to live in mine."

"Veil, is that ye? What the shite! What was that just now?"

"It does not matter. What is important is that from now on, as long as you don't draw undue attention to yourself, you'll remain hidden from sight."

"For how long?"

"As long as necessary."

"Seriously?!" I groaned. "And when were ye goin' to tell me about *this t'ing we could've done ages ago* to keep me from bein' hunted down by armed security guards and prison wardens from Hell? For Christ's sake, what about the Dark Horse spell? Are ye tellin' me ye could've kept me hidden from it, too?"

"What? Of course not. You saw it for yourself. The spell won't be denied by anyone or anything. You can run as far as you like, but you'll never escape it. As for the rest, well...you never asked."

77

Only once I'd thoroughly explained the core concept of volunteering information to the unusually taciturn Veil did I begin the laborious process of crossing the battlefield. Unfortunately, doing so was not an entirely risk free affair, as even hidden from sight I remained vulnerable to secondhand slaughter. I only barely managed to duck beneath the double-headed axe of a ginger Viking, for instance, as he attempted to decapitate a ferocious-looking bogart, which was to say nothing of the various projectiles and spells I had to avoid along the way—each somehow more deadly than the last.

That said, I did eventually manage to reach the mausoleum unscathed. The entrance had been blown wide open, leaving scattered debris and the bodies of would-be intruders spewed across the lawn like so much trash. Fortunately, it seemed the survivors of the break-in had neglected to appoint a guard, which allowed me to waltz right in.

Once beyond the gaping hole in the wall, however, I quickly determined staying hidden would only prove more difficult from now on; while the air was choked with smoke and dust, there was significantly less room to maneuver in the hallways should a pitched battle ensue. Worse, there was no sign of Kára or anyone else I might recognize—no sign of anyone at all, in fact.

Guessing the fighting had migrated to one of the adjoining antechambers deeper into the mausoleum, I began creeping down the hall in search of the Valkyrie and those who fought with her. I'd only made it some teen feet or so, however, when I happened to overhear a hushed conversation between two women. Pulse racing, I pressed myself up against the nearest wall, wary of a potential ambush.

What I discovered when I peered around the corner, however, was not a trap waiting to be sprung, but a heart wrenching display of affection: a mother and daughter laying huddled together against the alcove's statue, dressed as ordinary people, their faces stained with tears and dirt. Civilians caught in the crossfire, by the look of them. Shit.

"They're bound to end up dead if they stay here," I whispered to myself, disgusted by the prospect.

Unfortunately, I wasn't sure what I could do for them; I certainly couldn't protect them. Indeed, without Veil's shadow to keep me out of sight, I was little better than a glorified meat shield standing between the pair and certain death. As for escape, well, there were several armies between them and freedom.

"You will find them in the shadows where the dead lie," Veil intoned, her voice unusually gentle as she repeated Matthias' words back to me. "Lead them to the staircase that descends beneath the roots. Isn't that what the Maker said?"

I nodded, reminded not only of that recommendation, but also his warnings. But did that mean these were the two he intended for me to save? If so, did that make the daughter the child from the prophecy? It was all so confusing. And besides, it made no sense. There was no staircase here, and certainly no roots.

Unless he meant...

I turned to look farther down the hall, eyeing the path we'd need to take to reach the tiled mosaic with its jewels and the fountain that stood before it. To my surprise, the way appeared clear, suggesting either that the fight was happening elsewhere, or that it had ended. My money was on the former.

Of course, pursuing that course of action had its flaws—namely that I hadn't seen any evidence of a lower level when I'd been here last, let alone a stairwell beneath the mosaic. But at least it was a way forward, and therefore vastly superior to the alternative, AKA turning away from innocents in need.

"Well," I muttered, "here goes nothin'."

78

I turned and slipped into the alcove, my presence going unnoticed by either female until I was merely inches away from the mother, who appeared to be masking a great deal of pain for her daughter's benefit. I frowned, wondering how and when she'd gotten hurt. Sadly, I didn't have a chance to ask before I saw the raw panic spill into their eyes.

I clamped a hand over the mother's mouth to stop her from crying out, pressed a finger to my lips, and shook my head. "It isn't safe here. Follow me."

"Who are you?" demanded the daughter, thrusting herself forward. Which, considering the circumstances, was pretty impressive. After all, running afoul of any flavor of Freak was traumatizing enough without adding a war zone to the equation.

Unfortunately, we didn't have time for introductions; there was no guarantee the path to the fountain would remain clear, and certainly not for long. So, rather than answer the girl's question, I hooked an arm around her mother's waist and yanked the woman to her feet.

As soon as I did this, however, it became clear she was hurt worse than I could have imagined; the mother leaned heavily against me, one blood-soaked hand pressed to her belly as if that might somehow conceal the grevious wound beneath. When she caught me staring, however, she shook me off and straightened to take her daughter's hand.

"Thank you," she whispered through gritted teeth, leaving me to wonder whether I was being thanked for helping her up, or for keeping my mouth shut about her injury.

Either way, my plan did not change.

I nodded and gestured for them to follow. Together, the three of us crept farther down the hall, bypassing dozens of Temple statues—very few of which seemed to have survived unscathed—along the way. Occasionally, the clash of swords and cries of men and women could be heard echoing throughout the mausoleum, and yet, miraculously, we managed to reach the nave without encountering a single soul.

There, everything was more or less how I remembered it—albeit a little worse for wear. Thinking to get a closer look, I inspected both the floor and the fountain itself for signs of a staircase while the mother and daughter busied themselves admiring the bejeweled mosaic representing the Temple family tree.

True to Matthias' word, I discovered such a thing coiling downward from the base of the fountain's shallow pool, running parallel to some kind of waterslide. Both were admittedly odd features, and I couldn't be sure where either of them led, but there was no doubt in my mind that it was the only chance the pair stood of not being crushed underfoot by some clumsy troll or cut down by a bloodthirsty Norseman—especially the mother, whose wounds would soon make it impossible for her to move much less run. In fact, I wasn't sure she'd last long enough to survive the stairs.

"You'll be safer down there," I insisted, pointing to the slide.

The moment I suggested it, I could hear voices approaching from farther down the hall, accompanied by the rapid rattle of metallic feet on stone. We still had time before they arrived and spotted us, but not enough to risk an unnecessary delay. And so I insisted they hurry.

Vehemently.

The girl squeezed her mother's hand and nodded in another unprecedented display of courage under pressure. "We have no other choice, Mom."

For a moment, I thought the mother might argue, but then the pair clasped hands and climbed into the fountain. Once settled in the shallow water that perpetually spilled down the slide, they swung their legs round and froze, their apprehension plain.

"I've got no idea what you'll find down there," I confessed. "But whatever it is, try not to make any noise. That'll only bring trouble. Just keep quiet and stay hidden."

Hopefully long enough for me to find help, I added silently, my eyes drawn to the blood that stained the waters surrounding the mother. Of course, there were other factors to consider. Matthias' other predictions, for instance—specifically those regarding the fate of the girl.

"Are you sure—" her mother began, turning to me.

I held up a hand. "I'm sure. Your job is to protect your daughter, so focus on that. Trust me, she'll need it."

"What? Why would you say that?"

"There's no time," I replied, exasperated with myself for letting Matthias' prophetic nonsense get to me. Still, I supposed it was only fair to pass along what little I remembered, especially since there was no guarantee I'd see either of them again. "Just know that she's been marked, and that only the Dark Horse can save her, now."

"The Dark Horse?" the mother echoed, her interest piqued.

The voices at our backs grew suddenly louder, and I could tell we could expect visitors at any moment. Which meant this conversation had to end now, and that they had to get away while they still could. The question was, how could I convince them to take the risk? Or, if necessary, trick them?

That was when I recalled Matthias' leather pouch and the instructions that had come with it.

Use this if you must to keep them calm.

Thinking quickly, I retrieved the pouch and perused its contents. The sand within glowed as if burning with an internal fire, and I recognized it for what it was: pixie dust. The stuff happy thoughts were made of.

"What can I say?" I said at last, praying I was right. "Destiny can be a real bitch sometimes."

With that, I flung a handful of the powder over the pair, allowing it to descend over them like motes of dust. The instant the powder landed, both mother and daughter visibly relaxed. Indeed, they even began to eye the waterslide with something approaching eagerness.

Sensing my task was finished, I stepped back into the shadows and watched as the pair ultimately took the plunge and vanished from sight.

79

While I hid in the farthest corner of the room, busy grappling with the possibility that I'd just condemned two strangers on the word of a madman, a cluster of armored figures appeared at the entrance to the nave, their hulking silhouettes emerging from the smoke like wolves from the shadows. I recognized them as the black knights I'd seen in the Elder realm, though I only counted four of the six.

The knights advanced into the room without speaking, the rattle of their clanking armor barely audible over the commotion being raised outside. To my growing horror, they made a beeline directly towards the fountain and, once there, began a plodding descent down the stairs. I cursed under my breath, my stomach lurching.

"They'll be found in no time," I hissed. "What should we do?"

"Don't worry," Veil replied. "They took a different route, which means they're bound to end up in different places."

"I hope you're right. Because if you aren't, what happens next will be on me."

"Nonsense. You did everything you could for them."

"I know. But don't ye see? That's the problem. I'm basically power-less right now. Before this all began, back when I had Areadbhar and

Nevermore, I could've rescued both of 'em. Gotten 'em to a hospital or at least far away from here, instead of encouragin' 'em to crawl into a freakin' hole in the ground and wait for help."

"That is all true, yes. Which is why we waited to come here, last."

I frowned, disturbed by the implication that my role here hadn't been to rescue the two Regulars, but merely to guide them to the fountain. Of course, that wasn't the only shocking thing she'd said. "Wait, last?" I asked. "What d'ye mean, last?"

"I mean your part is almost finished. All that's left to do now is to use the tool I gave you and speak the words."

"Huh? What tool? And what words? For fuck's sake, Veil, haven't we been through enough yet for ye to trust me? Just tell me what's goin' on."

"You'll find out for yourself, soon enough. But first, you should bear witness."

"Bear witness to what?"

To my surprise, Veil answered my question by using my very own arm to point across the room. More upsetting still, when I attempted to ask how she'd managed this, I found myself unable to utter so much as a sound. Indeed, it was as if Veil's shadow were clinging so tightly to me that it was all I could do just to breathe.

And so, with no other choice but to do as I'd been instructed, I watched.

I watched, unable to move or speak, as a Gateway tore through the fabric of space and a host of both familiar and unfamiliar faces appeared some distance down the hall, startling a few wizards who'd wandered in with the intention of looting the place. I watched as one of those faces transformed into a diamond mask, and a pair of skeletal wings sprouted from the man's back like unsheathed blades.

I watched as a fifth knight raced past my hiding place and practically leapt into the fountain in his eagerness to join his companions, followed relatively shortly thereafter by an Elder and cat-like Faeling in armor as white as their quarry's was black.

I watched as the vast majority of the newcomers left to join the fray outside, while the few who remained fended off opportunists and sought out more of that strange armor. I watched as flashes of unholy light strobed through the hole in the mausoleum wall, followed by concussive roars and ferocious howls, then silence.

I watched as that entrance remained empty for five minutes, then ten, then thirty before someone finally reappeared.

I watched as that someone conferred with his friends in the hallway beyond before wandering into the nave, his attention so focused on the backsplash mosaic that he never even considered looking in my direction. I watched as he fell to his knees, joined moments later by his Valkyrie lover. I watched as he thumbed through a book that had appeared in his hands as if by magic, his expression increasingly tormented.

I watched as he rose and the others gathered around him, several of them dressed in the very suits of armor that had been so recently collected.

I watched as they each climbed into the fountain and disappeared beneath its shallow waters, one by one.

And then, just like that, we were alone.

80

"It's time," Veil said, disturbing the eerie silence that followed their departure. Moments later, I felt my legs begin to move against my will, propelling me across the room as though I were some sort of lurching automaton or lock-legged zombie in search of brains. I came to a stop at the fountain's edge, at which point I was able to see the defacement of the tree that had so troubled Nate.

Aiden, Mac's son.

There was that name again, graffitied boldly on the wall. Before I could dwell on what it could mean, however, Veil made use of my hand to rummage about in my pockets. Eventually, she produced and uncapped a familiar container—the one containing the speck of bone dust she'd retrieved from the trunk of the Hangman's Tree. Plucking the speck between two shadowy fingers, she held it out over the pool.

"Wait, stop!" I urged, surprised to find I could speak at last. "Don't do this."

Veil grunted. "And why shouldn't I? You don't even know what it is I intend to do, nor why I must do it."

"Then explain it to me," I insisted. "Or at least tell me why ye stopped me back there? Those were people I know. Friends. Nate. Gunnar. Kára. They might've been glad of me help."

"Which is precisely why I did what I did. Because it is in your nature to interfere, and because doing so might have jeopardized everything we've accomplished so far."

"Jeopardized it, how?"

"I remember who I am now, you know," Veil said after a moment's silence, veering off topic so suddenly I struggled to keep up. "What I am. It's been coming back to me, piece by piece. But once our bond was restored, the entire picture became clear."

"What bond? What are ye talkin' about?"

"Don't tell me you've forgotten, as well? How we used to meet and talk in the realm between realms? I admit I was not privy to the whole truth then as I am now, but I did try my best to guide you. Remember? We spoke of time, and of unconditional love, and of the power I was meant to bequeath to you. A power you would never be able to understand, much less control, and so you locked it away. Locked *me* away, and using a worthless trinket no less."

The longer she spoke, the more a festering suspicion grew. One person and one person only had talked to me of all those things and given me a power that routinely threatened to overwhelm me: my mother's ghost. But she was no more, gone the moment she passed on the last vestiges of my mother's power.

Or so I'd assumed.

"You're lyin'," I whispered. "Ye must be. What you're sayin' makes no sense. Ye couldn't possibly be her."

"Oh, but I am. I was fading. Running out of time. And yet we had to be sure you would continue to grow and gather what was needed. That you would live long enough to fulfill your purpose."

"Purpose? What purpose?"

"Ensuring the advent of the Omega War, what else?"

The Omega War? Something tickled the back of my mind at the mention of such a thing, but I couldn't place where or from whom I might have heard of it. Something Mordred had said, perhaps? Or was it Starlight? Did it have something to do with the Alpha and the

Omega mentioned in Matthias' Dark Horse prophecy? It had all become so jumbled, frankly.

"And how is it I'm supposed to do that?" I asked, finally.

"You've already done it. Or you will have, once you speak the words and finish what we started so very long ago."

While I was busy processing this baffling bit of information, Veil went ahead and dropped the speck of bone dust into the pool. It floated unremarkably for perhaps a second before being swallowed beneath the surface and vanishing from sight.

"Well, that was anticlimactic," I noted, wryly.

"Because you have not yet spoken the words."

"Jesus Christ, *what words*?! Don't ye realize by now I have no idea what you're talkin' about?"

Veil sighed. "I am talking about the words Calvin Temple gave to you when he told you how to close the door between this realm and the realm below. The speck is merely the lock, as it was always meant to be. It belonged to the first Temple ever to strike a bargain with the Elders, and so in a way is fulfilling its destiny. But then such has always been the wheel of fate."

Feeling a tad overwhelmed by the staggering deluge of information being lumped on me all at once, it took at least a minute before I was able to recall the brief conversation I'd had with Calvin Temple on the outskirts of his property. Come to think of it, he *had* mentioned the Elders, amongst other things.

"Wait," I said, struck by a disturbing realization, "won't lockin' the door mean trappin' everyone who went down there? What about the girl and her mother? Or Nate and his friends?"

"Such is their destiny. Just as it was Callie Penrose's destiny to meet Roland Haviar, the Shepherd, when she was most vulnerable. As it was Gunnar Randulf's to be given the means to break his curse before he could resent those who had none. As it was Brunhilde's daughter to serve alongside Special Agent Jeffries. As it was all those you have helped, or harmed, or simply born witness to."

A gnawing sensation worked at my stomach with each mention. Indeed, when she put it like that, it sounded like I'd been on some sort of quest. But then, according to her, I had: to make sure the Omega War took place, whatever that entailed.

"What if I don't want to start a war?" I asked. "What if I refuse to say the words? What then?"

"Don't be a fool. The Omega War has already begun. It began the very moment the first peace ended. We merely endeavor to wage it on our terms, to give everyone the fighting chance they deserve."

"Everyone meanin' whom, exactly?"

"Those you claim to care about, for starters. But also strangers. The residents of this world. Fae. Perhaps even the Vanquished, if they ever manage to find their way home."

"No pressure then," I muttered.

"Not for you, there isn't. Once this is finished, you will have done your part and can return to the place where all this began."

"Ye mean once I say the words, you'll send me home?"

Veil hesitated. "Home. Yes."

I'd have loved to say I waffled in that moment, that I was leery enough of this manipulative creature to wonder whether she could be trusted...but I didn't. Firstly, because I so desperately wanted to be finished with it all. To rest and process everything I'd seen and done. And secondly, because I had somewhere else I needed to be—something else that needed to be done.

And so I did as she asked.

"I will show ye fear in a handful of dust," I intoned, repeating aloud the fateful phrase given to me by Calvin Temple for just such an occasion. The very moment I said it, the water in the pool froze—not chemically, but chronologically, its undulating surface locked in place like a mold of transparent gelatin.

Veil let out a long sigh, and with it, I felt the pressure holding me in place ease. "It is finally done," she said.

"So you'll send me home, then? Like ye promised ye would?"

"Oh yes. And I will say goodbye, as well, for all that which once sustained me has finally run its course."

If Veil expected me to show remorse about that, she was sorely mistaken; no matter her reasons or the effectiveness of her methods, the bitch had played me far too often and pushed me way too far for me to regret the fact that we'd never see each other again. In fact, assuming she was telling the truth, I was relieved to be free of her—even if that meant bidding farewell to the godlike powers I'd come to think of as my own.

"Such a shame," I replied, instead. "Anyway, let's say we hurry this up, shall we? I'm pretty sure I left me door unlocked, and Boston neighborhoods aren't what they used to be."

"Oh, I am afraid you misunderstood me. You won't be going back to your aunt's house. I am sending you *home*, to the place where it all began. To the End of the World."

"What? But—"

"Good luck."

And with that, Veil disappeared, and I was set adrift once more.

81

"It is his legacy and her blood you have been given, and it is their will you are meant to impose."

82

I came to soaked and spluttering on a muddy, puddle-filled field covered in roiling fog. Instantly freezing, I sat up rubbing vigorously at my arms and suppressing the urge to shiver. Overhead, the sky was a seamless shade of grey, while in the distance I heard the pounding of the surf against a shore nestled between two cliffs.

"I sssee you have finally returned."

Startled, I rolled to my feet and raised my fists in preparation for a fight, only to find the speaker looped around a tree some twenty paces from where I stood, his alabaster white scales and blazing red eyes reflecting the light of a modest campfire. It took me a moment to recognize the beast as the enormous serpent I'd stumbled across not so long ago—though I was pleased to note he'd shrunk considerably since our last encounter.

"Come, you will be more comfortable sssitting by the fire," he insisted. *"I thought you might prefer me better thisss way. A little lesss threatening, perhapsss."*

I cocked an eyebrow. "A little less, aye. Though I don't suppose ye come in your standard garden snake size? Ye know, about yay big?" I held out my hands approximately six inches apart for emphasis.

"I do not."

"Worth a shot," I muttered. "So, I take it ye were expectin' me, then?"

"For sssome time now, yesss."

Which probably meant Veil had intended to send me back here all along, though the why remained a mystery. Frankly, I wasn't sure I cared; my goal at this point was to get back to my own life in one piece. Of course, I had a sneaking suspicion that would prove easier said than done.

"The person who sent me here," I began. "She called this place the End of the World. Why?"

"Becaussse it isss my home. The place where head and tail are dessstined to one day part. And becaussse sssome believe the war to end all warsss will be decided here."

"The Omega War."

"That isss one name for it, yesss. There have been othersss."

I nodded, teeth chattering as I tried to imagine an all-out war being waged across this bleak and unforgiving landscape. It wasn't hard to do, frankly—not with the dense fog that surrounded us making shapes out of nothing. But, if there was to be a war, who would fight it? The gods? Angels and demons? Men?

Realizing it was pointless to speculate, I turned back to the giant vertebrate. "So, d'ye have a name I can call ye?"

"Yesss. To mossst I am known asss Jormungandr. Though sssome call me the Midgard Ssserpent. You may decide for yoursssself which you prefer."

"Wait, not *the* Jormungandr? As in Loki's son?"

"Do you know sso many othersss?"

Good point.

Still, that was an unexpected twist. Unfortunately, uncovering the creature's identity only raised more questions. After all, I'd had very little to do with the Norse or their pantheon until relatively recently —though I had come across Jormungandr's mischievous father, drooling brother, and terrifying sister over that span. Perhaps that had something to do with it?

Either way, sensing Jormungandr was no threat to me—or at the very least that no amount of distance would make a difference should he prove otherwise—I decided to accept his invitation and approached the crackling fire. Once I stood basking in its glow, I spoke again, choosing a more direct tack this time.

"D'ye know why I was sent here?" I asked.

"I do, yesss. You were sssent to make a choice. And to hear the truth, though not necesssssarily in that order."

"And does the truth have somethin' to do with this place? The one who sent me called it my home. She said this was where it all began, whatever that's supposed to mean."

The sea serpent tilted his head. *"Not all. But you, yesss. Thisss isss where you were firssst conceived."*

"Conceived, as in...? Oh, God. Gross. What, like right here? Actually, ye know what, don't tell me. I don't want to know."

"You misssundersssstand. You were not born to a mother and father, but cassst. You are a being of pure magic. Old magic. Indeed, sssome might sssay you are the finessst conjuration to grace the world sssince the Jötunnar came down from their mountainsss. And believe me when I sssay that would be high praissse indeed."

"Sorry," I said, cupping a hand to my ear. "I must've misheard ye. D'ye just call me a *spell*?"

"I did."

"Right...okay, no offense, but how drunk are ye right now? Be honest. Believe me, I won't judge."

Rather than show appreciation for my little joke, the Midgard Serpent studied me with those baleful eyes of his, and somehow I could tell that he at least believed what he was saying, regardless of how outrageous it sounded.

"Okay," I said, sighing. "Look, whatever this is, can we just skip it? It's been a really, really long couple of days, and I just want to go home."

"I sssspeak the truth."

I rolled my eyes. "Really? Because it sure sounds like shite to me."

"Have you never wondered why you ssshed your own mind sso easily and sso often?" Jormungandr asked. *"Why you have ssswapped one power for another, time and time again? It isss becaussse from the very*

beginning you were meant to do one thing and one thing only: ssset the board."

"Set the board? What does that even—"

"It meansss you are no goddessss. No wizard or Valkyrie or ssseer. What you are, child, isss a conduit of power."

"I'm afraid I still don't follow," I confessed.

Jormungandr cocked his head. *"Do you not find it ssstrange that after ssspending but a few momentsss in a realm outssside time, you inexplicably learned to wield it? That you dissscovered you had magic the very moment you encountered a witch who could teach it to you? That you ssshared a dream with a godkiller and came away ssstrong enough to ssslay a Massster?"*

"I, uh..."

"Did you not find it curiousss," he went on, *"that you learned to harnessss night itsssself from the daughter of a Titan tasssked with chauffeuring the sssun? That from the moment you crosssssed into Fae, you were able to lay claim to their ssstrength? Did you never think to wonder at the sssheer coincedence of it all?"*

I opened my mouth to offer a viable explanation but simply couldn't find the words. "I guess it does sound a little too convenient, when ye put it like that," I admitted. "But it didn't seem like it at the time. It all just sort of happened."

"Of courssse it would ssseem that way." A film flicked horizontally across Jormungandr's eyes as he blinked. *"But that doesss not change the fact that you are by your very nature a chameleon. A creature forever changing her ssskin to sssuit the room."*

"I've been called worse," I replied, hoping to ease the growing tension and hopefully change the subject.

"Jessst all you like, child. But know that you were conceived by the Archwizard himsssself, fueled by the life force of a goddessss who could sssee no other way to sssave her people. That isss your legacy. Anything elssse you may have been told wasss a lie meant to disssstract you from uncovering the truth too sssoon."

"And what would that be?" I asked, my mouth suddenly bone dry.

"That you are and alwaysss have been powerlessss. That your child-

hood wasss not a childhood at all, but an incubation period. That every ability you laid claim to wasss merely a perfume you happened upon and wore for a time."

I drew a deep, ragged breath, allowing the air to invade my lungs until they ached, then locked eyes with the monstrous sea serpent. "I don't believe ye."

Jormungandr's tongue flicked out like a ribbon caught in the wind. *"Then I welcome you to depart thisss place with my blessssing. You will find ssshelter to the north, and even civilization beyond that. Unlessss you would prefer to sssave yoursssself the trouble and create a Gateway?"*

"Of course I wouldn't. I can't..."

Wait. Why not create a Gateway? I'd been able to once, though of course that seemed long ago, now. Indeed, I'd been able to do a great many things once. I'd wielded fledgling magic, for instance. Manipulated shadows. I'd even possessed the superhuman strength and stamina inimical to the Fae. And yet, it appeared none of it remained. Indeed, it seemed as if every ability I'd ever called my own had been translated into a language I could no longer read.

Which raised the question, was it possible Jormungandr was telling the truth? Was I truly nothing more than a spell, siphoning powers off of others like some sort of parasite?

"It can't be," I whispered, staring down into the fire. "I'm a person. I have thoughts and feelin's and emotions."

"That isss true."

I looked up. "Then why call me a spell?"

"Becaussse that isss what you are. The ssspell made flesssh. Not mortal, no, but no lessss a persssson for it."

"The spell made flesh?" I echoed, realization dawning. "Hold on! The box that started this whole mess. That t'ing that bit me, and the note. That was all ye, wasn't it?!"

"No, it wasss not. It wasss the one they call Merlin. I believe he felt we would be kindred creaturesss, each of usss destined to ssswallow our own tailsss. Or tale, in your particular cassse. Perhapsss that isss why he sssought me out. Why he assssked me to passss on hisss final wordsss."

"You're sayin' that, like, he's dead."

Jormungandr hung his scaly head, refusing for the first time to meet my gaze.

"Since when?" I asked through gritted teeth.

"It wasss quite a few yearsss ago, now. Not long after you were firssst created and sssent away. He went peacefully, if that isss of any comfort."

It wasn't.

"Ye said he wanted ye to pass along a message," I said through gritted teeth. "Was that to me, specifically?"

"Yesss, though only if you wissshed to hear it. He told me he would undersssstand if you did not."

I swallowed past a sudden lump in my throat and rubbed angrily at my eyes. For as long as I could remember, I'd hoped to find some way to connect with the man I thought of as my father. And yet, Merlin had proven himself nothing like the man I'd imagined—the figure I'd spent most my life searching for. Indeed, if Jormungandr was to be believed, he wasn't even my father at all, but rather my creator. Surprisingly, I hoped he was right; at least then the man had an excuse for what he'd done.

That said, I was no fool. Anyone could make something and discard it—even a parent.

"Tell me," I said, at last.

"He sssaid, 'I do not expect you to forgive me for what I did to you. To forgive either of usss. The fault will forever be oursss. But the fact that you are here meansss you are now free to become whatever you wisssh to be, and it isss my hope that you will not let our missstakesss ruin what comesss next."

"Ye told me before that I had a choice to make," I said after a prolonged silence, my voice so ragged with repressed emotion I couldn't be sure Jormungandr had even understood me until I met his eyes. "Once I'd heard the truth. What was the choice?"

"A sssimple one, I hope, compared to the othersss you have made lately. For all that you have been told and all you have done, you are to pick your next dessstination, and in return I am to sssend you there, no quessstionsss asssked."

I had already opened my mouth to insist the sea serpent send me home when another thought occurred to me. No matter how miserable I felt right now, Boston would always be there waiting for me. But a free ride to the place of my choosing? That was an opportunity I couldn't lightly pass up.

"What if I don't know where it is, the place I want to go?" I asked after careful consideration. "What if I want to find someone, instead? Could ye send me to 'em?"

"Possssibly. Who isss it you hoped to find?"

I told him.

"Ah, I sssee." Jormungandr turned away from me for the second time. *"I can do asss you asssk, but I ssshould warn you, you will not find there what you hope to find."*

"Let me worry about that. Please, just do it."

"Very well."

83

"The woman herself may have the answers you seek..."

84

Puffs of steam snaked past my lips as I hiked up the steep, snow-covered slope. Bright sunlight beat against my back, illuminating the trail of footsteps I followed to the top. What few rocks and bushes there had been protruding from the snow when I began my ascent had since disappeared, leaving me with nothing but the sounds of my labored breathing and the crunch of snow underfoot to keep me company on my march. That and the eagles; the majestic creatures wheeled high overhead, their wings occasionally blotting out the sun.

When at last I reached the hilltop, I saw that the footsteps I tracked curved off and to the left before vanishing at the threshold of a modest hut bathed in the golden light of dusk. Smoke trickled skyward from the far side of the thatched roof, and I swore I could smell the tangy aroma of cooked fish in the air.

Just as I was about to approach, a figure stepped out from the dark recesses of the doorway and into the sunlight with one hand shielding her eyes. She was armed with an axe at her hip, dressed in heavy furs, and wore her raven tresses in Nordic plaits that left one side of her face completely bare.

Still, I recognized her at once.

"Aunt Dez!" I called, waving.

The owner of the hut cocked her head, and—though I found some warmth in the woman's expression—I did not see the recognition I had expected. Instead, she returned my gesture.

"Did the Lady Freya send you?" she called back. "If so, please forgive me for being so unprepared. We don't get many visitors up here."

I froze in mid-motion, my smile fading. The voice sounded different with the accent gone, and yet it was still Dez's voice. But then why had she mentioned the goddess Freya, and what was she doing up here to begin with?

When Jormungandr initially agreed to ferry me to the location of my aunt's soul, I certainly hadn't expected to end up in a snowy glen in the middle of winter. Indeed, I'd fully expected to end up camped outside the Pearly Gates begging St. Peter to grant me an all-access visitor's pass. Instead, it appeared my aunt's soul was roughing it somewhere in the Norse realm.

"Aunt Dez," I called again as I approached, "it's me! It's Quinn! Quinn MacKenna."

The woman rested a hand on the head of her axe. "I'm sorry, but I'm afraid you have me confused for someone else. My name is Gisela. Are you sure you have the right lookout? There are several of us Valkyries up here, keeping an eye on the border between Fólkvangr and Valhalla. Perhaps I could signal one of them for you?"

Perplexed in the extreme, I had no choice but to halt in my tracks and gape at the woman. Had she just called herself a Valkyrie? But that was impossible. To become a Valkyrie, her soul would have had to be reborn...

"No..." I felt my legs go weak as I fell to my knees in the snow. "It can't be. It can't..." I slumped forward in a daze. "I came to save ye, to take ye back..."

I did not know how long I rambled on like this. All I knew was that the woman who called herself Gisela must have taken pity on me, because before I knew it I was being ushered into her home. She sat me in a chair, slung a blanket around my shoulders, and pressed a bowl of piping hot stew into my hands.

"Here. Eat. You'll feel better."

Though it took a great deal more prompting, I did eventually do as she asked. More than that, I allowed her to mother me the way she always had—proving the nurturing woman I'd known all my life was still in there, somewhere. I did not speak. I did not trust myself to speak; there was simply too much I wanted to say that Gisela would not understand. Amends I desperately wanted to make that she would not allow.

Eventually, however, it was she who spoke to me.

"Tell me," she said as she settled on the floor, propped up by a mound of furs, "did we know each other in my past life? The way you look at me...I do not believe we are strangers to one another, or that you came here by accident."

I perked up, my earlier reticence forgotten. "It wasn't an accident, no. And aye, we knew each other. Ye were—"

"Please." Gisela held up a hand. "Before you say too much, I must insist you tell me nothing of my past."

"But—"

"Let me finish, please," she interjected, sternly. Then, in a gentler tone. "I feel for you. I really do. It's obvious you came here because you thought the person I was would be waiting for you. But I am not her. And frankly, I don't want to be her. It's true I have no actual memories of my time before I entered the Lady's service, but I do still get the occasional flash. The odd feeling."

"What sort of feelin'?"

"Guilt, most often. But also regret. Longing. Loneliness." Gisela sighed. "I do not know the woman I was before, but I do not believe she was a happy person. As such, I fear talk of who I was would only make those feelings worse. I...hope you understand."

"I..." I swallowed past the lump in my throat and felt a tear slip down my face before I was able to speak again. "Yes, I understand. I'm sorry, I should never have come. I can see that, now."

"That wasn't—"

"No, it's alright. I should go."

"You don't have to leave…"

But I was already halfway out the door, my vision blurry with unshed tears. Though she called after me, the Valkyrie did not follow, for which I was grateful. The truth was I had no words for how I felt and feared what I would do if I lingered.

I should have been happy for her, obviously; the woman who'd cared for me all my life may have been gone, but her spirit was whole and at peace. Of course, hearing how she'd suffered until now was enough to make me want to curl up in a ball and cry, which was to say nothing of Jormungandr's soul-crushing revelations.

I just wanted it all to end, that was the truth.

I wanted to feel nothing. To remember nothing. To care about nothing.

What I needed, I realized, was a drink.

But not just any drink.

I needed something potent.

And so I reached into the lining of my leather trench coat and retrieved exactly what I was looking for. I raised the flask, listening to the river water as it sloshed within its metal container.

Too much of it and you may not remember your own name.

We would see.

I flung the popper the cap and tossed back the contents of Charon's bottle.

And that was the last thing I remembered.

85

"This is what you become. Not who you are."

86

Until, that is, I heard Nate's voice.

"Talk about a confusing cliffhanger," he said, staring down at me from the entrance to the well. The wizard cradled a ball of light in his left hand and a vaguely familiar scythe in his right. For a moment, I wondered how he'd found me, but then I remembered the strange storm I'd seen on the horizon before I descended below Yggdrasil.

His spell, no doubt.

I smiled, weakly. "Well, if it isn't the Dark Horse, himself. What took ye so long? Actually, nevermind. I don't care."

Nate's mouth fell open. "What are you—"

"Isn't it obvious?" I gestured to my bloodstained face, acutely aware of a terrible throbbing sensation that was bound to get worse the longer I left the wound unattended. As for the memories I'd traded the eye for, well, I had a feeling those would take a whole lot longer to recover from. "Anyway," I went on, "what are the chances ye have a flask on ye? Because I could really use a drink."

"Really? Because it looks to me like you could use an eye."

I grimaced. "Wow, too soon, dude. Way too soon."

"Sorry, sorry," Nate apologized as he raced down the steps to

SHAYNE SILVERS & CAMERON O'CONNELL

stand over me with his hand out, the ball of light hovering over our heads and casting strange shadows on the walls of the cave. "It's just when you know as many sight-challenged people as I do, the jokes really sort of tell themselves."

"I'll bet they do."

I took his hand and together we headed for the stairs, though of course that meant relying heavily on the wizard for help.

"I don't suppose ye could cast a healin' spell, or some such?" I asked, offhandedly. "Or, ye know, a basic antibiotic spell? I'm not sure what kind of infection ye get from tearin' out your own eye and throwin' it in a well, but I can't imagine it'll be pleasant."

"You did that to *yourself*? And you threw it in Mimir's Well? Why?"

"It seemed like a good idea at the time."

"Wow. Well, you know what they say. Hindsight is 20/20. Or, you know, 10/10, in your case."

"Hah hah. Laugh it up. You're the one gettin' blood on his shirt."

A pained expression flashed across Nate's face as he plucked at the fabric and exposed it to the light. "Yeah, that's not your blood."

"Shite, I'm sorry."

"Don't be, I'm sure it wasn't your fault. But hey, since we're on the subject of DNA, maybe you'd like to tell me how one of your hairs ended up on someone's shoulder down in the Elder realm?"

I grimaced. "I guess that depends. Whose shoulder was it on?"

"What?"

"Well, it was either the mother, the daughter, or Matthias. But the answer to your question would depend on the person."

Nate stopped in his tracks, his right hand clasped so tight around my arm it felt like he was trying to take my blood pressure. "Did you say Matthias?"

"Oy, that hurts, ye know."

Nate squeezed harder. "I know. Now talk."

"You're not the boss of me," I replied through gritted teeth. "But, yes, that's what I said. I ran into him there in some place he called the Reverie. Reminded me a lot of Chateau Falco, from what little I saw of it. Oh, and he also asked why ye weren't writin' him back? Not sure what he meant by that."

"He did?" The wizard released my arm, his expression completely slack. "Wait, *you* were inside Reverie? When? How?"

"It's a long story. And not one I'm particularly keen to tell just yet, if I'm bein' honest."

"Yeah, no offense, but I don't care. You have no idea the sacrifices that were made trying to figure out who left that hair behind. My friends could still be in danger because of it, and I think I deserve to know why."

A disturbingly large part of me wanted to reach out and slap the wizard in the wake of his little tirade. After all, what could he possibly know about sacrifice? But then, it was obvious he had no idea where I'd been or what I'd done or what I'd learned. What I'd given up.

What I'd very nearly lost forever.

"Ye should hurry and get back to 'em. Your friends. Leave me here. I'll find me own way out."

Nate sighed as if I'd taken the wind out of his sails, somehow. "Of course I'm not going to leave you here. Come on, we can talk more once we're topside. You can meet Grimm, assuming he hasn't wandered off. You'll like him. He curses like an Irish sailor had sex with a Boston whore."

"Jesus," I said, cringing at the image that painted.

"No, not Jesus. *Grimm.* G-R-I-M-M. Don't tell me you lost an ear, too?"

"Oh, fuck off."

Nate patted my back. "That's more like it."

87

Grimm was gone by the time we reached the surface, no doubt cavorting with Yggdrasil's resident rodent, Ratatoskr. Personally, I was glad; I was having a hard enough time keeping track of Nate with my one good eye, let alone a demonic bird horse with a chronic aversion to rainbows.

"Does it still hurt?" Nate asked.

"Not as much, t'anks."

The wizard had helped me to a soft patch of grass and proceeded to use his magic to partially heal my wound—enough so I'd stopped bleeding down my face, at least. It was a kind gesture, and one I very much appreciated in light of the circumstances.

"I'm sorry your spell led ye here to me," I said, though I didn't bother elaborating any further. Truthfully, I simply wasn't ready to talk about what I'd witnessed and done—not yet, and maybe not ever. I was still reeling from my brief encounter with a dead woman, not to mention the sickening revelation that my parents weren't my parents, at all, but puppet masters who'd used me to tug on the strings of fate.

"Here, use this to wipe your face." Nate tore a strip from his sleeve and passed it over to me.

"T'anks."

"Don't mention it. But I do need you to tell me something. And I need you to be very, very honest. Do you know a man named Aiden?"

"Hmm?" I frowned, forced to choose my next words carefully. "No, I've never met a man named Aiden. Why? What is he to ye?"

Nate was silent for a moment. "He's someone I am going to kill."

"Is that right? Well then, I'm glad I'm not that guy."

Nate studied me for a long time before finally appearing to relax. "You really don't know him. That's a relief."

Seeing the look on his face, I will admit I briefly considered mentioning the fact that I'd encountered a boy named Aiden, once. But in the end I realized that to do so I would have to open an entire trash can full of worms. Besides, I had no reason to believe they were one and the same.

"Not that I don't appreciate the help," I said instead, "but shouldn't ye be gettin' back to your friends now?"

"Soon. But first, I want to see what I can do about that eye of yours."

"What d'ye mean?" I asked, probing the tender flesh around the socket. "I thought ye healed it as best ye could?"

"That's true, I did. But I've never been much of a healer. I'm more of a maker. Or a breaker, depending on the circumstances."

Before I could reply, Nate leapt to his feet and began pacing along the base of the World Tree like a little boy hunting for Easter Eggs. I tracked him as best I could but found it increasingly difficult the farther he wandered in search of whatever it was he was hoping to find. Fortunately, it didn't take very long for him to return triumphant.

"Have you seen this stuff?" he called, hoisting a fist-sized shard of Bifrosted glass. "There's bits and pieces of it hanging everywhere along with a bunch of other random junk."

"Ornaments," I corrected. "They're decorations. For Yule. Ratatoskr put 'em up."

Nate paled. "Wait, did you say Yule? *Still?*"

"Aye. Why, what's wrong?"

"Um, nothing," he lied. "It's fine. I just seem to be losing track of time a lot lately, that's all."

I grunted in amusement. "Ye aren't the only one, trust me."

"Oh?" Nate eyed me sidelong but ultimately didn't press the issue, which I appreciated. "Anyway, on a scale of one to ten, how would you feel about having an amazing technicolor dreamcoat for an eyeball?"

I scowled. "As opposed to havin' no eye, at all?"

"Yeah, that would be the one on the one-to-ten scale."

"And what's the ten?"

"Having an eye, obviously. Wow, you're really struggling with this, aren't you? Should I try making you a new brain, too, while I'm at it?"

"Okay, look here ye—"

"No, *you* look *here*," Nate interjected, holding the shard up so that it completely dominated my field of vision. "And try to relax. This shouldn't hurt."

"Shouldn't?"

"What am I, a doctor for eyes?"

"Ye mean an optometrist?"

"Potato, tomato."

"That isn't even—"

A sudden burst of light and heat cut off what I'd been about to say as the shard in Nate's hands began to soften and shrink, its exterior smoldering beneath his fingertips. A brisk wind blew past my face to coil around the Bifrosted glass like a miniature tornado in the shape of a ball, smoothing edges and polishing the shard's chromatic surface to a brilliant shine.

Then, so quickly I didn't even have time to flinch, Nate clamped his hand over the right side of my face. Heat and pain followed, though it was more like pins and needles than anything. After a moment, the wizard pulled away and stepped back, his palm smoking as though he'd shoved it into a furnace.

At least, that's what I could see with my left eye.

With my right, I was witness to an entirely new world.

Everywhere I looked, things glowed. Some were objects hanging from the branches of the World Tree, their edges wreathed in black smoke or strobing neon red like a street light. More noticeable still were those items Nate wore on his person. A blazing white coin riddled with emerald fissures, a satchel that reminded me of a bottomless pit, and so much more. The brightest of all, however, was Yggdrasil itself, which burned with a golden aura so pure it was almost blinding.

"What was that?" I asked as the indescribable effect faded to something approaching normal. "What did ye just do?"

"Something potentially disastrous, I'm sure," Nate admitted, sounding oddly spent as he produced that scythe of his out of thin air once more. "But that's sort of what I do. Anyway, you can yell at me about it some other time. I really should hurry and find Grimm and get out of here, now that you're okay. You are okay, aren't you?"

"Better than I was before ye got here," I admitted, truthfully. As a matter of fact, Nate's visit had lifted my spirits higher than I ever could have hoped—so much so that I desperately wished I could repay him, somehow. If only...I reached up and snatched at Nate's sleeve. "Wait! I have somethin' for ye. Consider it a gift, in exchange for me eye."

"That isn't necessary—"

Whatever Nate had been about to say was forgotten the moment I placed the objects fetched from the inner lining of my pockets in his hand.

"The coins were a gift," I explained. "Ye can use 'em to call the Charon the Boatman, assumin' that's somethin' ye want to do. As for the vial, I have it on good authority it contains a fragment of the philosopher's stone. Apparently ye can use it to revive someone, so long as ye know where to find both their body and soul."

Nate sucked in a breath. "Are you being serious?"

I nodded.

"Right. Shit. Okay. And you're sure you want me to have them?"

I nodded, feeling a weight lifted from my shoulders I hadn't even known was there. "I am, provided ye promise me you'll put 'em to good use."

"Oh, I will," he assured me, closing his fist around all three objects, a glimmer of hope reflecting in his eyes. "I definitely will."

~

Quinn MacKenna will return...

~

DON'T FORGET! VIP's get early access to all sorts of Temple-Verse goodies, including signed copies, private giveaways, and advance notice of future projects. AND A FREE NOVELLA! Click the image or join here: www.shaynesilvers.com/l/38599

~

Turn the page to read a sample of **OBSIDIAN SON** *- Nate Temple Book 1 - or BUY ONLINE (It's FREE with a Kindle Unlimited subscription). Nate Temple is a billionaire wizard from St. Louis. He rides a bloodthirsty unicorn and drinks with the Four Horsemen. He even cow-tipped the Minotaur. Once...*

TRY: OBSIDIAN SON (NATE TEMPLE #1)

There was no room for emotion in a hate crime. I had to be cold. Heartless. This was just another victim. Nothing more. No face, no name.

Frosted blades of grass crunched under my feet, sounding to my ears like the symbolic glass that one would shatter under a napkin at a Jewish wedding. The noise would have threatened to give away my stealthy advance as I stalked through the moonlit field, but I was no novice and had planned accordingly. Being a wizard, I was able to muffle all sensory evidence with a fine cloud of magic—no sounds, and no smells. Nifty. But if I made the spell much stronger, the anomaly would be too obvious to my prey.

I knew the consequences for my dark deed tonight. If caught, jail time or possibly even a gruesome, painful death. But if I succeeded, the look of fear and surprise in my victim's eyes before his world collapsed around him, it was well worth the risk. I simply couldn't help myself; I had to take him down.

I knew the cops had been keeping tabs on my car, but I was confident that they hadn't followed me. I hadn't seen a tail on my way here but seeing as how they frowned on this kind of thing, I had taken a circuitous route just in case. I was safe. I hoped.

Then my phone chirped at me as I received a text.

I practically jumped out of my skin, hissing instinctively. "Motherf —" I cut off abruptly, remembering the whole stealth aspect of my mission. I was off to a stellar start. I had forgotten to silence the damned phone. *Stupid, stupid, stupid!*

My heart felt like it was on the verge of exploding inside my chest with such thunderous violence that I briefly envisioned a mystifying Rorschach blood-blot that would have made coroners and psychologists drool.

My body remained tense as I swept my gaze over the field, fearing that I had been made. Precious seconds ticked by without any change in my surroundings, and my breathing finally began to slow as my pulse returned to normal. Hopefully, my magic had muted the phone and my resulting outburst. I glanced down at the phone to scan the text and then typed back a quick and angry response before I switched the cursed device to vibrate.

Now, where were we?

I continued on, the lining of my coat constricting my breathing. Or maybe it was because I was leaning forward in anticipation. *Breathe*, I chided myself. *He doesn't know you're here.* All this risk for a book. It had better be worth it.

I'm taller than most, and not abnormally handsome, but I knew how to play the genetic cards I had been dealt. I had shaggy, dirty

blonde hair—leaning more towards brown with each passing year—
and my frame was thick with well-earned muscle, yet I was still lean.
I had once been told that my eyes were like twin emeralds pitted
against the golden-brown tufts of my hair—a face like a jewelry box.
Of course, that was two bottles of wine into a date, so I could have
been a little foggy on her quote. Still, I liked to imagine that was how
everyone saw me.

But tonight, all that was masked by magic.

I grinned broadly as the outline of the hairy hulk finally came
into view. He was blessedly alone—no nearby sentries to give me
away. That was always a risk when performing this ancient rite-of-
passage. I tried to keep the grin on my face from dissolving into a
maniacal cackle.

My skin danced with energy, both natural and unnatural, as I
manipulated the threads of magic floating all around me. My victim
stood just ahead, oblivious to the world of hurt that I was about to
unleash. Even with his millennia of experience, he didn't stand a
chance. I had done this so many times that the routine of it was my
only enemy. I lost count of how many times I had been told not to do
it again; those who knew declared it *cruel, evil, and sadistic.* But what
fun wasn't? Regardless, that wasn't enough to stop me from doing it
again. And again. And again.

It was an addiction.

The pungent smell of manure filled the air, latching onto my
nostril hairs. I took another step, trying to calm my racing pulse. A
glint of gold reflected in the silver moonlight, but my victim remained
motionless, hopefully unaware or all was lost. I wouldn't make it out
alive if he knew I was here. Timing was everything.

I carefully took the last two steps, a lifetime between each,
watching the legendary monster's ears, anxious and terrified that I
would catch even so much as a twitch in my direction. Seeing nothing, a fierce grin split my unshaven cheeks. My spell had worked! I
raised my palms an inch away from their target, firmly planted my
feet, and squared my shoulders. I took one silent, calming breath, and
then heaved forward with every ounce of physical strength I could

muster. As well as a teensy-weensy boost of magic. Enough to goose him good.

"*MOOO!!!*" The sound tore through the cool October night like an unstoppable freight train. *Thud-splat!* The beast collapsed sideways onto the frosted grass; straight into a steaming patty of cow shit, cow dung, or, if you really wanted to church it up, a Meadow Muffin. But to me, shit is, and always will be, shit.

Cow tipping. It doesn't get any better than that in Missouri.

Especially when you're tipping the *Minotaur*. Capital M. I'd tipped plenty of ordinary cows before, but never the legendary variety.

Razor-blade hooves tore at the frozen earth as the beast struggled to stand, his grunts of rage vibrating the air. I raised my arms triumphantly. "Boo-yah! Temple 1, Minotaur 0!" I crowed. Then I very bravely prepared to protect myself. Some people just couldn't take a joke. *Cruel, evil,* and *sadistic* cow tipping may be, but by hell, it was a *rush*. The legendary beast turned his gaze on me after gaining his feet, eyes ablaze as his body...*shifted* from his bull disguise into his notorious, well-known bipedal form. He unfolded to his full height on two tree trunk-thick legs, his hooves having magically trans-formed into heavily booted feet. The thick, gold ring dangling from his snotty snout quivered as the Minotaur panted, and his dense, corded muscles contracted over his now human-like chest. As I stared up into those brown eyes, I actually felt sorry...for, well, myself.

"I have killed greater men than you for lesser offense," he growled.

His voice sounded like an angry James Earl Jones—like Mufasa talking to Scar.

"You have shit on your shoulder, Asterion." I ignited a roiling ball of fire in my palm in order to see his eyes more clearly. By no means was it a defensive gesture on my part. It was just dark. Under the weight of his glare, I somehow managed to keep my face composed, even though my fraudulent, self-denial had curled up into the fetal position and started whimpering. I hoped using a form of his ancient name would give me brownie points. Or maybe just not-worthy-of-killing points.

The beast grunted, eyes tightening, and I sensed the barest hesitation. "Nate Temple...your name would look splendid on my already long list of slain idiots." Asterion took a threatening step forward, and I thrust out my palm in warning, my roiling flame blue now.

"You lost fair and square, Asterion. Yield or perish." The beast's shoulders sagged slightly. Then he finally nodded to himself in resignation, appraising me with the scrutiny of a worthy adversary. "Your time comes, Temple, but I will grant you this. You've got a pair of stones on you to rival Hercules."

I reflexively glanced in the direction of the myth's own crown jewels before jerking my gaze away. Some things you simply couldn't un-see. "Well, I won't be needing a wheelbarrow any time soon, but overcompensating today keeps future lower-back pain away."

The Minotaur blinked once, and then he bellowed out a deep, contagious, snorting laughter. Realizing I wasn't about to become a murder statistic, I couldn't help but join in. It felt good. It had been a while since I had allowed myself to experience genuine laughter.

In the harsh moonlight, his bulk was even more intimidating as he towered head and shoulders above me. This was the beast that had fed upon human sacrifices for countless years while imprisoned in Daedalus' Labyrinth in Greece. And all that protein had not gone to waste, forming a heavily woven musculature over the beast's body that made even Mr. Olympia look puny.

From the neck up, he was now entirely bull, but the rest of his body more closely resembled a thickly furred man. But, as shown moments ago, he could adapt his form to his environment, never appearing fully human, but able to make his entire form appear as a bull when necessary. For instance, how he had looked just before I tipped him. Maybe he had been scouting the field for heifers before I had so efficiently killed the mood.

His bull face was also covered in thick, coarse hair—he even sported a long, wavy beard of sorts, and his eyes were the deepest brown I had ever seen. Cow-shit brown. His snout jutted out, emphasizing the golden ring dangling from his glistening nostrils, and both glinted in the luminous glow of the moon. The metal was at least an inch thick and etched with runes of a language long forgotten. Wide, aged ivory horns sprouted from each temple, long enough to skewer a wizard with little effort. He was nude except for a massive beaded necklace and a pair of worn leather boots that were big enough to stomp a size twenty-five imprint in my face if he felt so inclined.

I hoped our blossoming friendship wouldn't end that way. I really did.

Because friends didn't let friends wear boots naked...

≈

Get your copy of OBSIDIAN SON online today! http://www.shayne-silvers.com/l/38474

≈

If you enjoyed the BLADE or UNDERWORLD movies, turn the page to read a sample of DEVIL'S DREAM—the first book in the new SHADE OF DEVIL series by Shayne Silvers.
Or get the book ONLINE! http://www.shaynesilvers.com/l/738833

Before the now-infamous Count Dracula ever tasted his first drop of blood, Sorin Ambrogio owned the night. Humanity fearfully called him the Devil...

TRY: DEVIL'S DREAM (SHADE OF DEVIL #1)

God damned me.

He—in his infinite, omnipotent wisdom—declared for all to hear...

Let there be pain...

In the exact center of this poor bastard's soul.

And that merciless smiting woke me from a dead sleep and thrust me into a body devoid of every sensation but blinding agony.

I tried to scream but my throat felt as dry as dust, only permitting me to emit a rasping, whistling hiss that brought on yet *more* pain. My skin burned and throbbed while my bones creaked and groaned with each full-body tremor. My claws sunk into a hard surface beneath me and I was distantly surprised they hadn't simply shattered upon contact.

My memory was an immolated ruin—each fragment of thought merely an elusive fleck of ash or ember that danced through my fog of despair as I struggled to catch one and hold onto it long enough to recall what had brought me to this bleak existence. How I had become this poor, wretched, shell of a man. I couldn't even remember my own *name*; it was all I could do to simply survive this profound horror.

After what seemed an eternity, the initial pain began to slowly ebb, but I quickly realized that it had only triggered a cascade of smaller, more numerous tortures—like ripples caused by a boulder thrown into a pond.

I couldn't find the strength to even attempt to open my crusted eyes, and my abdomen was a solid knot of gnawing hunger so overwhelming that I felt like I was being pulled down into the earth by a lead weight. My fingers tingled and burned so fiercely that I wondered if the skin had been peeled away while I slept. Since they were twitching involuntarily, at least I knew that the muscles and tendons were still attached.

I held onto that sliver of joy, that beacon of hope.

I stubbornly gritted my teeth, but even that slight movement made the skin over my face stretch tight enough to almost tear. I willed myself to relax as I tried to process *why* I was in so much pain, where I was, how I had gotten here, and...*who* I even was? A singular thought finally struck me like an echo of the faintest of whispers, giving me something to latch onto.

Hunger.

I let out a crackling gasp of relief at finally grasping an independent answer of some kind, but I was unable to draw enough moisture onto my tongue to properly swallow. Understanding that I was hungry had seemed to alleviate a fraction of my pain. The answer to at least one question distracted me long enough to allow me to think. And despite my hunger, I felt something tantalizingly delicious slowly coursing down my throat, desperately attempting to alleviate my starvation.

Even though my memory was still enshrouded in fog, I was entirely certain that it was incredibly dangerous for me to feel this hungry. This...*thirsty.* Dangerous for both myself and anyone nearby. I tried to remember why it was so dangerous but the reason eluded me. Instead, an answer to a different question emerged from my mind like a specter from the mist—and I felt myself begin to smile as a modicum of strength slowly took root deep within me.

"Sorin..." I croaked. My voice echoed, letting me know that I was in an enclosed space of some kind. "My name is Sorin Ambrogio. And I need..." I trailed off uncertainly, unable to finish my own thought.

"Blood," a man's deep voice answered from only a few paces away. "You need more blood."

I hissed instinctively, snapping my eyes open for the first time since waking. I had completely forgotten to check my surroundings, too consumed with my own pain to bother with my other senses. I had been asleep so long that even the air seemed to burn my eyes like smoke, forcing me to blink rapidly. No, the air *was* filled with pungent, aromatic smoke, but not like the smoke from the fires in my—

I shuddered involuntarily, blocking out the thought for some unknown reason.

Beneath the pungent smoke, the air was musty and damp. Through it all, I smelled the delicious, coppery scent of hot, powerful blood.

I had been resting atop a raised stone plinth—almost like a table—in a depthless, shadowy cavern. I appreciated the darkness because any light would have likely blinded me in my current state. I couldn't see the man who had spoken, but the area was filled with silhouettes of what appeared to be tables, crates, and other shapes that could easily conceal him. I focused on my hearing and almost instantly noticed a seductively familiar, *beating* sound.

A noise as delightful as a child's first belly-laugh...

A beautiful woman's sigh as she locked eyes with you for the first time.

The gentle crackling of a fireplace on a brisk, snowy night.

Thump-thump.

Thump-thump.

Thump-thump.

The sound became *everything* and my vision slowly began to sharpen, the room brightening into shades of gray. My pain didn't disappear, but it was swiftly muted as I tracked the sound.

I inhaled deeply, my eyes riveting on a far wall as my nostrils flared, pinpointing the source of the savory perfume and the seductive beating sound. I didn't recall sitting up, but I realized that I was suddenly leaning forward and that the room was continuing to brighten into paler shades of gray, burning away the last of the remaining shadows—despite the fact that there was no actual light. And it grew clearer as I focused on the seductive sound.

Until I finally spotted a man leaning against the far wall. *Thump-thump. Thump-thump. Thump-thump...* I licked my lips ravenously, setting my hands on the cool stone table as I prepared to set my feet on the ground.

Food...

The man calmly lifted his hand and a sharp *clicking* sound suddenly echoed from the walls. The room abruptly flooded with light so bright and unexpected that it felt like my eyes had exploded. Worse, what seemed like a trio of radiant stars was not more than a span from my face—so close that I could feel the direct heat from their flare. I recoiled with a snarl, momentarily forgetting all about food as I shielded my eyes with a hand and prepared to defend myself. I leaned away from the bright lights, wondering why I couldn't smell smoke from the flickering flames. I squinted, watching the man's feet for any indication of movement.

Half a minute went by as my vision slowly began to adjust, and the man didn't even shift his weight—almost as if he was granting me time enough to grow accustomed to the sudden light. Which...didn't make any sense. Hadn't it been an attack? I hesitantly lowered my hand from my face, reassessing the situation and my surroundings.

I stared in wonder as I realized that the orbs were not made of flame, but rather what seemed to be pure light affixed to polished metal stands. Looking directly at them hurt, so I studied them side-long, making sure to also keep the man in my peripheral vision. He had to be a sorcerer of some kind. Who else could wield pure light without fire?

"Easy, Sorin," the man murmured in a calming baritone. "I can't see as well as you in the dark, but it looked like you were about to do something unnecessarily stupid. Let me turn them down a little."

He didn't wait for my reply, but the room slowly dimmed after another clicking sound.

I tried to get a better look at the stranger—wondering where he had come from, where he had taken me, and who he was. One thing was obvious—he knew magic. "Where did you learn this sorcery?" I rasped, gesturing at the orbs of light.

"Um. Hobby Lobby."

"I've never heard of him," I hissed, coughing as a result of my parched throat.

"I'm not even remotely surprised by that," he said dryly. He extended his other hand and I gasped to see an impossibility—a transparent bag as clear as new glass. And it was *flexible*, swinging back and forth like a bulging coin purse or a clear water-skin. My momentary wonder at the magical material evaporated as I recognized the crimson liquid *inside* the bag.

Blood.

He lobbed it at me underhanded without a word of warning. I hissed as I desperately—and with exceeding caution—caught it from the air lest it fall and break open. I gasped as the clear bag of blood settled into my palms and, before I consciously realized it, I tore off the corner with my fangs, pressed it to my lips, and squeezed the bag in one explosive, violent gesture. The ruby fluid gushed into my mouth and over my face, dousing my almost forgotten pain as swiftly as a bucket of water thrown on hot coals.

I felt my eyes roll back into my skull and my body shuddered as I lost my balance and fell from the stone table. I landed on my back but I was too overwhelmed to care as I stretched out my arms and legs. I groaned in rapture, licking at my lips like a wild animal. The ruby nectar was a living serpent of molten oil as it slithered down into my stomach, nurturing and healing me almost instantly. It was the most wonderful sensation I could imagine—almost enough to make me weep.

Like a desert rain, my parched tongue and throat absorbed the blood so quickly and completely that I couldn't even savor the heady flavor. This wasn't a joyful feast; this was survival, a necessity. My body guzzled it, instantly using the liquid to repair the damage, pain, and the cloud of fog that had enshrouded me.

I realized that I was laughing. The sound echoed into the vast stone space like rolling thunder.

Because I had remembered something else.

The world's First Vampire was *back*.

And he was still *very* hungry.

～

Get the full book ONLINE! http://www.shaynesilvers.com/l/738833

Check out Shayne's other books. He's written a few without Cameron helping him. Some of them are marginally decent—easily a 4 out of 10.

MAKE A DIFFERENCE

Reviews are the most powerful tools in our arsenal when it comes to getting attention for our books. Much as we'd like to, we don't have the financial muscle of a New York publisher.

But we do have something much more powerful and effective than that, and it's something that those publishers would kill to get their hands on.

A committed and loyal bunch of readers.

Honest reviews of our books help bring them to the attention of other readers.

If you've enjoyed this book, we would be very grateful if you could spend just five minutes leaving a review on our book's Amazon page.

Thank you very much in advance.

ACKNOWLEDGMENTS

From Cameron:

I'd like to thank Shayne, for paving the way in style. Kori, for an introduction that would change my life. My three wonderful sisters, for showing me what a strong, independent woman looks and sounds like. And, above all, my parents, for—literally—everything.

From Shayne (the self-proclaimed prettiest one):

Team Temple and the Den of Freaks on Facebook have become family to me. I couldn't do it without die-hard readers like them.

I would also like to thank you, the reader. I hope you enjoyed reading *SNAKEBITE* as much as we enjoyed writing it. Be sure to check out the two crossover series in the TempleVerse: **The Nate Temple Series** and the **Feathers and Fire Series**.

And last, but definitely not least, I thank my wife, Lexy. Without your support, none of this would have been possible.

ABOUT CAMERON O'CONNELL

Cameron O'Connell is a Jack-of-All-Trades and Master of Some.

He writes The Phantom Queen Diaries, a series in The Temple-Verse, about Quinn MacKenna, a mouthy black magic arms dealer trading favors in Boston. All she wants? A round-trip ticket to the Fae realm...and maybe a drink on the house.

A former member of the United States military, a professional model, and English teacher, Cameron finds time to write in the mornings after his first cup of coffee...and in the evenings after his thirty-seventh. Follow him, and the TempleVerse founder, Shayne Silvers, online for all sorts of insider tips, giveaways, and new release updates!

Get Down with Cameron Online

facebook.com/Cameron-OConnell-788806397985289

amazon.com/author/cameronoconnell

bookbub.com/authors/cameron-o-connell

twitter.com/thecamoconnell

instagram.com/camoconnellauthor

goodreads.com/cameronoconnell

ABOUT SHAYNE SILVERS

Shayne is a man of mystery and power, whose power is exceeded only by his mystery...

He currently writes the Amazon Bestselling **Nate Temple** Series, which features a foul-mouthed wizard from St. Louis. He rides a bloodthirsty unicorn, drinks with Achilles, and is pals with the Four Horsemen.

He also writes the Amazon Bestselling **Feathers and Fire** Series —a second series in the TempleVerse. The story follows a rookie spell-slinger named Callie Penrose who works for the Vatican in Kansas City. Her problem? Hell seems to know more about her past than she does.

He coauthors **The Phantom Queen Diaries**—a third series set in The TempleVerse—with Cameron O'Connell. The story follows Quinn MacKenna, a mouthy black magic arms dealer in Boston. All she wants? A round-trip ticket to the Fae realm...and maybe a drink on the house.

He also writes the **Shade of Devil Series**, which tells the story of Sorin Ambrogio—the world's FIRST vampire. He was put into a magical slumber by a Native American Medicine Man when the Americas were first discovered by Europeans. Sorin wakes up after five-hundred years to learn that his protégé, Dracula, stole his reputation and that no one has ever even heard of Sorin Ambrogio. The streets of New York City will run with blood as Sorin reclaims his legend.

Shayne holds two high-ranking black belts, and can be found writing in a coffee shop, cackling madly into his computer screen while pounding shots of espresso. He's hard at work on the newest books in the TempleVerse—You can find updates on new releases or chronological reading order on the next page, his website, or any of his social media accounts. **Follow him online for all sorts of groovy goodies, giveaways, and new release updates:**

Get Down with Shayne Online
www.shaynesilvers.com
info@shaynesilvers.com

facebook.com/shaynesilversfanpage

amazon.com/author/shaynesilvers

bookbub.com/profile/shayne-silvers

instagram.com/shaynesilversofficial

twitter.com/shaynesilvers

goodreads.com/ShayneSilvers

BOOKS BY THE AUTHORS

CHRONOLOGY: *All stories in the TempleVerse are shown in chronological order on the following page*

PHANTOM QUEEN DIARIES

(Set in the TempleVerse)

by Cameron O'Connell & Shayne Silvers

COLLINS (Prequel novella #0 in the 'LAST CALL' anthology)

WHISKEY GINGER

COSMOPOLITAN

MOTHERLUCKER (Novella #2.5 in the 'LAST CALL' anthology)

OLD FASHIONED

DARK AND STORMY

MOSCOW MULE

WITCHES BREW

SALTY DOG

SEA BREEZE

HURRICANE

BRIMSTONE KISS

MOONSHINE

YULETIDE PUNCH

SNAKEBITE

NATE TEMPLE SERIES

(Main series in the TempleVerse)

by Shayne Silvers

FAIRY TALE - FREE prequel novella #0 for my subscribers

OBSIDIAN SON

BLOOD DEBTS

GRIMM

SILVER TONGUE

BEAST MASTER

BEERLYMPIAN (Novella #5.5 in the 'LAST CALL' anthology)

TINY GODS

DADDY DUTY (Novella #6.5)

WILD SIDE

WAR HAMMER

NINE SOULS

HORSEMAN

LEGEND

KNIGHTMARE

ASCENSION

CARNAGE

SAVAGE

DARK HORSE

FEATHERS AND FIRE SERIES

(Also set in the TempleVerse)

by Shayne Silvers

UNCHAINED

RAGE

WHISPERS

ANGEL'S ROAR

MOTHERLUCKER (Novella #4.5 in the 'LAST CALL' anthology)

SINNER

BLACK SHEEP

GODLESS

ANGHELLIC

TRINITY

HALO BREAKER

ANGEL DUST

CHRONOLOGICAL ORDER: TEMPLEVERSE

FAIRY TALE (TEMPLE PREQUEL)

OBSIDIAN SON (TEMPLE 1)

BLOOD DEBTS (TEMPLE 2)

GRIMM (TEMPLE 3)

SILVER TONGUE (TEMPLE 4)

BEAST MASTER (TEMPLE 5)

BEERLYMPIAN (TEMPLE 5.5)

TINY GODS (TEMPLE 6)

DADDY DUTY (TEMPLE NOVELLA 6.5)

UNCHAINED (FEATHERS...1)

RAGE (FEATHERS...2)

WILD SIDE (TEMPLE 7)

WAR HAMMER (TEMPLE 8)

WHISPERS (FEATHERS...3)

COLLINS (PHANTOM 0)

WHISKEY GINGER (PHANTOM...1)

NINE SOULS (TEMPLE 9)

COSMOPOLITAN (PHANTOM...2)

ANGEL'S ROAR (FEATHERS...4)

MOTHERLUCKER (FEATHERS 4.5, PHANTOM 2.5)

OLD FASHIONED (PHANTOM...3)

HORSEMAN (TEMPLE 10)

DARK AND STORMY (PHANTOM...4)

MOSCOW MULE (PHANTOM...5)

SINNER (FEATHERS...5)

WITCHES BREW (PHANTOM...6)

LEGEND (TEMPLE...11)

SALTY DOG (PHANTOM...7)

BLACK SHEEP (FEATHERS...6)

GODLESS (FEATHERS...7)

KNIGHTMARE (TEMPLE 12)

ASCENSION (TEMPLE 13)

SEA BREEZE (PHANTOM...8)

HURRICANE (PHANTOM...9)

BRIMSTONE KISS (PHANTOM...10)

ANGHELLIC (FEATHERS...8)

CARNAGE (TEMPLE 14)

MOONSHINE (PHANTOM...11)

TRINITY (FEATHERS...9)

SAVAGE (TEMPLE...15)

HALO BREAKER (FEATHERS...10)

ANGEL DUST (FEATHERS...11)

YULETIDE PUNCH (PHANTOM...12)

SHADE OF DEVIL SERIES

(Not part of the TempleVerse)

by Shayne Silvers

DEVIL'S DREAM

DEVIL'S CRY

DEVIL'S BLOOD

DEVIL'S DUE (*coming 2022...*)

83242936R10193